# The Queens of New York

# The
# Queens
# of
# New
# York

## E. L. SHEN

Quill Tree Books
An Imprint of HarperCollinsPublishers

Quill Tree Books is an imprint of HarperCollins Publishers.

Library of Congress Cataloging-in-Publication Data

Names: Shen, E. L., author.
Title: The queens of New York / E. L. Shen.
Description: First edition. | New York : Quill Tree Books, [2023] | Audience: Ages 13 up. | Audience: Grades 10-12. | Summary: Seventeen-year-old inseparable best friends Jia, Ariel, and Everett navigate first love, grief, racism, and Asian American consciousness during one life-changing summer apart.
Identifiers: LCCN 2022031721 | ISBN 9780063237957 (hardcover)
Subjects: CYAC: Best friends—Fiction. | Friendship—Fiction. | Summer—Fiction. | Asian Americans—Fiction.
Classification: LCC PZ7.1.S51425 Qu 2023 | DDC [Fic]—dc23
LC record available at https://lccn.loc.gov/2022031721

Typography by Erin Fitzsimmons
23 24 25 26 27  LBC  5 4 3 2 1
First Edition

*For the Chopstick Chicks—my queens of New York.*

*And for Mom, Diana, and Grandma, always.*

# June

# 1
# Jia

There are three parts to every perfect dumpling: the skin, the meat, and the water.

Ariel is the skin—the delicate foundation that can make something beautiful out of nothing.

Everett is the meat—tough, juicy, and packed with spice.

And me? I guess I'm the water, the one keeping us all together.

The yellow awning letters that spell out *Lee's Dumpling House* are chipped and faded (Dad still needs to repaint), but the kitchen is bustling. Sesame balls cover the counter, anxious to be deep-fried, while sweaty chefs awaken hundreds of char siu bao from their frozen slumber.

In the booth by the window, Ariel yawns.

"You can sleep on the plane," Everett says, swatting her head.

Ariel sticks out her tongue and loudly slaps meat onto the fragile wrapper.

"Don't mess up my dumplings," I tease.

"Your *parents'* dumplings," Everett corrects. She gestures to our large assembly line. "And we're basically free labor, so you can't complain."

I make a show of rolling my eyes but my heart dips. I'm going to miss all of this. Our early-morning dumpling masterpieces and lazy bike rides through Flushing Meadows. Sketching anime boys, Everett's soft humming fanning the pages. Watching Ariel decimate her opponents at every debate and cheering on Everett at all her musicals. And then, ending the night squished into sleeping bags, falling asleep next to leftover fried pizza and half a dozen sheet masks.

When we met, we were seven-year-olds prancing through Queens's annual Lunar New Year festival in our fluffy winter coats and fuzzy earmuffs. Back then, everything was simple. Our parents were volunteers, so we got there early, whizzing past closed storefronts and messing around with confetti cannons until Dad yelled at us. When it was time for the parade, we lifted our chins and marveled at the massive red dragon dragged through the streets by neighbors now part of something magical. Ten years later, we still feel that magic—in our city and in our friendship. Everett goes to her fancy private school in Manhattan and Ariel naturally placed into the best public high school in Queens, so during the school year, we only see each other on weekends.

But the summers? The summers are special. The summers are for us.

That is, of course, until they both decided to ditch me.

I want to be mad at them, but I'm not. Everett is making her dreams come true; tomorrow she'll fly to Ohio to sing her brains out at a top-notch musical theater institute. And Ariel? Well, maybe she needs the time away. After Bea's accident, she hid herself in homework, and Netflix, and vacuums of unread text messages. All her studying must have paid off, though, because she graduated a year early and got a full scholarship to Briston University in California. She starts in late August, but her parents are shipping her there today for an eight-week precollege program. I wish I could carry her through the San Francisco waves, but instead I'm stuck at home helping Mom and Dad with the restaurant until the heavy Queens air thins and the leaves ache for change.

As if Everett can read my thoughts, she nudges my shoulder, her hands still pinching dough folds. We crane our necks toward Ariel, who has stopped spooning meat and is staring out the window with wide, glassy eyes. The rising sun streaks her pale cheeks. Even though she's here with us, I know she's somewhere else entirely.

Everett stencils a question mark into the flour and we play our daily game of *Who should bug Ariel first?* I shake my head and she relents. Placing her finished dumpling on the platter, she clears her throat.

"Um, you okay, girlie?"

Ariel snaps toward us and immediately grabs a wrapper. "Oh," she says, "sorry, didn't mean to stop our production train."

Her smile is Barbie doll plastic—a look she's mastered since last fall.

Light begins to flood the restaurant. Seventy-five dumplings stand at attention, like little boats that might float away with Ariel into the Pacific.

"You know," I whisper, reaching across the table to touch her sleeve, "Bea would be really proud of you."

But Ariel won't look at me. "Yeah," she says, and then, standing up abruptly, "Mrs. Lee, we're all set here!"

My mother comes out from the back in her cashmere sweater and tan slacks, permed curls grazing the nape of her neck. As hostess, she always tries to look professional even if that means wearing her one good sweater every single day. Buying another would be lang fei. Money exists to pay the bills. Riches, Mom always says, are merely a dream in the night.

Now she nods approvingly at our dumplings. "Not bad. Maybe you'll all work here one day."

She's joking, but heat crawls up my necks and prickles my ears. This is *my* future, I know. But not Ariel's or Everett's.

Ariel wipes her hands on a cloth napkin and pushes the platters forward. "Nowhere else we'd rather be, Mrs. Lee."

She glances down at her phone and then looks back at us, lips drawn tight.

"Time for you to go, isn't it?" I say.

Ariel nods, shifting out of the booth. Everett is already weeping, silent tears trickling down her chin. As we walk to the front entrance, Mom dashes for the tissues, crushing them in her palms before flinging them toward Everett. Crying is my mother's least favorite activity, followed by goodbyes.

"Good luck in California, Ariel," she says, hurrying to the back, trays of dumplings folded between her arms.

I crouch behind the counter and pull out three large suitcases.

"We'll text and video-chat all the time," Ariel promises, "and email."

"Ooh, *email*," Everett gushes, "like we're old-fashioned and writing letters to each other. I like it."

"Okay," I say, "every day?"

"Ariel can't even answer her messages every day when she's *home*." Everett sniffs, and then, realizing the weight of her words, swallows hard.

But Ariel doesn't seem to notice. "Hey," she laughs, "I've gotten better."

"Every *week*," I amend.

"Okay," the girls agree, "every week."

Everett throws her arms around Ariel's waist, squishing her small frame.

"Help, can't breathe!"

Everett is unyielding. "Meet lots of cute guys for us, okay?"

"Oh, for sure. I'll just ditch all my classes for college boys."

"That's my girl."

We make our way onto the street, hiding from the thick summer heat under the awning's shade. Flushing is beginning to stir. Colorful Chinese signs crowd the block. Mr. Zhang slides up the glass protector on his food cart, revealing salted tofu pudding and sweet soy milk. The stench of decades-old steam stacks and stale cigarettes waft through the early-morning air.

Ariel calls a rideshare, and a sleek sedan appears within minutes. She piles her suitcases into the trunk and gives us one last squeeze.

"Eight weeks," she says, "and then we'll be together again."

It seems like a lifetime and no time at all. Everett rests her head in the crook of my neck and we wave and wave until Ariel is just a dot on the horizon.

And then, she's gone.

# 2
# Jia

If there's one thing I know about Everett Hoang, it's that she despises the heat. So we unlock our bikes and pedal from the collection of whirring fans cramming the restaurant walls to the icy blast of Everett's air-conditioned house.

It's a short ride through the park, yet the city seems to transform. When we reach the promenade, I brake to stare up at the Unisphere, a massive steel sculpture of the earth encircled by skateboarders and drooling babies. It quite literally marks the line between one universe and another: the hungry, haggling streets of Chinatown, where old ladies hunch over squeaky carts filled with plastic bottles, and the dreamy Tudor homes of Forest Hills Gardens, where the sprinklers are automatic and the trash is out of sight.

Everett heaves all the way there, one hand on the bike, the other fanning herself with a takeout menu she stole from the counter. And then, the park gives way to toasted ceramic roofs and tree-lined streets and we're here. Everett unbuckles her helmet and smooths down the flyaways poking out of her French braids.

"God," she says, inspecting her crop top, "I'm gonna need to shower again."

We wheel our bikes up to her garage and enter the mudroom. Even though I've been to Everett's house probably six hundred times, I always feel like a tourist in a royal palace. The Hoangs hired an interior designer so the house resembles a prettier, more modern version of Mr. Bingley's home in *Pride & Prejudice*. Columns frame the doorways, flanking Persian carpets and crystal chandeliers. Bay windows overlook the garden, where the landscaper hunches over a hydrangea bush, rings of dirt lining his sleeves. He examines me and smiles, his eyes crinkling like we know each other, like we're friends from the same world.

Everett follows her labradoodle, Watkins, into the living room and plops down onto the couch, one leg swinging over the edge.

"Ariel's going to be okay, right?" she asks as I smooth out the carpet and settle beneath her feet. Watkins flops across my lap, anxious for a belly rub.

"I don't know," I answer truthfully. "I hope so."

"Well, even if she weren't, she wouldn't tell us anyway." She rolls her head to the ceiling and groans.

We have the same conversation every day: Ariel detached, Ariel unresponsive, Ariel lost in her own mist. But now she's gone for real, and there's nothing we can do. I nudge Watkins off my lap and squeeze onto the couch beside Everett.

"Cheer up," I say. "Think about tomorrow."

Everett cracks a smile and bolts up so she's sitting on her knees. "Jia, it's going to be *so* great. They'll announce the show on the first day, and I have a feeling it will be something really, you know, emotionally resonant. Like *Cabaret*. Or *Ragtime*. Oooh, or maybe something artsy, like *Merrily We Roll Along*."

"Or *The Sound of Music*."

Everett throws a pillow at me and I yelp as it brushes the side of my face. She hates *The Sound of Music* because she detests anything that's—in her words—*cheesy and simplistic*. That girl could spend years talking about the symbolism of the gorilla costume in *Cabaret* or the complicated morals about art and sacrifice in *Sunday in the Park with George* (yes, she's ranted enough that I remember). To her, musicals aren't just about two people falling in love. They're about the meaning of life.

"You're going to have so much fun," I say. "You and all those cornstalks."

"And all those *boys*." She wiggles her eyebrows.

"You never end up dating theater guys, Everett."

She opens her mouth to offer some witty comeback but she can't because it's true. Everett has always wanted a boyfriend, but her theater friends are usually girls or too tied up in drama for her to date. She had one, Richie, in ninth grade, but the relationship lasted exactly two makeout sessions and three after-school Starbucks hangouts before they called it off. I know she wants this to be *her* summer though—the one where she has some salacious fling with a farmer's-tanned guy from Montana or a charming hipster from Oregon. I can see her fantasizing about it right now, absentmindedly petting Watkins, her eyes drifting toward the garden.

"Jia?"

"Yeah?"

She smiles to herself. "This is going to be the best summer ever."

I can't help it. Needles of jealousy prick my skin and course through my veins. I stare at the space between my feet where tufts of carpet peek out from under my socks. Everett immediately swoops toward me, her chin on my shoulder.

"I'm sorry," she says, "that was insensitive."

"No." I shake my head. "You *will* have the best summer ever. I'm just being pathetic."

"Jia Lee? Pathetic? Pretty much impossible." Everett kisses my forehead and lies back down on the sofa.

I *am* being pathetic though. If Dad were here, he'd tell me, "The torment of envy is like a grain of sand in the eye." It's an old Chinese proverb he loves. He repeated it the day I cried because I couldn't go on the class trip to Boston. All I could think about were Paul Revere's black shutters, the Battle of Bunker Hill obelisk my classmates would Snapchat in front of, late-night gossip under hotel sheets, and bus ride movies no one wanted to watch but everyone secretly enjoyed. Dad told me I could learn all those things from Wikipedia and that we needed the trip's cost for next month's rent. "Remember what's important," he warned.

I breathe in the smell of expensive perfume and hydrangeas

and try to remember. What's important is that Nai Nai's Parkinson's is getting worse and she needs my help. If she falls or forgets to take her pills, I won't ever forgive myself. And CeCe is only six, still playing hopscotch, and picking trash off the subway floor, and screaming whenever I don't pay attention to her for five minutes. I have jobs to do this summer. I have a *destiny* to fulfill. It's all part of Mom and Dad's master plan: community college, where I'll earn my associate's degree, shadow my parents, and eventually run the dumpling house so they can retire. My future is as crystal clear as the Hoang family's chandelier.

Everett and I sit in silence for a moment—just us and Watkins and the gentle whir of the air conditioner. Her parents are working and her older brothers are in college doing summer internships, so the house feels peaceful and still. Maybe nothing will change and we'll stay like this forever.

As I lean down to let Watkins lick my hand for traces of scallion, Everett pushes my head aside and points toward the foyer.

"Ice cream truck," she says, and soon enough, I hear it too. The faraway, sparkly melody inching closer and closer.

She grabs my arm and practically yanks me from the couch, racing toward the foyer. We slip on the wood floors like speed skaters lurching on ice. Everett digs her palms into fistfuls of dollar bills from the tin by the door and jets down the steps, motioning for me to keep up.

I pant behind her. Everett's second favorite thing after theater? Ice cream.

We make it to the street just as the truck pulls up—blue and white with the classic Mister Softee cone-head logo, like it's a city delicacy instead of three-dollar watered-down milk and sugar. Forest Hills Gardens is one of the only neighborhoods in Queens where the ice cream truck actually comes to your doorstep. At the dumpling house, we walk two blocks over and cross a busy inter-section, hoping for treats after a long, stuffy shift frying shaobing and pouring oolong tea.

Everett and I aren't the only ones with ice cream on our minds. A curly-haired boy hands the child next to him a swirled pink cone.

The boy and the child turn. Everett waves as we jog up to them.

"Oh, hey!" She pulls me out from behind her shadow. "Jia, meet my new neighbors." Everett gestures to the little boy, his mouth coated in strawberry ice cream. "Masud Abboud."

I follow her gaze up to Masud's brother, tall with impossibly gray eyes.

"And Akil Abboud."

Akil looks down and then back at me, offering a wide-toothed smile. My insides are humming with bees. It's not like I haven't seen cute boys before. And I've certainly seen lots of them in Ever-ett's neighborhood, strutting around in pastel polos and khaki shorts. They're just usually more Everett's type, not mine.

"I'm Jia. Jia Lee. Nice to meet you." I crouch down to Masud, liquid ribbons now streaking his striped T-shirt. "How's the ice cream?"

Masud grins. "Yuuuuuummmy."

Akil rolls his eyes. "Hopefully worth the mess he's making."

Masud skips around us in circles, forcing me to step closer.

I shake my head. "I understand. My sister's six. She's a pain."

"She's adorable," Everett counters.

"An *adorable* pain."

Akil laughs, and I watch the muscles bounce up and down beneath his jersey shirt. The bees tickle my throat even as I try to force them down.

"Masud is five," Akil says as his brother happily digs his face into his cone. "And he definitely loves his ice cream."

"Ah, just like Everett."

Everett fake scowls, crossing her arms over her chest. "Hardy-har-har." She marches up to the server. "One chocolate cone, please."

Akil's brother skips farther and farther away from us, rounding the cul-de-sac.

"Well, I should probably go get him." He groans, running a hand through his curls. "Nice meeting you, Jia. See you around, Everett."

I watch as Everett's new neighbor steers his little brother into a massive brick house covered in tendrils of ivy. It looks like something from a fairy tale. A beautiful home for a beautiful boy.

Everett links her arm in mine, smirking between licks of chocolate.

"Maybe your summer won't be so bad after all." She winks.

I shake my head, pulling her back toward the driveway. "I don't know *what* you're talking about."

But the bees are still swarming.

From: arielunderthesea_29@gmail.com

To: everetthoang24601@gmail.com; jialee@leedumplinghouse.com

5:03 PM

Subject: The land of crocs


Dearest Jia and Everett,

   Aren't you proud of me? I texted when I landed *and* I'm writing you an email. On the same day, no less. I think I'm turning a new leaf. Now that I'm in San Francisco, I would like to report that it is freezing. In the middle of June. Like, put on a heavy coat and shiver. Also, I counted and have already seen five guys wearing Crocs on the street. It is not okay. Please save me. I miss you both.

XO,

Ariel

# 3
# Ariel

This is what I know: San Francisco is dull and cold. The buildings here are gray. Umma and Appa have already texted me fifteen times. They want to call later. Sandwiched between **How was the flight?** and **Are you hungry? Go buy a sandwich on the debit card in case the cafeteria is closed** is a message I'm trying to ignore: **We're so proud of you.**

The lady at the front desk is wearing a horrible neon green shirt and a gold lanyard. I realize I've forgotten that these are the school colors. Briston University. My future for the summer, and the next four years. Cold, gray San Francisco forever. Hurrah.

Everett and Jia are probably loafing around, licking ice cream from their fingertips until Everett's flight tomorrow. What I'd give to be with them in Queens even though it smells like pee and garbage and rat feces. At the very least, I could have squeezed them in my suitcase to make this all a little more bearable.

When I won the scholarship, I tried to put on a happy face. I tried to be the Ariel from before. The one who picked out which picture frames went best with her high school awards and mulled over whether to buy a glass cabinet or a bookcase for her debate trophies. I chose the cabinet. Now I wanted to smash all that glass with a baseball bat. I text Appa and Umma: **all good, checking in now** and turn off my phone.

"Hi! Are you here for the precollege program?" Front Desk Lady is far too cheery. She smiles wide and I can see the plastic invisible braces lining her teeth.

My hair is too long and drapes over the table. I stuff it into the back of my shirt and nod.

"Great," she says. She pulls out a binder with five dozen laminated pages. "What's your name?"

"Ariel." I stare down at my chipped nail polish. "Kim."

Front Desk Lady flips through the pages so ferociously, you'd think there was a million-dollar check hidden in there with her name on it. Finally, she reaches *K*.

"Wonderful. ID?"

I rummage in my backpack and fish out a leather wallet. Bea gave it to me the day she left for South Korea. Over a year ago now. It was March, slushy and freezing, the worst time to travel. We were in the kitchen. Umma and Appa weren't speaking to her. And I was frustrated. I remember leaning my elbows on the granite island and parroting that she wasn't *applying herself*. She could do better, if she tried. She didn't have to ditch America. Ditch us.

Under the harsh kitchen lights, Bea's face looked freckled and sallow—free of her usual makeup. She winced at my lecture, like I had burned her with a frying pan instead of telling her the truth. Or what I thought was the truth. Then she pulled out the wallet from her jacket pocket. It had a little gold bee engraved on its center. She said she bought it at the flea market. *A bee for Bee*, she explained, *so you won't forget me*. She squeezed my arm and told me she'd be back soon.

My license clatters to the ground. Front Desk Lady is all elbows and knees. She snatches my ID and matches it to my face. Then she brightens. Her plastic braces catch the glare from the window.

"Oh, you're one of our matriculating students!" she squeals. "And I see you're part of our *prestigious* science and technology summer program. How wonderful. Your parents must be so proud." I wait for her to pinch my cheeks like the ajummas at church.

"Thanks," I say. I shove the license back into my wallet and dump the whole thing in my backpack. It lands with a heavy thud. Front Desk Lady starts droning on about summer dorm rooms, and schedules, and keys. But I can only think of my sister's freckles. The way her shoulders heaved when she dragged her luggage to the front door. Did she look back before she left? I swear she did. I hope she did.

I try to focus on Front Desk Lady's small, chipper voice. When she finally finishes, I make the long trek across campus. Most of the Briston students have left for the summer so it's just us precollege kids. Girls cluster under a lamppost like cyclopean fireflies. I overhear them buzzing about the upcoming guest lecture on Rosalind Franklin's pioneering DNA research. They must be in my STEM program. I've never seen anyone bond over DNA before. Except for the boys in my high school's science research club, but they shoot spitballs at each other and make inside jokes that I don't understand.

Someone yells "Incoming!" and a soccer ball flies over my head and somersaults onto the grass behind me. I should go and kick it back, but I don't. Instead, I count my footsteps and repeat *amygdala* under my breath. It's my favorite part of the brain. If I focus, I can picture it smothering each fear receptor until I feel numb. *Amygdala.* The syllables stick to my throat.

By the time I reach my dorm room, I almost forget about Bea. I almost forget that she's dead.

From: everetthoang24601@gmail.com

To: arielunderthesea_29@gmail.com; jialee@leedumplinghouse.com

10:16 AM

Subject: One step closer to BROADWAYY

To my best friends forever and ever and ever,

Ariel!!!! I'm so glad that you made it to San Fran okay. And yes, v proud of you for the email AND the text. You deserve a trophy.

Though we do need a follow-up on all those dudes in Crocs. This is a tragedy and you need to teach them some fashion sense, stat. Give them your best New York crash course, girl!! And Jia, hold down the fort for us. Maybe with Akil???? (Ariel, to recap, this is my new neighbor who Jia is DEFINITELY in love with, 900%.)

Anyway, this is a PSA that I've made it to nowhereeeeee, Ohio!!! I think I'm in a relationship with corn now. I might buy a straw hat and live here forever with my farmer husband, hehehe. But in all seriousness, this is my time to SHINE. Don't worry, I'll still remember you when I'm rich and famous.

Much love,

Everett

# 4
# Everett

In the magazines, you read about actors who've really made it, who are rolling in millions and cherry-picking their roles, and they always talk about that formative moment when they were seventeen and had some amazing teachers and met some soon-to-be-legends and two years later—BAM. They transformed. They became stars. Well, that's going to be me. And this is my Extremely Amazing Summer of Seventeen.

Except maybe not right this second, while I'm trying to wipe sweat from my armpits with the paper towels in the communal bathroom. Jia *did* warn me about how ridiculously hot it was going to be here. I mean, has Ohio ever heard of air conditioners? They're apparently big supporters of recycled hot air blasting in my face all day long. Catch me swimming in a humidifier filled with seventy-five mosquitoes feeding on my skin. I run my hands under the faucet and splash flecks of cool water on my face. They should rename it Ohio: Earth's Swamp.

No matter. I take a deep breath and focus on the name tag in my reflection: EVERETT HOANG in large, typed letters, and then underneath: *The Lucius Brown Performing Arts Institute*. Actually, they messed up, so it really says EVERETT HANG, but I squeezed in an *o* with a marker I stole from the check-in desk.

In Flushing, everyone's last name is Hoang. There are the Hoangs who own the phở place in the mall—they always try to speak Vietnamese to me and laugh when I remind them that the only language I speak is English. There are the Hoang twins who sit in front of me in math class. And then there are the hundreds of other Hoangs whose names are on every sign, and attendance sheet, and soccer jersey.

So Ohio misspelling my name? It just means I'm original. Here, I'm the only Everett Hoang you need to know.

A girl with a fuchsia lipstick smile swings open the bathroom door. She adjusts her halter top and squints at my name tag.

"Everett? Room 202B?"

I glance down at the sopping information sheet sitting in a puddle next to the sink.

"Yup."

"I'm Valerie. Your roommate!"

She rushes toward me with a wave of floral perfume and loose curls. I hug her back, trying to make sure my sticky armpits aren't suffocating her. When I process the face attached to the hair, I realize that my new roommate is basically a glossy headshot come to life—like if Elle Woods and Glinda the Good Witch had a child and she decided to go to acting camp. This is not the kind of girl you see at the Queens supermarket, in black pants and a black leather jacket, glued to her cell phone, talking vaguely about corporate policy. As Aladdin would say: *I'm in a whole new world.*

Valerie releases me from her clutches.

"I'm so excited!" I babble. "Although, I *should* tell you, I already nabbed the bed by the window."

"It's okay, I like to be by the door. Closer to the boys." She laughs and winks at me.

I already know we're going to get along splendidly.

Together, we leave the bathroom and the dorms and head to the auditorium where Abel Pearce, the director, is finally, finally, *finally* going to announce the show (okay, it's only been like an hour and twenty minutes since we arrived at camp, but it feels like forever). On the way there, we chat about our hometowns (Valerie is from South Dakota, which is wild because who lives in South Dakota?), and what age we started voice lessons (age twelve for the both of us, and I judge people who ruin their voices by taking them any earlier), and our favorite type of dance (tap), and our *least* favorite type of dance (ballet, I don't care to tendu five days a week, thank you), and what we think the musical will be, although neither of us truly has any clue. The gnats keep chewing on my skin, but I swat them away and try to take in the wild yellow fields in the distance, and the tall archway of trees, and the colossal stone buildings. Who knew that nowhere, Ohio, would look like an enchanted forest? I can't believe people go to boarding school here and just live in this magical bubble all year long. Taxi cabs and car alarms must seem like ancient city relics to them.

When we reach the auditorium, we climb a million stairs until we're greeted by swarms of students louder than the buzzing flies outside.

Valerie and I grab the first free seats we see. She gets the end spot so now I'm shoulder to shoulder with some gross boy. Wait. Recalibrate. Gross Stranger is actually a very hot dude with incredibly cute dimples and blue-green lagoon eyes I could *absolutely* get lost in. He turns and smiles at me. I try to smile back and hope my forehead sweat isn't trickling down my face. So what if Jia says I never date theater guys? No better time than now to break the cycle.

I can't focus on Hot Stranger for long though, because a man is walking up to the podium. I know it's Abel Pearce before he even speaks—I've pretty much memorized every wrinkle on his face from the camp brochure. He clears his throat into the microphone.

Like any semi-famous director with a niche fan club, Abel Pearce gives a long, self-important monologue filled with dramatic pauses and pointed stares. He goes on and on about how Lucius Brown is one of the best summer musical theater programs in the country, and how we've all been hand-selected, and how we should use this experience to *enrich our minds and souls*. Then he seems to wrap up by declaring that this program is designed to push boundaries, and give theater new life, and cultivate the next generation of Broadway actors, which is fantastic because I'm *great* at pushing boundaries (I mean, I played the lead role of Bobby in a gender-bent version of *Company* in ninth grade and I am *not* afraid to don a lacy corset and stilettos when the role requires it), and obviously, I belong on Broadway. Even my high school theater director wrote that in my Lucius Brown recommendation.

But just when I think he's finished, he starts running through a list of every Broadway composer he's ever met (yes, it's *so* cool that he got coffee with Lin Manuel Miranda that one time), and I swear it's never going to end, when finally, FINALLY, he says, "Now, I know that you're all wondering what the musical is this summer."

Hot Stranger and I both lean forward. Valerie is biting her nails. Abel Pearce smiles slowly like he's a villain in a superhero movie confessing a series of devastating murders.

"Well, instead of telling you, I thought I'd *play* it for you."

He pulls his phone out of his pocket, makes a show of scrolling through it, and then holds it up to the podium microphone. A brassy chorus erupts from the mic, followed by some extraordinary belting from what sounds like Sutton Foster, although I can't be sure. The room is erupting. The girls in front of me whip their hair so violently, their strands nearly slap me in the face. Valerie screams with them while Hot Stranger flops his arms over the back of his chair and starts humming along to the music. Meanwhile, I'm just sitting here still trying to figure out what the heck this show is. The music sounds familiar, like something I heard once when I was six and still sampling Broadway songs on my brother's old iPhone.

Abel Pearce clears his throat once more and the room quiets.

"Welcome to 1922!" he bellows. "If you didn't know from the music, this summer's production is the one and only *Thoroughly Modern Millie*."

Valerie jumps up to her feet like Abel Pearce is Beyoncé and she's a single lady. The girls with the long hair are back on their very dangerous whipping train, forcing me to drop to my knees. While I'm ducking, I taste the words on my tongue. *Thoroughly Modern Millie.* Of course it's that musical with Julie Andrews from the 1960s. I don't know too much about it except that it's supposed to be a comedy—which isn't really my thing unless Abel Pearce revamps it to be something raw and wonderful like the 2019 Broadway revival of *Oklahoma!* Which, you know, he probably will. After all, just minutes ago, he announced his first goal was to *push boundaries.*

And besides, I can tell from the music that there's a good deal of tap dancing and belting—both of which I'd consider my strong suits. I stare at the dried gum speckling the backs of the hair-whip girls' seats. In my head, I'm already donning berry lipstick, a red flapper dress, and silky finger waves, curtsying to a standing ovation. The audience will yell *Encore!* and I'll say *No, really? Well, if you insist* before belting a rendition of whatever the heck these girls in front of me keep scream-singing. The *New York Times* arts critics will be like, *Even though it's not on Broadway, we just couldn't pass up a chance to review this standout cast featuring a very talented Miss Everett Hoang!*

I press my fingers against the smeared *o* on my name tag and try not to hit my head on the wooden seat. Millie, whoever you are, I'm coming for you.

# 5
# Jia

Everett has texted us more times than I can count. My phone blinks with emojis, details about some show I've never heard of, and a boy that Everett unsurprisingly thinks is Hercules sent from Olympus. I smile down at her series of messages—the way they seem to flood our kitchen with joy. They stand in stark contrast to CeCe's math workbooks, which bury the kitchen table, smudgy handprints the only sign she's written anything in the past few hours. At least she's good at origami. While I'm hunched over *her* workbooks, CeCe is curled up on a folding chair, making paper birds out of scraps she's supposed to use to practice addition and subtraction.

I let out of a big gust of air and watch my bangs flutter against my forehead. I can't believe Mom and Dad are making me teach CeCe math this summer, like my meager brain cells are suddenly going to transform her into a genius. They'll never admit it, but I know they're hoping she's their second chance, their protégé—the one who will make our ancestors proud with a Harvard degree and a fancy job at Google.

I lay my chin on the table. Ariel should be the one teaching CeCe, not me. I glance back at my phone. She hasn't answered any of our texts—besides her arrival message and that lone email, she's lost to the Silicon Valley Crocs and Einsteins. I never know what she's thinking when she goes radio silent. Maybe she's zipping around Victorian townhouses in trolley cars, too busy feeling alive to answer us. Or maybe she's in her basement of Bea, a steel cage she'll never reveal. I text Everett.

Anything from A?

Everett is typing the second I press send:

Nope.

Mom says I should let Ariel be, that there's no point in talking about Bea anyway, that the dead need to rest. Once you've bowed your head and burned the incense, the grief locks inside the coffin, shrouded underneath new grass and fertile soil. But I don't think Ariel has any grass at all.

"Jie Jie, look!"

CeCe peeks up at me with chocolate doe eyes, her origami bird pressed to her lips. She plunges it in the air.

"We're flying!"

I sigh. She can't do math to save her life, but she really *is* excellent at folding paper.

I get up from the table and scoop her into my arms, twirling her in circles around the kitchen, following the path of her bird. She's getting too big for this. Still, I love watching her belly-laugh as we dip over the ceramic tiles and career into the living room. I set her down on the carpet and she rolls around, hiccupping through giggles.

"Ai ya, what are you doing?"

I look up to find Mom scowling as she tries to jam the front door shut. She's in her good sweater and pin curls, sleeves scrunched up to her elbows. Sesame oil and soy sauce waft through the doorway and curve around the thin apartment walls.

My mother sets her purse on the table and crosses her arms.

"This does not look like math."

CeCe bites her lip and clumsily crawls back into the kitchen, trying to hide under the chairs.

"I see you."

My sister snatches her paper bird and giggles. Mom clucks her tongue, pattering to the living room. Her skirt is wrinkled, her hair now wilted and loose. Despite her efforts, the front door stretches its limbs and yawns, revealing a stained carpet hallway and patchy brown walls. Downstairs, Dad barks orders and crunches numbers even though the lunch crowd is long gone and the dinner rush has not yet arrived. Now only the old Chinese men stay sunken in booths, spooning liquor into their tea, watching their wives scribble on crossword puzzles and collect orange peels. Dad will never make them leave. *The fabric of home*, he tells me.

Mom props her feet up on the coffee table. CeCe scurries out from under the chairs and nestles beneath her arm. My mother can pretend she's mad, but she holds my sister close and kisses the top of her head.

"Where's Nai Nai?" she asks.

"Taking a nap."

It's where she is most days, huddled in her and CeCe's bedroom with the curtains drawn, walker pushed against the nightstand. She's lived with us since the beginning of summer—when the Parkinson's disease got bad and Dad insisted a Chinatown studio was no longer safe for his mother. Mom and Dad and I all take turns caring for her: spooning egg drop soup between her lips and ferrying her to the toilet and bath every few hours. Usually, Dad tries to be Nai Nai's primary caretaker, but since her medical bills are high and the waiters need raises, he spends every waking moment in the restaurant, turning the register inside out, counting every dollar.

Mom switches on the television and flips to the only cable news station in Mandarin. I try to quietly slip my sketchbook and pencils out from their hiding places on the bookshelf. My mother hears me anyway.

"Go," she says, still staring at the television, CeCe now asleep in her lap.

"Seriously?"

"Be back before dinner."

I jam my pencils in my shorts pocket and jet out of there before she can change her mind.

The sun is buttery gold by the time I unlock my bike and roll down Forty-First Avenue. Cars zip past, and an old lady in a hot pink puffer jacket skitters out of my way when I skim the edge of the sidewalk. I brake at the Unisphere and park myself on the benches circling the metal sculpture. Here, the pigeons reign, pecking at my feet while skateboarders roll past. I grab my sketchbook from the bike basket and open to my half-finished sketch of Itachi Uchiha. He's my favorite character in *Naruto*. While I've nailed his scowl, I'm having a harder time with his deep-set ruby eyes and long choppy hair. I want to get it just right. I want to show how complex a villain he is, how his poor decisions are only a product of his desperation to protect his village. After I shape his hair, I start in on his irises—tortured, stoic.

"Hey!"

I jump up, shoulders punching my ears, sketchbook flying across the gravel. Strange hands reach out to grab my drawings. I connect the hands to the arms, and the arms to the body, and the body to the face. Akil. Staring at me. Holding my sketchbook.

"Crap," he says, "I'm so sorry. I didn't mean to scare you. I was just, uh, exploring the neighborhood."

I smooth down my shirt and try to avert my gaze from the sweat dribbling down his neck. "Oh," I say, "I mean, it's fine. Did you, um, run here?"

Akil wipes off his upper lip with his shirt. "No," he laughs, "I do this thing called urban hiking."

"Urban hiking?"

"Yeah, it's like regular hiking but, like, in a city."

"Isn't that just . . . walking?"

He shakes his head, mussing his curls. "You walk faster than regular walking. It's hard to explain. I do it when I'm anxious. My mom says endorphins are good for anxiety. Got to let it all out, you know?" I can see the blush creeping up his neck. "Sorry, I don't know why I'm telling you all this."

"No, it's okay." I eye my sketchbook wrapped between his hands as he swings his leg over my bike to sit beside me on the bench. Together, we're two dots under a giant metal world.

His knee trembles, his foot vibrating against the concrete. I open my mouth to say something but I can't seem to find the words. It doesn't matter though, because Akil is examining my sketchbook, his nose inches from Itachi Uchiha's incomplete eyes.

"Whoa, this is cool." He cocks his head to the side. "Really different."

My face flushes. "It's anime."

"Anime?"

"Yeah, like, uh, cartoon characters. But not, you know, cartoons for *children*. The character is based off a Japanese TV series I really like. It's not a big deal."

"Well," he declares, gingerly pressing the sketchbook back into my palms, "it's awesome."

"Thanks."

He grins and I can't help but grin back.

"So," I say, trying to choose my words carefully, "why do you feel anxious? I mean, you don't have to talk about it. Only if you want to."

Akil shrugs. "You know, the usual. New neighborhood. New school. I goofed off a lot in Chicago, and my parents didn't like it too much. They keep saying I have to *behave* here. I dunno. They think I'm weird."

"You seem totally normal to me."

"Why thank you," he replies, folding over to bow deeply. He forgets he's sitting and almost topples to the ground.

"Okay," I laugh, "maybe not *totally* normal."

Akil sits back up and makes a show of straightening out his shirt. The sun's midafternoon glow turns hazy, muted amber enveloping my skin. I never talk to boys. But perched under the Unisphere with Akil and the pigeons feels easy, feels right.

"What school are you going to?"

Akil scrunches his nose. "A place called Farrow Academy? Ever heard of it?"

My stomach sinks. Of course I have. Last October comes rushing back in a stream of shame—the girls with their acrylic nails, their lip-gloss smirks, my best friend pushing them out the restaurant door. "Yeah," I say, "Everett goes there."

Akil doesn't miss the falter in my voice. "Is it weird? Terrible? Is everyone super mean? 'Cause I had, like, a bad feeling but my parents saw the ranking and *insisted*—" He pauses. "Sorry, I'm talking too much again."

"No." I plaster on an encouraging smile. "It's great. And Everett will be there, so you'll already have a built-in friend."

Akil narrows his eyes but he doesn't question me further. "All right," he says, "if you say so."

I am desperate to change the subject. So we talk about his friends from Chicago and the pranks they used to play on their teachers. I tell him about all the hidden art buried in New York City's corners and alleys—street-corner manga, under-the-bridge graffiti, and even the little doodles people leave on subway car walls. He tells me that his family moved here because his mom is now chief of surgery at NewYork-Presbyterian Queens. I imagine her face on one of those banners they blanket the hospital with: her pearly white smile and heavy lab coat, metal scalpel in hand. When he asks what my parents do, I say *business*, and try not to think about the Farrow girls with their chiffon blouses and Gucci backpacks. I wonder if Akil can smell the cooking grease permanently plastered to my clothes.

He talks about what he wants to be when he grows up. He thinks English teacher, or historian, or politician—but not one of those slimy ones. When he asks what I want to be, I tell him *I'm not sure* even though swimming pools of hoisin sauce and fryer oil flood my mind.

Soon, the sky turns rusty pink, and the pigeons start to splinter off, searching for shelter.

"I should probably get home," I say, standing up and nudging the kickstand with my sneaker.

"Yeah, me too. Can't be late for dinner or the boss will kill me."

"Your parents?"

"No," he says, "Masud."

I crack a smile. "Ah, of course."

I put my sketchbook in the bicycle's basket and plant a foot on the pedal. My ribs ache from laughter and too much talking.

Akil curls his fingers around my handlebars. "Wait. We should exchange numbers. In case, you know . . . you want to go urban hiking."

He bites his lip, eyebrows crinkled. In my head, Everett is doing that wriggly victory dance she always does when she knows she's right. *Maybe your summer won't be so bad after all.* Maybe. Or maybe this is just a glitch in an otherwise completely boring June.

Still, I take out my phone and offer it to him. Akil punches in numbers and returns it to me. "Awesome. I'll see you around, Jia."

"See you."

As I bike away, the world seems to turn faster and faster. I know he's headed in the opposite direction, toward an ivy-tendril home, surgeon parents, and girls who have perfect nails and the right designer bags. I know where I'm headed, too.

I stuff my phone in my pocket and don't dare look back.

## WORLDGAB GROUP CHAT

**Ariel:** Hey

**Everett:** Oh my god. She speaks!!!

**Ariel:** It's only been like, three days

**Everett:** Yeah but did you hear that I saw THE HOTTEST GUY EVER

**Ariel:** Is he really the hottest guy alive or does he just look like Harry Styles

**Everett:** WOW BURN

**Jia:** Ariel! Hi! We were worried about you

**Ariel:** You guys are like my mom 😉

**Everett:** Ya ya ya anyway tell us about California

**Ariel:** It's fine

**Everett:** Just *fine*? How are your classes? Have you cured cancer yet??

**Ariel:** It's a science and technology program, not med school, E. And besides, you know I only really like psych

**Everett:** Well you could cure someone's BRAIN

**Jia:** Yes! The best future psychiatrist in all the land!

**Ariel:** Ha, no. Anyway, enough about me. I want to hear about you. Other than hottest guy alive, how's camp, E?

**Everett:** Awesome! I love it

**Jia:** That's great! Thoroughly Modern Millie, right?? Is that a good musical

**Everett:** I think so! The music seems good! The plot is a lil weird tho but it's okay, I'm sure they'll adapt it. That's what Farrow did when we put on Carousel sophomore year

**Jia:** Weird how?

**Ariel:** Too many jazz hands

**Everett:** You suck

**Ariel:** You're so great at jazz hands tho 😊

**Everett:** Oh I'm gonna blow that audition AWAY

**Jia:** Yes girl you'll kill it!!! When is it

**Everett:** Not for a week

**Ariel:** Well keep us posted 🙂

**Everett:** Ofc!!! I haveto go coz I have tap class now, but I'll text you after! And Ariel you are required to answer our messages more often plz and thank u!!!

**Ariel:** I will, I will. Love you too

**Jia:** Sending so many virtual hugs, xo

# 6
# Ariel

When Umma and Appa video-chat me for the fifth time, I know I have to answer. It's been five days since I started the precollege program. I've gotten away with texting them delicately crafted phrases every day like "Things are great!" and "So busy! STEM mixer." But Umma won't let me disappear for too long. I can't end up like Bea.

I press the Accept button. Suddenly, there they are: wide noses pressed to the camera, slivers of our living room in the background. I know this house well. I don't have to see it. The couch. The money tree. And on the windowsill, a framed photo of our whole family—me, Bea, Umma, and Appa. We're on a vacation in the Bahamas. Umma is wearing a floppy straw hat to shield her porcelain skin from the sun. Bea has on a bikini. Her mouth is open in mid-laughter. When she died, Appa hid the photo behind the curtain so he didn't have to look at it all the time.

Now they wave wildly, like they are a cruise ship and I am the land they long to reach. They are too happy. They are on Disneyland drugs.

"Ariel! You finally picked up!"

Appa pushes his glasses up his nose so he can get a better look at me. Umma is inspecting the dorm room behind my head. I force a smile.

"Hi, Umma, Appa, I miss you."

"We miss you too," Appa says.

Umma starts in on her twenty questions: How are your classes? How's San Francisco? Have you made any friends? Do you have enough to eat? How is the dining hall food? Should we ship you some SPAM from Queens?

I answer her like a good girl. I am obedient. I am great. Everything is dandy. The food is tasty and the classes are interesting; I am so lucky to be at this school. I am grateful.

They are pleased with my answers. Umma moves on to their life in Queens—how things are going at the bank, how Appa stepped in dog poop and it took her forever to clean it off, and how Charlotte Ajumma never sent us a thank-you note for the birthday pears we mailed her, isn't that rude? I tell her: Yes, that is so rude. Wow. Dad says: Charlotte Ajumma is going senile. Cut her a break.

Umma insists on a room tour and then wants to know why I haven't decorated at all. She says that it looks like a bomb shelter. When I start school for real in August, she will come down and make it homey and nice so all the girls will want to paint their nails in my room. I do not want to paint my nails with Briston girls. I want to eat dumplings with Everett and Jia and rewatch *Little Women* and laugh when Everett ad-libs over Teddy's proposal to Jo. I want to cuddle under blankets and listen to my breath, and not have to speak at all.

Finally, I tell Umma and Appa that I have class, which is actually true. I have Developmental Psychology in five minutes.

"I love you," I say.

Umma hugs herself around the chest. "Hug through the phone."

For a second, I choke up. But it's just a reflex. I can make this go away. I end the call.

Class is on the other side of campus, so I swing my backpack over my shoulder and run down the stairs. The buildings are still gray and the weather is still cold, but if you stand on top of the hill, you can see the cable car wires and pastel townhouses. If you squint, you can make out the Golden Gate Bridge. On the second day of orientation, the resident assistants took a bunch of students to see it. Apparently, it was so windy that three girls lost their scarves to the ocean, but no one seemed to mind because they got good pictures for Instagram. I didn't go. Instead I put on two sweatshirts and sprawled out on the Great Lawn. I spent hours staring at the palm trees and wondering how they survive this weather.

It seems like I made a mistake. The Golden Gate Bridge excursion was a pivotal moment in summer clique formation. When I reach the auditorium, the lost scarf girls are canoodling in the corner. The Ultimate Frisbee bros take up the entire back row. The ultra-nerds—the ones who are more excited about science than humanly possible—are jammed in the front row. It's been less than a week and I am already alone at sea. My phone pings. Jia's sent a photo of her sister with marker all over her face. I smile just a little. After class, I will be a good friend. I will text her back.

I settle into an end seat. The psychology professor is a seventy-five-year-old lady with white hair tied in two Princess Leia buns. She has a very pointy noise and excellent posture. She looks like someone who sleeps on a board at night and heats her house with kettles of hot water.

Professor Leia Buns dims the lights and we settle in for a forty-five-minute lecture about Erik Erikson's stages of psychological development. I already know these from last summer when Jia, Everett, and I trekked all the way to Roosevelt Island and picnicked behind the smallpox hospital ruins. Everett thought they were creepy and Jia was too busy trying to find the cat sanctuary. But I marveled at the carved-out windows and looming stone walls. The way they seemed caught in a different time. We spent hours on the island that day. Jia drew anime. Everett read Stephen Sondheim's autobiography. They both teased me when I cracked open *Childhood Disrupted*. It used to be my favorite book. If I close my eyes, I can remember that entire summer. Every detail I washed down with bubble tea and New York rain. My world before the accident.

Erik Erikson's eight stages of development:

1. *Infancy: the baby must learn to trust their mother.*
2. *Early childhood: the toddler starts to gain basic control of their environment.*
3. *Preschool: the child finds purpose.*
4. *School age: the child develops social, physical, and academic skills.*

Professor Leia Buns says, "Stage five. Adolescence: the teenager transitions from childhood to adulthood. They develop a sense of identity."

The image on the screen is of a cartoon baby becoming larger and larger until they are a teenager with a ginormous face. I try to focus on the weird morphing baby but when I blink, there's a different person in front of me. Bea. Seven-year-old Bea insisting bunny loops are the best and only way to tie your shoes. Her death-defying performance at the middle school talent show, screaming Avril Lavigne's "Sk8r Boi" while I hid under my sweatshirt in embarrassment. That time she dyed a strip of her hair neon blue in the bathroom, and then panicked and dunked her head in the sink. When Bea's teacher called to tell Umma and Appa she was failing calculus and she'd have to go to summer school or not graduate. The night I tried to tutor her, but didn't understand why she didn't understand, and she stormed out of the house. Our parents screaming at Bea in the kitchen as I dutifully finished my English essay upstairs. Telling everyone at school that my sister was "studying abroad" when Bea had disappeared to Imo's house in Busan. Bea video-chatting me the day before Chuseok, insisting she couldn't come home, not with Umma and Appa still clucking their tongues and clipping their words every time she called.

Professor Leia Buns flips to the next slide. The Ultimate Frisbee bros snort at the stock photo of an emo sixteen-year-old fake scowling at the camera.

"Adolescence is characterized by risk-taking behaviors," Professor Leia Buns says. "Failure to take dangers seriously. This is a result of immaturity in the prefrontal cortex." She shakes a finger at us. "At your age, your brain still has a lot of growing to do."

I look down at my empty notebook. When we got the call, I could not imagine Bea in that glass water, hand reaching for the sky. I could not picture her at all. I could only think of the pontoon flipped on its belly like a beached whale. Faceless friends with salty knees scattered on the sand.

Umma and Appa flew to Busan and stayed there for two weeks. They came back with a dead body and no answers. All they said was *Bea had a boating accident. She was being reckless. We should have never let her go.* Then we buried her. Umma slept until she had to go back to work. Appa said *Thank you very much* when all the church ajummas cried about how terrible they felt and then whispered about the scandal behind his back. So I learned about my sister's death from the Korean news, and from Imo, who knew as much as the articles did. I tried to reach out to Bea's friends but couldn't find their numbers. And none of them called. Not a one.

Before I know it, the lights come up. Professor Leia Buns says we have an exam next week, but we shouldn't worry about it too much and enjoy our weekend. This Saturday there's a trip to

Fisherman's Wharf, where you can watch all the seals sleep on the docks and get their summer tans. Afterward, one of the scarf girls is throwing a party in her suite. She put an invite on the group chat, which technically means I'm invited and should go. *Make friends. Ace your classes. We are so proud of you.* If Bea were here, she'd wear a strappy black top and boyfriend jeans. She'd chat up the scarf girls, and the Ultimate Frisbee bros, and the ultra-nerds. She'd tell the story about the time she farted and accidentally crapped her pants during benediction and had to subsequently go pantyless for church lunch. Everyone would laugh. Everyone would love her.

From: jialee@leedumplinghouse.com

To: arielunderthesea_29@gmail.com; everetthoang24601@gmail.com

12:24 PM

Subject: Your bestie misses you

Everett and Ariel,

I can't believe it's been a week since you both ditched me! I hope it was worth it. Just kidding—you know I'm so proud of you both. I have already bragged to everyone at the restaurant wondering where you are. I'm like, haven't you heard about my brilliant friends? You're practically famous.

Nothing much is happening at home. The dumpling house is super busy so I'm either there or with Nai Nai and CeCe. CeCe is bored out of her mind and therefore peak annoying, so I took her and Nai Nai to the zoo yesterday. My sister's new obsession is sea lions. We legitimately spent 45 minutes staring at them. She named every single one. Now she thinks that we can convince Mom and Dad to get us a sea lion as a pet. She says we can blow up the kiddie pool and put it in the living room and the sea lion will live there. Even Nai Nai laughed at that one. Personally, I'm partial to the cows. They're fluffier.

Literally nothing else interesting to report back. Oh, well, I ran into Everett's neighbor, Akil, at the park. Contrary to what Everett says, I am not "900% in love with him." I'm not even 1% in love with him. He is just nice to look at, that's all. We talked about art.

I miss you both and hope you have wild tales to tell me. I wait with bated breath . . .

xx,
Jia

# 7
# Everett

"Ev, you ready?"

When you want to have a good time in the city, you sneak into Dizzy Cat, the only bar in Queens that lets in teenagers (though they won't let you drink), and tell your parents you're at a sleepover. Or you take the 7 to Manhattan and listen to the train rattle across the bridge as you hug your oversized wool coat around your shoulders and pretend you're in *Gossip Girl*. When you want to have a good time in Ohio? You trek through acres of corn and try to remember your Girl Scout training.

Valerie is not even batting an eye. Which is impressive considering her false eyelashes shoot up to her eyebrows. I'm still sitting on the dorm bed, scrolling through Jia's email. *Nothing to report back? I call bullshit.* I'll have to interrogate her later though, 'cause Valerie is waving her patent leather purse in my face.

"Earth to Evvvvvvv."

No one calls me Ev except my brothers, and Ariel and Jia, but I think Valerie means it in like a "we know each other so well, we have nicknames for each other," way, so I'll take it as a compliment. I put my phone in my pocket and smooth out my lacy crop top—the one that's just a *little* bit see-through.

"I'm ready."

I was not kidding about the corn trek. It's like two miles long, and we're in heels. We should have left earlier so we could have gone with the group, but I had to FaceTime my brother, Sean, while he was making some bet about a yacht, and Valerie spent like ninety-five minutes in the bathroom.

The corn reaches the top of our heads. The whole way there, we pretend we're Dorothy and Toto (I'm Dorothy, she's Toto, duh) on the yellow brick road and sing through the entire soundtrack. Valerie is a very whiny Toto though, because she's upset that there won't be alcohol at this party. I mean, it's a camp-sponsored "mixer," which is just another word for a very safe, adult-supervised event in which no one will get their stomach pumped or get pregnant, lest you die at the hands of the Ohio theater gods. I'm not mad. Even though we could theoretically sneak liquor into Dizzy Cat, Jia is perpetually worried she'll die of alcohol poisoning and Ariel is way more interested in the pool table. Me? I come for the jazz, the cabaret, and the dancing. I don't think there will be any saxophones at *this* party.

When we finally arrive, Valerie heads over to Sofia and Rae, the infamous hair-whip girls. She gestures for me to follow her, but I trail behind. I'm here to scope out the situation. In the middle is

the bonfire and the s'mores table, which I'd totally be down for if
there weren't a Times Square–worthy crowd gathered around it.
Also, I'd like to point out that there's no ice cream here, and there
should be. In this humidity? Cookies 'n' cream in a waffle cone is
a necessity.

The karaoke kings are by the speakers, also known as Ariel's least
favorite kind of people, and honestly mine too. They literally cannot stop singing show tunes. In harmony. Don't get me wrong, I
love musical theater, but it is *a lot*. The counselors are in the far-left
corner, hiding behind the bushes and probably dishing out college
gossip. I'm sure their drama is *way* more interesting than ours, but
I don't think I'd be welcome in their little counselor circle.

That's when I spot him. Hot Stranger. By the ice bucket. I've
been holed up in the practice rooms for days, and we don't have any
scene study or dance classes together, so this is the first time I've
seen him since orientation. He's just as hot as I remember. Surfer
waves. Breezy T-shirt. Dimples ten out of ten. It looks like he's just
finishing up a conversation, so now's my shot. *Time to roll your dice,
Everett.*

I dot rollerball perfume on my wrists and try to casually circle
the ice bucket. I have the urge to make a joke about water, which
is terrible and cheesy as hell, so I don't say anything. Instead I just
smile.

"Hey."

Hot Stranger looks up from his cider and smirks. He points to
the clearing of corn I just came from. "I saw you over there giving
everyone a once-over. Are you secretly a talent scout?"

I take a tiny step closer. *All right, Dimples. Game on.*

"Only the best. But I'm not so impressed by this corner."

He gasps in fake shock. "Really? Should I tap for you? Rap? Belt 'Giants in the Sky' at the top of my lungs?"

"Definitely belt 'Giants in the Sky.' Give the karaoke kings a run for their money." I nudge my head toward the group, who've moved on to "Mamma Mia."

Hot Stranger shakes his head. "Yikes, I think I'm out."

"Damn. So much lost potential."

"I'll have to win you over next time."

I shift in my heels and try not to grin too hard. "I'm Everett."

"Cheney."

He awkwardly shakes my hand like we're at an interview, and we both laugh.

He's definitely my type, and judging by the way he's lowered his cider and is looking me up and down, I think I'm his, too. Even Ariel would be impressed.

"So where are you from, Everett?"

"New York City. You?"

"Maryland." He tilts his head. "Where were you from before that?"

"Oh, I've lived in Queens my entire life. A New Yorker through and through." I toss my braids behind my shoulder, showcasing the teeny-tiny spaghetti straps clinging to my top.

"Nice, but I mean where are you *from* from? Like, your parents. Your grandparents. Your family."

Why does it matter where my grandparents live? They're both

dead, and when they were alive, we barely talked because they
didn't speak English and were always chastising my parents for
making my brothers and me too *Western*. But Cheney is clearly on
the Everett train, and God, he's even cuter up close, so I swallow
my thoughts.

"My parents are also from the city. My grandparents immi-
grated from Hanoi."

Cheney fist-pumps the air. "Ah, I knew it!" He beams. "You'd
make a great Kim in *Miss Saigon*."

He says it so fervently, I actually believe him, even though he's
never heard me sing or dance. Kim *is* the lead role and an objec-
tively great part. She has some fantastic solos. But she's kind of a
problematic character. The whole play basically exoticizes Vietnamese women and the entire Vietnam War. I pick at my nail
polish. Maybe Cheney's never met anyone Vietnamese before. I
mean, I've never really met anyone from Maryland. The closest I
got was that time my high school friends and I went to the cherry
blossom festival in D.C. and Madison flirted with someone from
Silver Spring. Maryland is probably, like, an endless row of boring
suburban houses and cutesy main streets.

"Who'd make a great Kim?" Valerie asks.

Sofia and Rae squeeze in so we're shoulder to shoulder.

"Everett," Cheney says. "Don't you think?"

"Definitely," Valerie replies. "I'd love to be Ellen in that show,
but my voice is too high."

"Ooh, have you ever done *Little Shop* though, Val? I could
totally see you as Audrey."

The girls start naming off their dream roles and even Cheney is drowned out by their tittering. He rolls his eyes at me, as if we're in on a secret. Once again, I'm beaming like a fool.

The conversation turns to *Thoroughly Modern Millie*. Sofia and Rae talk about the tap numbers and Valerie gushes about the great female roles in the show. We dance around the fact that we all want to be Millie. The chorus girls don't hold a candle to the lead.

"I'll save Millie for the rest of you," Sofia says, finally addressing the elephant in the room. "I'm going for Mrs. Meers."

"Ooh," Valerie replies, the relief palpable in her voice, "you'd be perfect for that role. I can totally see you rocking a kimono."

"A kimono?" I ask. "Why would she be wearing a kimono?"

Sofia sighs, the macaroon cream ruffles on her blouse flopping in the breeze. "Because she's pretending to be Asian. You've read the summary, right?"

Of course I've read the summary. I've done so much research, I could name every part down to the last Hotel Priscilla girl (Ethel, to be exact). But Mrs. Meers is pretending to be *Chinese*, and Chinese people don't wear kimonos. In fact, that whole role still doesn't make sense to me. From what I understand, she's the show's antagonist, who pretends to be an old Chinese lady running an all-female boarding house. But then—surprise, surprise—she actually reveals herself to be a white lady luring girls in so she can sell them into sex slavery. It's a musical from 2002 but I don't think it's been updated since the movie it was based on came out in 1967.

The hair-whip girls have moved on to gossiping about the worst singers in the camp, but I can't seem to shake Mrs. Meers from my head.

"She's kind of a weird villain," I say. "Mrs. Meers, I mean. She speaks in a fake Chinese accent and basically runs a white slavery ring."

Valerie pauses midsentence, her pink lips frozen into a tiny O. "It's a joke," she replies, "and besides, it takes place in the roaring twenties, so it just fits with the time."

In the 1920s, white ladies pretended to be Chinese ladies and started a human trafficking campaign to smuggle American girls into "the Orient"? Did I miss a crucial part of U.S. history?

I press harder. "But it's the twenty-first century," I say, remembering Abel Pearce's orientation speech about *pushing boundaries* and *giving theater new life*. "I bet Abel will update the script."

"Sure." Valerie shrugs.

The girls go back to ranking the worst singers in the camp (none of *us*, obviously), and Cheney adds that doe-eyed Annalise Dewan can't hold a note—there's a rumor going around that she got in because her cousin is Timothée Chalamet.

I think back to Abel's booming voice over the podium microphone, his declarations about modernizing theater, the sleek Lucius Brown website with its cursive slogan: *Today in Ohio, tomorrow on Broadway.* He must have chosen this musical for a reason. There hasn't been a revival on Broadway since it premiered in 2002—maybe *this* is the start of a new era of *Thoroughly Modern Millie.* Maybe he looked at Mrs. Meers, at Millie, at the talent he's fused together in these Ohio cornfields, and thought, *We can inspire the next generation. We can bring new life to the 1920s.* He probably has a bunch of producer friends who will come to the show, be blown away by its fresh take, and give at least a few of us our equity cards.

I should review my notes tonight and talk through ideas with Abel the next time I run into him. After all, I'm a pro at this—my high school, Farrow, is no stranger to modernizing old shows. Now I can use my talents for a bigger stage. Just like I promised Jia before I left for camp. Just like I promised myself.

The bonfire crackles, jolting me back to reality. Cheney's sleeve brushes against the goosebumps prickling my arms. The bugs are blessedly not nipping at my skin, and the flames from the fire seem to dress us in gold. It's a perfect night.

From: arielunderthesea_29@gmail.com

To: jialee@leedumplinghouse.com; everetthoang24601@gmail.com

1:53 AM

[No Subject]

J and E,

I'm not going to send this. I don't want you to worry. Also, I know I haven't answered any of your messages this week so you're probably annoyed at me anyway.

Theoretically, Briston is great. There are palm trees and oceans and parties. All the students are California chill. And friendly. A couple of girls tried to talk to me in the dining hall yesterday. But I hate it. I hate all of it. Every time I look up at the giant Briston banners, I want to vomit. Sometimes, I pick up my phone to tell you how I'm feeling. But you guys are so excited about theater and crushes and the city and I want to be excited for you. I really do. So I don't say anything. I don't want to bring you down.

Sometimes I wonder how Bee would fit in here. She'd be a lot better at this than me. She'd make a crap-ton of friends. Remember that time she was voted prom queen even though she basically missed half the school year? And then she let us try on her sash and crown afterward? You looked fantastic, Everett, wearing that plastic diamond tiara. And Jia, you were so worried you were going to rip her sash. As if Bea cared. She loved when you tried on her stuff. It made her feel wanted.

I heard they don't do prom court anymore at Queens Academy. Guess they lived and died with Bee. Just as well.

Ariel

# 8
# Ariel

I delete the email. I'm sweating. The clock on my phone blinks two a.m. Fifty-three unread messages from Everett and Jia. **Did you go MIA again? Ariel? Did you meet someone and fall in love and start a new life? Ha ha ha. Seriously, hello?** I turn off my notifications.

Night sweats are usually caused by hormonal changes. Menopause. Low blood sugar. An overactive thyroid. Overheating. Worst-case scenario: Leukemia. Lymphoma. I know I don't have any of these. My room is as cold as the biting night air. Still, liquid drips from my neck and curves down my spine.

When we were little, Bea and I used to share a room. We had bunk beds—her on the top, me on the bottom. Bee always conked out on the couch after marathoning *Avatar: The Last Airbender.* Our Appa used to scoop her up in a blanket and wrap her in a cocoon. He'd climb all the way up the ladder and place her on the bunk bed. She never stirred. In fact, she was quite the snorer. She constantly woke me up in the middle of the night. Once, she was so loud, I thought there was a dog barking outside our window. But no, it was just Bea, rambunctious even in sleep. Sometimes I would just lie there and listen to her. Feel her breath above me. When Bee was asleep, it felt like we switched roles. She was the baby sister and I was the older sibling. I was the protector.

If Bea were here, she'd say I never protected her. When I was twelve and she was fifteen, we moved to a bigger house. We had separate rooms. Separate lives. She drowned in hers. I polished trophies in mine.

I check my pulse. One hundred and twelve beats per minute. I could call Umma and Appa but then they would think that something was wrong with me. They'd make me video-chat Pastor Kwan. Pastor Kwan is just a middle-aged Korean guy with an undercut, but my parents think he's direct access to God. The day after Bea's death, he came to our house and recited, "'He will wipe away every tear from their eyes, and death shall be no more, neither shall there be mourning, nor crying, nor pain anymore, for the former things have passed away.'" Umma looked up at him in awe like he hadn't just said the most clichéd Bible verse in history. The circles under my eyes were blue and purple. My mother said, "See Ari-ya, you shouldn't cry so much. You'd make your sister unhappy."

I could video-chat Everett and Jia. But then I'd have to explain too much. I couldn't even send them my email.

So I do what I always say I won't do.

When Imo picks up, she groans.

"Ariel, shouldn't you be asleep?"

"Yes."

She inspects my face in the darkness. Behind her is a cloud of fuzzy light. It's six p.m. in Busan, South Korea. Golden hour.

"I couldn't sleep."

"I can see that."

"Please just show me."

Imo shakes her head. She looks just like Umma when she does that. Red lipstick, pinched cheeks, crinkled forehead. But that's where the similarities end. Imo and Umma may be sisters, but they are nothing alike.

"Okay," she relents. She wraps her shawl around her shoulders. "Only because I love you, Ariel."

She traipses out to the living room. The video shakes as she jiggles the balcony door and slides it open.

I get a shot of her feet on the stone. She walks out farther, her phone inches from the railing. She pulls the camera up and there it is.

The ocean.

The sea where Bea swam. The water she died in.

I inhale with the waves flooding the shore. They are easy. They are mine. I can feel my heartbeat slowing. Bea may be in Queens underground, but for now, she is here. We are little girls again, on this shore together. Just for a moment.

# 9
# Everett

"I'm going to murder her."

Jia sighs from the other side of my phone screen, blinking away early-morning dust and New York smog.

"It's only been ten days. Ariel's probably busy with classes. And anyway, you can't murder her if she doesn't answer the phone."

"*Eleven* days," I correct her. "And not true. I could fly to California, demand that she check her messages, and *then* murder her."

I set Jia down on the hallway radiator and bend down to rebuckle my character shoes. Everyone else at Lucius Brown is headed to lunch after a very sweaty, very grueling dance class, but not me. I have important things to do.

1. *Find Ariel and tell her to answer her flipping texts.*
2. *Ambush Abel Pearce in whatever office he's hiding out in.*
3. *Force the karaoke kings to stop hogging the practice rooms so I can rehearse my thirty-two bars for next week's audition.*

My buckle gets caught on my sock, and a sweat stain on my wrap sweater pools into my leggings. Okay, perhaps number one should be "Get my shit together."

"Ev," Jia's voice rings out. "You all right?"

I grunt in response, pushing my buckle prong through the loop and tightening aggressively. How am I supposed to be *all right* when I don't know if Ariel's shacked up with some hot college guy or been eaten by a shark? Jia would say the latter is statistically unlikely, but what does she know? Bea drowned and no one expected that.

As if Jia can read my thoughts, she sits up and tucks her hair behind her ears. "We can't force Ariel to talk to us if she's not ready. It's a hard time of year for her."

"Every time is a hard time of year for her."

"Everett."

I wave a hand in Jia's face like I'm swatting a fly. "Yeah, yeah, I know."

She gives me one of those trademark therapist smiles. The kind she used when I got mad at Mrs. Callahan for casting me as Tree #3 in the fourth-grade play. And the look she mastered when I was about to kill Ariel for leaving my fifteenth birthday party early to work on her science research project (apparently she had to present it to a panel of judges the next day, but whatever). Jia is magical when it comes to calming me down and generally being right about things.

I stand up, the reject audition songs in my backpack rustling against my shoulders.

"I just want her to know that we're here for her. That we love her."

"She knows, Ev." Jia bites her lip. "She's basically a genius. I think she's aware that her best friends care about her."

I groan. The ironic part is that Ariel really *is* a genius. In tenth grade, she literally won the Future Genius award. The teachers created it especially for her after she ranked number one in every class from calculus to flag football (who knew she had such an arm? Like, that girl can do anything). At the award ceremony, Mr. and Mrs. Kim were in the front row, sitting so straight you'd think someone was holding a ruler to their backs. They took us out for hot pot afterward. Ariel was over the moon, guzzling down pork like she'd never eat again, her gold plaque gleaming on the seat beside her. Even Bea video-chatted from Busan for a few minutes, looking as stylish as ever, though no one seemed to care. Mrs. Kim was too busy reaching over the table to pat Ariel's hand, practically dipping her sleeve in soup oil. I didn't know it then, but that was the last time I'd see Bea before the accident. The last time I'd hear her voice. I should have spent more time with her, grilled her on Korean fashion designers, asked if she'd run into Hyun Bin yet. Instead, all I could think about was how my own mother would never risk an oil stain just to pat my hand. An affectionate gesture was certainly not worth the price of her Balenciaga blouse.

My heels click down the empty tiled hallway, aimless in their search for Abel Pearce. Last night, I reviewed everything I had learned about *Thoroughly Modern Millie*. I read more about Mrs. Meers, cringed at YouTube videos of high school kids doing fake

Chinese accents, rolled my eyes at her ridiculous henchmen. I brainstormed ways to make the show fresher, more interesting, less potentially problematic. I tried to memorize bullet points so I'd be prepared like Ariel before her debates.

I whirl my body this way and that, searching for my mysterious bearded director. Phone-Jia swings from wall to wall.

"I'm going to vomit if you keep doing that," she warns.

"Oh, sorry."

I pause, breathing in musty, post-sweat air and old leather.

"I should go then. If Ariel calls you first, promise you'll tell me right away, okay?"

"Of course," Jia says. "Don't worry."

We both know I'll worry anyway. I blow her kisses until she ends the call and zaps back to Queens.

Now it's just me in an eerily silent converted dance studio. Valerie and the hair-whip girls are probably out on the lawn, sunbathing and eating bad cafeteria pasta. I wonder what Cheney's up to. Maybe he's practicing his audition song or running that dance combo again. (It is hilarious how surprisingly bad he is at dancing. Guess theater guys aren't always triple threats.) Or maybe he's downstairs in a Terrapins jersey and basketball shorts just high enough so you can see his thigh muscles and glimpse the ripple of abs above his drawstring. *I was waiting for you*, he'll say. *Do you want to get out of here? And by out of here, I mean the post office or the only diner on Main Street?* And then of course I'll say yes, and he'll tell me that I'm a wonderful actress and that we'll *obviously* be cast as Millie and Jimmy because we're meant to be—

My fantasies are crushed by tufts of white hair flashing in the doorway window. Abel Pearce. I found him.

I roll down my scrunched-up leggings and straighten my wrap sweater so that my boob isn't popping out. In my head, I run through my speech one more time. *Hi, Mr. Pearce.* (Do I call him Mr. Pearce? Or Abel? How have I not heard one student address him since the start of camp?) *I'm Everett Hoang. Yes, I'm a Farrow Academy student; you may have heard about my performance as Jo in* Little Women *last year? Nathan Lane's best friend, who happens to be an off-Broadway choreographer, called my performance "stunning" in the local paper. Oh yes, I wrote about that in my application essay to Lucius Brown. Anyway, I wanted to talk to you about—*

"Miss Hoang? Is that you?"

So he *does* know my name. Abel Pearce is leaning back in a rolling chair, spectacles sliding down the bridge of his nose. He eyes me through the sliver of glass and waves me in. *You are a bold, talented actress, Everett.* That's what Jia said to me on the phone the other day. Time to show off my skills.

"Hi," I begin. "I, um, I didn't mean to disturb you."

"You're the first person to find me here," he replies, swiveling to pick up a tattered book from the desk behind him. "It's just been me and *Notes on Theatrical Craft.* This is a welcome distraction."

Abel cocks his head and surveys my frizzy ponytail and smudged makeup. "What can I do for you?"

I think I'm losing all my bullet points one by one. I can see them teetering off the edge of a tall, tall cliff.

"Well, I actually wanted to talk to you about *Thoroughly Modern Millie*," I say.

"Ah, doesn't everyone? If you're trying to bribe me for the lead, you're not going to get very far."

He laughs at his own joke and brushes crumbs off his tartan shirt. *Yes, you are so funny, Abel Pearce. You should think about a career in standup.* I shift from one character shoe to the other.

"No bribing, don't worry," I answer, forcing a laugh. "I was just thinking about the history of this show."

"The history?" Abel echoes.

"Yeah. You've probably thought about this already, but the show was written such a long time ago, and I'd love to brainstorm with you on how to modernize—"

"It was written in 2002," Abel Pearce interrupts, pushing his glasses up his nose. "Which is not that long ago."

"Well, yes," I say, trying to stifle my surprise at the coldness in his voice, "but it's based off a movie from 1967. And 2002 is still—"

"Modernize how?" Abel asks. "Put your teenage slang in? Perhaps Millie should say, 'Yo, I'm walking here, dawg' when she runs into Jimmy?"

God, that isn't even remotely correct. The joke, or the slang. I guess Abel *didn't* think about the Asian characters in this show. Or maybe he did and I'm just not explaining it well.

"I mean, um, in terms of characterization. Like Mrs. Meers, for example, is kind of a caricature with her intense Chinese accent—"

"That's for comedic effect. She's *supposed* to be over the top."

I am running out of steam, my bullet points now diving head-first into the abyss. If he would just listen for one second, I know we'd see eye to eye. The Farrow directors loved when I brought suggestions to the group, and they were always game to do something different, something fresh.

"I understand that," I say carefully, "and Mrs. Meers *is* very funny. But I also wonder how her character will be received by, like, a modern audience. And her henchmen too—Ching Ho and Bun Foo? They're a little stereotypical with their broken English and stuff. I don't know, they all seem a little one-note. I . . . I just have a couple of solutions on how to make them more believable. I'd love to share them with you if that's okay."

Abel Pearce doesn't respond, and I find myself unable to look at him, too anxious to see the expression on his face. I can tell I've made him annoyed. And the one thing I've learned from my years in musical theater is that an annoyed director won't cast you as the lead. No matter how talented you are.

I have about three minutes to turn this around.

"For example," I begin slowly, "there are a couple of lyrics in Mrs. Meers's songs that we could change slightly, to make them more satirical, you know? And I think we could hint to the audience that trafficking in East Asia isn't even that big of a thing. Because obviously it isn't. So maybe we make it clear that only Mrs. Meers . . . does it. Or tries to do it. And with Ching Ho and Bun Foo, I wonder if we can change just a couple of their lines to make their dreams more nuanced." I pause. "If that makes sense."

Abel Pearce stands up, the swivel chair rolling back and

bumping into the desk. I finally glance up at his face, his expression unreadable.

"Those are interesting points, Miss Hoang," he says. "Why don't you send them to me via email and I'll look over your ideas?"

"You will?"

"Of course. Lucius Brown is a boundary-breaking apprenticeship program designed to push young people to their theatrical limits. So you can come out of this stronger. *Wiser.* A better actress."

I nod, the words *theatrical limits* and *a better actress* swirling in my head.

Abel Pearce continues. "And this show may test those limits. But I know"—he steps toward me, his enormous frame looming over mine—"that it will all be worthwhile."

With that, my theater director snakes his arm around my back to turn the doorknob. It swings open.

"Now if you'll excuse me, I have a chapter to finish before all you hooligans come running back in for class. I look forward to your email."

"Yes," I say, somehow out of breath even though I haven't moved a muscle. "I'll send it right away. Thank you, um, Abel. Mr. Pearce."

"Abel is fine. See you later, Miss Hoang."

"Bye."

I take a step back, the clack of my heels bouncing off the empty hallway walls. Well, that conversation sort of spun out of control, but I got it back on track, right? Like I always do. I mean, he listened to some of my ideas and he genuinely wants to consider them. I call that a win. In fact, he said the program was *boundary-breaking*. And maybe he thinks I'm impressive for reaching out to him directly. That has to give me a leg up. I pinch the sides of my ponytail holder, tangled between strands of obnoxiously thick hair. I wish Ariel were here. She'd help me write the perfect email. She's the smartest person I know.

Too bad she's missing in freaking action.

# 10
# Jia

My bedroom may be small, but sunlight curves through every crevice and streaks my legs with honey. Summer afternoons like these make everything a little better. For a moment, nothing exists: not Ariel's empty silence, not Everett's frustrated threats, not even my own shoelace anxiety crisscrossing my insides. Tucking my phone and sketchbook under my armpit, I crack open the window and squat down to reach the fire escape. I settle onto the sloped metal slats and look out at the world.

Mom hates that I come out here. She says it's too dangerous—I could trip and slide between the railing and the slats, collapsing onto piles of week-old restaurant trash. But I don't care. This is my favorite spot. And at least the stale red bean buns and egg cartons would cushion my fall.

CeCe and Nai Nai's room is bigger, but their window faces a brick wall. The fire escape overlooks the new food court complex my parents despise but has tasteful pruned trees out front and a cobblestone courtyard that the street sweepers come and clean every night so it always looks pristine. Across the way, I can see Mr. Sa on his balcony, puffing cigars in his tank top, leaning against a stack of vinyl lawn chairs. Sometimes he waves and I wave back.

If I drew my neighborhood like an anime show, there'd be pot-bellied Chinese smokers on their balconies, restaurant owners and waiters in aprons underneath, and between us, giant glass buildings sprinkled with couples in yoga pants and expensive half-zip pullovers. Then an explosion would happen. And one character from the tower and one from the kitchen would have to team up and save the day—all while falling in love, of course. And Flushing, Queens, would turn on its head. I tuck my knees under my oversized shirt. My life will never turn on its head.

My phone pings and I sit up, hoping it's Ariel telling us she's all right. But it's not. Instead, a new name appears on my screen.

Hey Jia, it's Akil!!!

His exclamation points are sharp and eager, buzzing through my body like fizzy lemonade. I try to keep my palms steady as he continues typing.

My mom says there's a farmer's market today outside the botanical gardens and I'm a sucker for fresh fruits and veg. You've probably been, but maybe you can give me the grand ole tour? Promise to be a good tourist 😊

I stare at the winky face, and then I blink and look again. My throat feels dry and crackly. Part of me wants to immediately melt into the fire escape. But the other part—the *braver part*, Everett would say—imagines me fifteen minutes from now in a blue floral sundress and strappy sandals, marching toward a boy with the sweetest smile I've ever seen.

I bury my face in my shirt. It's like he knows that the farmer's market is my favorite summer activity. I never have money to buy anything, but I love sitting on the bench amid the plastic-wrapped bouquets and pastry displays—sketching ripe tomatoes, flaky croissants, children in strollers, and the shopkeepers who always give me pie samples even though they know I can't afford a whole slice. I could sit there and draw and draw until my hands go numb.

My fingers hover over my phone. Mom and Dad are downstairs in the restaurant, Nai Nai's asleep, and I haven't heard CeCe scream for a while. I might be able to leave with little fanfare. But I don't have an excuse for going to the farmer's market—at least not a good one—and I can't ask Mom for money, not when the registers are half empty and the waiters are muttering about their tips. What will Akil say when he fills his tote bag with artisan bread and watermelons and I fill mine with nothing?

"Ai ya, Jia, what are you doing?"

My mother flies into my bedroom, her arms crossed, a dirty rag draped over her shoulder. She pushes open my window and sticks her head into the fire escape.

"How many times do I have to tell you, huh?" She pulls on my arm so that I'm half in, half out. "That thing is flimsy. You'll get hurt."

Mom successfully grabs both wrists, and I dangle my feet over the window ledge until I'm back in my room, tumbling onto the floor.

"I'm fine," I insist.

My mother shakes her head. "I came in here to say that I'm going on break early. So I can watch Nai Nai and your sister."

"Really?" I ask, failing to hide the excitement bubbling in my throat.

"Yes, really," Mom says, squinting at me in my rumpled pajamas. "Don't even ask. I already know what you want. You have one hour off. *One hour*, okay? And then you have to be back here. Otherwise I miss my shift."

"One hour," I repeat, "absolutely."

This has to be fate. I throw off my shirt and slide into that frilly, baby-blue dress before my mother can change her mind and force me to endure CeCe scribbling more marker on her face. Grabbing my sketchbook and backpack, I race out of the bedroom and into the hall. Mom's slippers patter behind me.

"Where are you running off to so quickly?" she asks. "China?"

"Just the farmer's market," I mumble, barely registering what I'm saying as I type out a message to Akil. "Going to draw some stuff." I hold up my sketchbook as proof and slip into the hall before she can discover the guilt in my voice.

I decide to walk to the botanical gardens rather than bike. The heat sizzles against my back, and the old Chinese ladies' shopping carts hum down the sidewalk like music boxes. I am Akil's *tour guide*. I will talk so much, he won't realize I haven't bought anything. I will show him my favorite corners of the farmer's market and tell him about the time the Vu and Gonzales families got into a fight over the last pair of fuzzy peaches. I will ask more questions about the pranks he and his best friend, Luis, used to play on their teachers, and debate which type of art is the best. We will laugh and laugh until the hour is up.

As I approach the market, I see him—the real Akil, flesh and blood. His mouth is moving, and at first I think he's calling to me. But then I realize that his body is turned, his feet pointed toward someone else blocked by the trunk of a maple tree. No, not just one person, multiple people: a group of girls in ripped cutoff shorts and silk camisoles, giggling at a story he's telling them. My feet freeze on the pavement. I know these girls just from their acrylic nails and Prada sunglasses. They're Farrow girls. They're Everett's old friends.

I duck behind a postbox and press my shoulders against the hot metal. The memory rushes back in tidal waves—the crunchy orange leaves outside the restaurant and Everett's animated texts. She couldn't wait to bring her Farrow friends to the dumpling house. It was all she talked about for weeks. She insisted they'd be so impressed with the tender soup dumplings and pillowy pork buns. One of their fathers was a food editor at the *New York Times*, so maybe once the girls saw the restaurant, the *Times* would come and do a feature or an interview. It would be great publicity.

Everett and her friends showed up on a Tuesday night in plaid uniform skirts and ribbed socks that came up to their thighs. I was on hostess duty while CeCe was curled up under my feet, yanking down the hems of my pants because she thought it was funny. The restaurant was half full, a decent showing for a week-day, though never enough for my parents. The door swung open and Everett waltzed in, button-down cinched at the rib cage to show off her belly button. Her friends followed her while she proudly announced that this was her favorite restaurant. I watched the girls' faces one by one, slow-motion close-ups as each surveyed the store. It started with the crinkle of a nose, a glance at the frayed red seats, a push of a loafer into the carpet. Then, one of our regulars, Mr. Tsiang, who has hair sprouting from his ears and can't see more than a foot from his face, spit his chewing gum into a porcelain teacup. *Oh my God*, one of the girls whispered, loud enough for both CeCe and me to hear. My sister looked up from her hem pulling while Everett flounced toward me. *This is my best friend*, she said, *Jia Lee*. They stared blankly for a moment, as if they could not picture the friendship between a grease-stained girl and a future Broadway star.

Then I seated them. The girls nibbled on one tray of fried dump-lings, timidly biting into the half-moon corners, before scooting out of the booth. Everett's eyes flickered when they left, but she didn't say a word. As autumn fell away and winter slushed through the streets, Everett posted fewer and fewer pictures of her school clique on social media. By junior prom, the girls had disappeared from her camera roll altogether. We never talked about it again.

When I step out from behind the postbox, Akil spots me and eagerly waves. He is alone. The girls with their silk halters and lip-gloss smirks have somehow disappeared, lost to the botanical

gardens ticket booth crowd. For once, I am thankful to live in
such a busy city. Hurriedly, I adjust my bangs and weave past
strollers and bikes until I am inches from Akil Abboud's face. He
breaks out into a grin so deliriously happy, my cheeks flush. We
hug, a tangle of warm skin and bony limbs, an awkward dance of
*Is this okay? Is this what you want?* I try to erase the restaurant from
my brain as his arm skims the edge of my sketchbook.

"Ready for the tour?" I ask.

Akil links his elbow through mine. "More than ready."

## *WORLDGAB GROUP CHAT*

**Ariel:** Hey friends, sorry I've been MIA.

**Everett:** WELL LOOK WHO IT IS

**Ariel:** Okay, I deserved that.

**Jia:** Ariel! Are you okay? We were a little concerned

**Ariel:** Yeah I'm okay. Just had back-to-back classes this week.

**Jia:** See, Everett, I told you Briston was just keeping her busy!

**Everett:** Hmmpppph

**Ariel:** I'm really sorry I made you worry

**Jia:** Oh, it's ok. How are your classes going?

**Everett:** More importantly, how are the PARTIES? Have you met any cute boys yet? Have you made any new friends? Are we going to be REPLACED

**Ariel:** First of all, you could never be replaced

**Everett:** Obviously

**Ariel:** And second of all, parties + boys + Ariel = no dice

**Everett:** PARTY POOPER

**Ariel:** Your resident killjoy

**Everett:** Le sighhhhhh

**Ariel:** Anyway, how are you? How's the musical stuff going, Everett? And Jia, how's Akil? Have you guys talked more . . . 😉

**Everett:** It's going pretty well! The director told me I could email him some ideas on how to modernize the musical so I sent them last night 🙂 And auditions are tomorrow!! I'm in the practice rooms as we speak

**Jia:** Ahhhh good luck!

**Ariel:** You got this! You're a star!

**Everett:** Thank you, thank you! And YES JIA how's Akil?? We want DEETS

**Jia:** Actually, we went to the farmer's market yesterday

**Everett:** ??????!!!!!

**Ariel:** Well now you have to tell us more.

**Jia:** It wasn't a big deal! He said he'd never been and wanted me to show him what it was like

**Everett:** UH HUHHH no boy needs a TOUR of a farmer's market!!! HE LIKES YOU

**Ariel:** I have to agree.

**Everett:** SEE

**Jia:** We just hung out and talked. 🙂 It was very casual.

**Everett:** That is not nearly enough information

**Jia:** Well maybe we can video-chat later and I'll tell you more hehe

**Everett:** I'm down!! Tomorrow night?? 8 PM eastern? Will Ariel show up, I wonder???

**Ariel:** Yeah, yeah! I will.

**Everett:** You better write that in blood, missy

**Ariel:** How medieval of you.

**Jia:** Tomorrow night sounds good 😊 And Ariel, if you can't make it, just let us know 🖤

**Everett:** Do not enable her.

**Ariel:** I am writing 5 PM PST in blood as we speak

**Everett:** Good!!! Meanwhile I'll just be here singing JIA AND AKIL SITTING IN A TREE

**Ariel:** K-I-S-S-I-N-G

**Jia:** I hate you both

**Everett:** Heh

# 11
# Everett

Things you tell yourself before an audition:

1. *You're gonna kill it.*
2. *Even though you are very passionate about intersectional femi-
   nism and hope all the girls going for Millie sing their best, at
   this very moment in time, you would like to CRUSH THEM
   ALL. This part is yours.*

What are those lyrics again? *I'll march my band out, I'll beat my
drum.* It's *drum*, right? We're sure about that?

3. *Emotion is key! You are Barbra Streisand and Barbra Streisand
   is you. EMOTE OR DIE.*
4. *Wait, is there lipstick on your teeth?*

"Valerie Johnson? You're next."

Valerie squeezes my hand so hard, I'm worried she's trying to extract blood from my fingertips. She jumps up to her feet, red flapper dress shimmying as she follows Scary Lady with Clipboard into the audition room.

I bite my lip. The two dozen girls packed in the hall are also, of course, wearing flapper dresses and an array of gloves and fake pearls. How they somehow thought, *Ah yes, I'm going to pack 1920s costumes for summer camp* is beyond me.

The best I can do is an ice-blue shift dress Mom bought me from Bloomingdale's last spring. I remember she was feeling particularly charitable because she missed my performance as Sally Bowles in *Cabaret*. She and Dad were on a business trip that lasted "longer than they thought." They own a boutique bridal shop chain that was supposed to have just three locations—Queens, Atlanta, and Los Angeles. But then Mom got a call from England, and business was booming, so she *had* to expand internationally, and soon the humble Lillian's had outposts in London, Paris, and Milan. To them, Ohio is a quaint, faraway land they use for small talk when chatting up business partners. When I texted them to tell them I'd arrived, Dad wrote **Great, honey!** and asked exactly zero follow-up questions, because he's really trying to win an award for Parent of the Year. At least Ariel and Jia's three hundred good luck texts this morning make up for my parents' radio silence.

The accompanist starts playing the opening measures and even though I *should* give Valerie some privacy, I lean in as she belts to the brassy music. She's singing the first chorus of *Anything*

*Goes*, which is literally what half the girls before her also sang. She's not bad, but she's not great either. She's flat on the high note but recovers well. I'd rate her a solid six out of ten.

A hand taps me on the shoulder and I jump and spin around to face Cheney. His hair is slicked back with too much gel. It's cute that he's trying so hard to fit into the roaring twenties.

"Didn't mean to scare you, Millie Dillmount," he says.

"Not Millie *yet*."

"Well, I wouldn't want to play Jimmy opposite any of these other girls."

God, he's smooth.

The door bursts open and Valerie struts out smiling. I offer her a thumbs-up but she doesn't see me, too enraptured with the hair-whip girls, who have immediately circled her like a pack of hyenas.

"Everett Hoang. You're up to bat."

I think I'm going to throw up.

Cheney lightly touches my cheek. "Break a leg."

The audition room is an old classroom with wood panels that creak when you step on them. A long table and chairs are arranged in front of the window. Men (and a singular woman) with very pale skin and wire-rimmed glasses look up with such vacant stares that you'd think someone dragged them out to Ohio and was like, *If you don't cast this teen musical, I'll shoot.* In the middle sits Abel Pearce. His stare is just as quizzical as it was in his office the other day. I can still picture his puffed-out chest and round gold glasses perched on his nose. I wonder if he's read my email yet. *It will all be worthwhile*, he promised. If I'm Millie, it will be.

"Good afternoon," I say cheerily.

"Good afternoon, Miss Hoang." Abel's voice is monotone and serious. "What will you be singing for us today?"

I fumble with my binder, and it falls to the floor with a splat. Grimacing, I crouch to the ground and try to smoothly pass it off to the pianist. *Come on, Everett, buck up.* When I close my eyes, I imagine Ariel and Jia with pom-poms behind the window, painted signs pressed to the glass that say *Chin up, you got this! Show Abel Pearce what you're made of!* I straighten my shoulders.

"I'll be singing the last section of 'Don't Rain on My Parade' from *Funny Girl*."

"Wonderful. Start when you're ready."

The pianist bangs out the first two ascending bars. I pretend they are trumpets.

When I open my mouth, I am no longer Everett Hoang. I'm Fanny Price. As I sing *Get ready for me, love, 'cause I'm a comer*, I really mean it. I *am* a comer, and I *will* win the role of Millie Dillmount. My ribs expand. My lungs vibrate. I belt that last "parade," my note arching above the casting directors' heads and hitting the top of the ceiling like a clear, ringing bell.

The pianist and I end in triumphant unison.

The casting team is clapping. No one has ever clapped for me at the end of an audition before. My smile is so wide it might take up my entire face. I. Freaking. Crushed it.

"Excellent," Abel says, nodding and writing rapidly. "Wonderful job."

"Thank you."

Imaginary Ariel and Jia are rolling in the grass with glee. Before I leave, I give them a wink.

Who needs a flapper dress to nail an audition? I can just picture Abel Pearce right now—stroking his beard, turning to his stupefied colleagues, utterly astonished as he says:

*Wow, that Everett Hoang. Ten out of ten.*

# 12
# Ariel

Bethany Barnes is standing outside my door with a six-pack in one hand and a bottle of wine in the other.

When she smiles, her teeth are so white she could be in one of those Crest commercials. She points her wine bottle at the door across the hall.

"We're having a party tonight. Room 8C. Ten p.m."

We had an exam this morning, so naturally everyone is celebrating. I should be honored they're inviting me. Relieved. After all, Everett and Jia encouraged me to go to more parties when we video-chatted the other day. *Have more fun*, they said.

On Thursdays, Bethany and the other girls have carrot stick lunches. They call it that because they're obsessed with root vegetables for some reason. They chomp and chomp and test each other on brain biology. It's open to everyone. Sometimes I pass by them when they're working and Bethany waves. She's honestly very sweet. One of those girls that Everett would tell me to be friends with.

Bethany studies my face. I pull back my lips like the Cheshire Cat. I am flirty and bubbly. I love parties.

"Thanks," I say, "I'll be there. Should I bring anything?"

This is a silly question because there is literally nothing I can bring. What shall I do? Steal cookies from the dining hall? But it's a habit Mom and Dad have instilled. Always bring a gift when you're a guest. Manners are key.

Bethany laughs. "Oh no, we're good." She holds up her alcohol. "Got this from some of the upperclassmen still on campus."

Sometimes I forget that I'm going to be a permanent Briston student in September. One day, *I* will be an upperclassman. When I got my official acceptance letter in the mail, Umma immediately pinned it to the fridge. She took down my old tests to make room. This letter deserved the entire metal canvas. It was the culmination of all my hard work, all my high school accomplishments. It was the thing I had desperately wanted so many moons ago. Now I don't even know why I'm here.

If Bea knew about Briston, she'd cross her arms and tell me, *College isn't everything, you know.* Then she'd proceed to list the names of famous entrepreneurs who had skipped university or dropped out. Bea always said she was going to be just like them. She was going to somehow get seen at New York Fashion Week, become mega-famous, and open her own fashion line. She wasn't just a silmang like Umma and Appa thought. She was going to prove them wrong.

Bethany is craning her neck toward the next set of doors. I've been silent for so long, she probably thinks I'm a freak.

"Awesome," I say, mustering all my pep, "see you later."

I close the door before I can make a bigger fool out of myself.

Throwing on a sweatshirt, I cuddle under my comforter. I have a whole two hours before Bethany's party. I could video-chat Everett and Jia and spend my time picking out the perfect mesh crop top and boyfriend jeans. I could swipe on cherry lip tint and barely used mascara. I could blast whatever music is hot right now and pregame by myself in my dorm room.

Instead, I scroll through social media. I grab a bag of Cheetos that Umma and Appa packed for me. I feel the orange dust crust under my fingernails.

The last thing Bea posted was a photo of herself at a club in Busan under purple neon lights. I have it memorized. Her face half shaded in darkness. She is looking to the side at one of her friends, smirking, like the photo is candid even though I know it's not. You can see the straps of her black halter top digging into her neck.

Bea was constantly on Instagram. If you were a stranger following her account, you'd think you knew her so well. Partying all the time, wearing cute outfits, smiling on the beach, her calves covered in sand. You'd never realize that you in fact didn't know her at all.

Once, Bea video-chatted me from Busan, unprompted. I hadn't talked to her in weeks. After all, I was the golden child. If my parents shunned her, so did I.

She was drunk. It was four a.m. in Korea. She bragged that she had arrived home so late because she'd secured some sort of secret business deal. Imo had gone out for the weekend with her book club, so my sister was free to stumble around as she pleased. I told Bee that no one good does business at four in the morning. But she just laughed at me. She told me that they meant to call it a night at eleven but they were having too much fun. They were "making magic," she said. Even her friends were impressed. Where were they, I questioned, when she walked back to the apartment alone? These so-called friends? Didn't they worry about a potential murderer on the loose like I did whenever Bea snuck out of the house? My sister pursed her lips and told me: *You don't know anything* with a tone meant to sting. It was the last time we talked before she died.

Now I promise myself I won't look at her Instagram and then return to her shrine like an addict. The picture is still there. As are all the other ones—always the same two friends against the backdrop of a club, an ocean, an artsy street. Haejinloveslife and Carl_Kisses. I've thought about messaging them. Asking them why they left my sister in the ocean to drown. Why they never called, or emailed, or texted. *You don't know anything.* These people spent the last eighteen months of my sister's life with her. I want to know what they know.

I am elbow-deep in Cheetos. I drop my phone on the bed and close my eyes for a minute, but it ends up being hours. When I wake up, it's ten thirty. Bethany's friends are prompt. I can hear the thump of the speaker and the muffled laughter behind the door. I take a long time putting on jeans and a navy bustier—the one Everett made me buy when we went to that sample sale together. Bless Everett for making me purchase my only party-worthy clothes.

It is amazing how teenagers can fit fifty people in one dorm room. And also how a single resident assistant has not shut this down. Bethany is weaving through the crowd. She makes sure everyone has a drink and someone to chat with. She is also dragging people toward the "bar"—a scratched-up desk covered in beer cans and a giant bowl filled with red mystery punch. One of the Ultimate Frisbee bros is spooning out his drink with a baseball cap.

When Bethany sees me, she waves. I read a statistic that 5 percent of Briston precollege students become Fulbright scholars. Bethany is an intelligent person and an even better networker. She'll be a shoe-in. I pour a beer into a red Solo cup so I am not empty-handed.

Everyone is talking. If they're not talking, they're dancing. But the room is too packed, so they're really just swaying. I am standing right behind a scarf girl. She is chatting to another girl whose shirt says *Freudian slips happen to the breast of us*. I can't help but let out a snort. A different Ariel would buy this shirt in black and wear it on the bus to debate practice until Umma told her it was inappropriate to wear outside.

Somehow, even with the music hammering, Freudian slip girl hears me. She turns and smiles. Scarf girl steps to the side. They are opening the circle. They are letting me in.

"Hi," I say, "I'm Ariel."

Scarf girl tips her cup to mine. "Sarah."

"And I'm Simi."

They finish their conversation about the Exploratorium. It's a museum they went to last week that has all these activities and exhibitions about science. Simi's favorite part was the biology exhibit on identical twins.

"It's basically a jigsaw puzzle where the pieces of the twins' faces are mixed up," she explains, "which is so interesting because even though they may ostensibly look exactly alike, they really have key defining features."

"That is very interesting," I admit.

Sarah sighs happily. She takes a swig of her beer. "Isn't it so great that we can talk about this stuff?"

She swings her orange fingernails in my direction.

"Like, I can tell that you genuinely care about the biology of identical twins, unlike *my* family, who just says, 'That's nice, Sarah' and moves on to boring stuff, like work."

I shrug. I gush about science to Jia and Everett all the time. And they always listen attentively. Everett is particularly riveted when I drone on about Freud's oral, anal, and phallic stages. Mostly because she likes to say the word *phallic*.

Simi starts talking about her brother, who's fourteen and leaves the room any time she mentions her science research project.

"Oh my God, *yes*," Sarah says, punching her drink empathically in the air. "One time I showed my sister a picture of the mice I was experimenting on and she said she was gonna barf."

They laugh and I join them. We are in a club full of big brains and riveting research. When I take a sip of beer, it almost feels refreshing. I am in the circle. I am a bare-shouldered girl giggling with friends.

"Ugh, siblings," Simi says. She turns to me. "Do you have any?"

I choke on my beer. Simi and Sarah stare as I cough and cough. My face is red.

"Are you good?"

I nod yes, even though I'm still hacking away. The room feels unbearable. My skin feels unbearable. Unconsciously, I hold out a hand as if to say *Stop, red light, please no more questions.* Simi and Sarah step back. I am out of the circle.

I shake my head. When I can finally speak, I say: "Sorry, I think I just need to go back to my room for a little bit and drink some water."

Sarah smiles sympathetically. "Of course."

The music is pounding against my temples. I pummel through the beer pong crowd. The girls whispering cross-legged on the floor. The punch-stained baseball caps and beer-battered door-knobs.

Finally, I'm out. When I make it to the end of the hall, I unlock my door and fling myself onto the bed. I take a deep breath.

Sarah and Simi are nice. They are sharp-tongued. They think in experiments and hypotheses. They are *my* people.

But they are also *not* my people. And this is not my place. This is not my school.

It's becoming clearer to me every minute.

This is not where I belong.

From: everetthoang24601@gmail.com

To: arielunderthesea_29@gmail.com; jialee@leedumplinghouse.com

11:36 AM

Subject: Audition Update!!!

LADIES, LADIES, LADIES,

I am here to announce that I *killed* that audition. Like smashed it to pieces. They even clapped at the end! We all thought they'd announce callbacks today but Abel Pearce said that they're "so sure of their choices" that callbacks are unnecessary. SO SURE OF THEIR CHOICES. They better be *so sure* that I'm Millie Dillmount.

Speaking of Millie, our dearest director still has not answered my email yet. But he's probably super busy with the aforementioned casting and the dance showcase. Abel says that he wants to wait to tell us our roles until *after* the showcase as to not "distract us from our performances." I just think he wants to see if our dancing is up to par since the show is so tap-heavy. He also instructed us to "think outside the box" because I QUOTE: "We'll be doing even more of that in *Millie*." Sooooo maybe he *has* read my email? I mean I offered so many fabulous ideas. He's probably just trying to figure out which ones to pick.

While I'm withering away waiting for the cast list, I've been hanging out with Cheney. He's a *great* distraction. And yes, Ariel, before you make fun of me again, this is the same dude who kinda looks like Harry Styles. But not really. He's cuter. 😊 And at auditions, he truly CARESSED MY CHEEK.

CARESSED it, I tell you. If that isn't proof that he's into me, I don't know what is. Shall keep you all posted on all these thrilling developments.

Hugsssss,
Everett

# 13
# Jia

"Do you think," Akil says, holding a scowling illustration of Togusa to his face, "that I look like this dude?"

Akil does his best impression, mussing his curls so they pile on his forehead and frowning so intensely that the rolls under his chin reach his collarbone. I laugh at his dimpled cheeks and scrunched shoulders.

"To be honest," I say, "you look like you're constipated."

"Rude," Akil yelps, shoving my arm. Just the feeling of his skin on mine makes my heart jolt into my throat. I look down at the floor and pretend I'm very interested in the comics scattered across the tile.

I'm still surprised that Akil agreed to come, that he *wanted* to come, to Manga Palace. It's my favorite manga store—hidden between thickets of restaurants and tourist shops and shoved in the basement of a nail salon like a secret hideaway. Rows and rows of colorful spines coat the narrow halls, while games and action figures in shiny plastic boxes fill the front display. In the back, middle-schoolers kneel on the carpet and play Yu-Gi-Oh! Mr. Kimura always lets them stay for hours. Part of the culture—just like the old men sipping tea in our dumpling house.

I have exactly eighteen minutes before I have to get back home. Nai Nai has a doctor's appointment that both Mom and Dad want to attend, so I'm playing restaurant hostess for a few hours. If I'm lucky, CeCe will spend the next few hours under a dim sum cart, playing with her Barbie dolls until she falls asleep. I peek at my phone and check the time—seventeen minutes, all quiet. No one barking for me to come home just yet.

Akil looks up from Togusa's inky face. "You okay?" he asks. "Do you have to go?"

A manga page slices the corner of my finger, leaving an angry line puckered with blood. I make a fist and the blood smears all over my palm. Akil's eyebrows furrow, and I can't tell if he's concerned about my paper cut, or the fact that I keep checking the clock on my phone every five minutes.

"Not yet," I say. "I just . . . I just have to be somewhere later."

"Where?"

I knew my answer was too vague, yet it spilled out of my mouth anyway. *Where* is so easy—I could say Chinatown, the rolling hoisin duck bao carts, the hostess stand and the customers lined up in the alleyway between the restaurant and the convenience store. But then I think of the Farrow girls, their lips pursed, picking at their dumplings before pushing the tray to the side. I wonder if Akil's parents would look at me the same way—the girl in the stained apron who attends public school, who has no future beyond her family's restaurant walls. Farrow has wide wooden staircases and fundraiser parties where the prizes are Caribbean vacations and Broadway shows. Their graduates attend Ivy League universities, elite liberal arts colleges, or premier arts programs if they're talented like Everett. I am no match for Akil's future classmates. Maybe, then, I am no match for Akil, either.

So I tell him: "A restaurant. My parents are taking CeCe and me out for an early dinner." I am surprised at how easy it is to lie, how quickly the guilt hardens in my lungs.

Akil doesn't notice a thing. "Oh," he says, "cool." He drops the book on the ground and flattens his stomach against the carpet, his chin resting on Togusa's cheeks.

I breathe in the musty, magical smell of old books and Japanese candy. For these next several minutes, this is the only thing that matters. Akil, in front of me, Farrow-free. I crawl down the aisle and thumb through the bottom shelf of manga, landing on a volume of *Fullmetal Alchemist*.

"This series is my favorite," I say, sitting down to show Akil. "I actually have a drawing of Winry Rockbell in my backpack." I pull out my sketchbook and flip to the page filled with her wide eyes and signature green bandana.

Akil traces the outline of her face, his touch impossibly gentle. "I wanna hear all about her."

I can't help but smile. Even Ariel and Everett tune me out when I start talking about anime too much. I tell Akil that Winry loves machinery, the smell of oil—in fact, she's essentially a machine prodigy, making metal prosthetics in the blink of an eye. She's tough yet kind, a stubborn and passionate go-getter, the kind of girl who astonishes people everywhere she turns. And the best part is that she's normal. She doesn't have any superpowers like most manga characters.

"She's awesome," I continue. "She follows her dreams even if they're random. Like one time, she delivered this woman's *baby*. An entire baby!"

I realize I'm babbling, and blush, hiding the heat splotching my forehead under my bangs.

"Sorry, I just love her so much." I sigh. "If I could be anyone in the world, I'd choose to be her."

Akil cocks his head at me. "So why don't you?"

"Why don't I what?"

"Be her?"

I roll my eyes. "Yes, I'll just magically learn how to make metal prosthetics and deliver people's babies with no effort."

"Well, not *no* effort." He jumps to his feet, pacing around me in circles. "But you could become as accomplished as her. I mean you already have the foundation. You're tough *and* kind. You just have to put your skills to the test." When I scrunch my nose, Akil yanks my arm and spins me around on the carpet.

"I'm gonna get rug burn," I laugh.

But Akil isn't listening. "C'mon, Jia, you can be anything you want. You can be, like, a surgeon—though, to be fair, I don't recommend it. Or a world-renowned artist, since you're so good at drawing. Or hell, even a mechanic!"

He starts miming the different professions, twisting his body into outlandish poses. The more I laugh, the more dramatic he makes them. He shouts, "A therapist!" before pretending to sit on an invisible couch with a notepad. As he squats, he wobbles backward.

"Akil, wait—"

Akil crashes into the shelf, his shirt flying upward as he ricochets against the hardwood. Dozens and dozens of books plummet to the floor, landing with a loud *splat*. Winry's face is now squished by a mountain of half-bent manga.

"Oh God," Akil says, his voice small.

The Yu-Gi-Oh! kids hike up their glasses and peer out from the back corner. One boy in a too-small polo shakes his head. "Mr. Kimura is gonna kill you."

Akil is pacing again—this time for a different reason. "Oh God," he repeats. "Crap, crap, crap, crap, crap."

I stand and gingerly make my way through the maze of fallen books. "Hey," I say, watching sweat sprout on his collar, "it's fine. I'll just pick them up."

I bend down but Akil pushes me aside. "No," he replies, "this is my mess. I'm really, really sorry. This is your favorite store and I caused a scene. That's what my mom always says I do—*cause a scene*. I'm so sorry."

He starts rapidly scooping up manga and piling them on top of one another. "I don't know the order. Is it alphabetical? Or by section? Crap, half of these are in Japanese. Okay, well, I'll just—"

"Akil." I grab him firmly by the shoulders. "It's okay. You're okay."

Finally, he stops moving, the tower of books teetering in his hands. His eyes pool with water. I jut my head out toward Mr. Kimura, who is completely oblivious as he squishes his cell phone between his ear and shoulder.

"See, he didn't even notice."

Akil follows my sight line and watches Mr. Kimura energetically tell his wife that he wants tori katsu for dinner. The room is silent except for his voice and the flick of trading cards. The color starts to return to Akil's face, his breathing slower.

"You all right?" I whisper.

Akil nods. "Yeah," he says, "sorry. Sometimes I just . . . panic."

He sheepishly looks down at the manga curled between his arms.

"Don't worry about it," I say.

"Okay," he whispers.

"Okay."

Instinctively, my fingers reach out to fondle the cuff of his sleeve. We are standing so close, I can smell the sunscreen on his skin and see the freckles dappling his nose. Akil reaches up and puts his hand over mine. For one brief, impossible moment, I wonder if he'll kiss me. If he does, will it be strange? Wonderful? The last boy I kissed was Harvey Miller during a middle school game of Spin the Bottle. It hardly counts. I should have prepared—should have practiced on a pillow or watched embarrassing tutorials like Everett always wants me to do. I should have added up our time together: mulling about the farmer's market, his insistence on buying me a carton of cherry tomatoes, coming to Manga Palace on a moment's notice. The silence seems to clear a hole in my heart. Everett and Ariel were right. This silly, beautiful boy might actually like me. *Me.* Nobody, Jia Lee.

And then, he takes a step back. He lowers the books to the floor.

"It's almost four thirty. You have to go, right?"

"Oh," I say, my countdown long lost to the bookshelves, "right."

"Come on, I'll walk you out."

The bell tingles against the glass as we step onto the street.

"I'll text you when I get home," he says.

"Okay," I respond, barely aware that I am speaking.

Akil's curls flop over his forehead and he inhales sharply like he has something more to say. But instead, he just waves goodbye and heads back into the store. I stand frozen on the street, wishing I had Winry's courage.

*Next time*, I promise her. *Next time I'll be braver.*

From: arielunderthesea_29@gmail.com

To: jialee@leedumplinghouse.com; everetthoang24601@gmail.com

2:48 PM

Subject: Miss you 🖤

J and E,

Sending an email so you won't spam me over text again. Haha. I miss you both very much. So much, I'd make 1,000 dumplings at 5 a.m. every day for the rest of my life if I could make them with you. Yes, I'm being serious. Jia, your parents can write me up a contract.

Today, in psych lab, we spent 90 minutes observing a group of toddlers through a two-way mirror. Technically, we're doing an observational experiment on matched gender play, but honestly, we were just watching them roll on the floor and throw dolls. Is it strange that I was almost jealous of them? I want to be that little. To not care about anything except what toy I'm going to play with. Their lives are simple. And happy.

Anyway, on that note, I want to hear about your lives. Everett, can't wait to hear the cast list results. Let us know if Abel responds to your email. And Jia, that cryptic text about Akil and the manga store was not nearly enough! I expect a full recap soon.

XO,
Ariel

# 14
# Everett

Two summers ago, my ridiculous brothers rented a jet on a whim and forced a trainee pilot to fly us from New York to Bermuda. While that sounds exciting, it was actually terrifying as hell. The three of us squeezed into two leather seats, the boys spilled beer all over the carpet, and I got motion sickness and vomited on my white Saint Laurent sneakers. Ultimately, my brothers are wimps, so they called Mom and Dad as soon as we landed, and, naturally, they made us turn right around. The only slice of Bermuda life I received were a couple of palm trees swaying on the tarmac. Riveting.

Last summer, Ethan and Sean convinced me to go scuba diving with them in Aruba on half a tank of air. While I did see tons of fish and a supposedly legendary shipwreck, I also almost died. Let me tell you, swimming to the surface with an empty tank strapped to your back and goggles filling with water is not enjoyable. The boys laughed and laughed. They told me that this was an adventure I wouldn't forget. The most exciting thing I'd ever do in my entire life.

As per usual, they were wrong. Jetting off to Bermuda is not the most exciting thing I've ever done. Almost drowning while scuba diving is definitely *not* the most exciting thing I've ever done.

I'm doing the most exciting thing I've ever done right now. I'm racing forty-five jittery teenagers on a three-foot path to a large brick building. What's in the building? Oh, just a very, very scary piece of paper. The cast list.

Valerie's sequin shirt keeps reflecting the early-evening sun and blinding me, so I'm falling behind. We need to keep up with the pack.

"Walk on my left side," I tell her, but she just bumps my shoulder and yells, "WHAT?" over the rumble of the crowd.

"Left side," I repeat, "so you can stand in my shadow."

Valerie proceeds to halt in the middle of the road, causing a domino of girls to crash into our backs. Excessive screaming ensues. It's worse than a *Wicked* reunion concert.

"Everett," she says, "I love you, but I'm not going to *stand in your shadow*."

"No." I take Valerie's head and bring her ear to my mouth we stumble forward. "I just meant your sequins—your SEQUINS— are bouncing the light and blinding me. If you just move to the left—no, the LEFT—we can—stop poking me, Sofia, I'm WALKING—move faster. You know?"

She has no clue.

I've decided that the casting directors are even more dramatic than the students. Normally, the team puts up the list in the early morning, or in the middle of the night, and students trickle in and check their names when they wake up. But no, Abel Pearce decided to email us at five p.m. and tell us that he was going to unlock the theater doors precisely at six—no earlier, no later. It's 5:59. I bet the casting team is watching from the classroom windows and cackling.

The first wave of hopefuls burst through the double doors and skitter down the hall. I crane my neck to look at the mob behind me. Cheney is trailing the mob, at least twenty feet behind the last flock of girls. How nice it must feel to know that you've already nabbed the lead role. There are only six guys in the entire cast, and Cheney is by far the best singer. He's probably as chill as a jazz solo, smirking back there as he watches us run. I find this both extremely irritating and extremely hot.

Finally, Valerie and I make it in. The locusts ahead begin to swarm the list. I take Valerie's hand and jostle our way to the front.

At first, I can't see anything. And then, with Sofia digging into my shoulders and Valerie's chin collapsing onto my head, I spot it. Fat black letters in the middle of the page.

CHING HO—EVERETT HOANG

Ching. Ho.

Ching Ho is one of two henchmen that help Mrs. Meers run the white slavery ring.

Ching Ho is Chinese.

Ching Ho barely speaks in English, and when he does, it's broken and messy.

Ching Ho is not Millie Dillmount.

Valerie dives forward to fling her arms around my waist and I cough on chunks of curls and Bath & Body Works perfume.

"I'M MILLIE!" she shrieks.

She's jumping up and down as the girls snap toward her like they just discovered that she's the queen of Magical Musical Theater Land and they are nothing but her minions. I turn back to the list. Sure enough, there it is.

MILLIE DILLMOUNT—VALERIE JOHNSON
JIMMY SMITH—CHENEY WHITAKER ALDRICH

"Congratulations," I hear myself say, though my head feels heavy and I'm scanning the room for any sign of Abel Pearce. He's a bearded man in a horde of teenage girls, so he should be easy to spot.

But Abel Pearce, like any wise director, is nowhere to be found. He must be in his office. I push past the hair-whip girls and the karaoke kings and until I reach the tail end of the crowd. Cheney is standing there, staring aimlessly at the ceiling. He sees me and waves.

"So, can I call you my Millie?"

I don't say a word. I just continue down the corridor, trying to remember which nondescript room is his. Then I see him. A blurry, faraway man reclining in a swivel chair.

I spit out one of Valerie's hairs and knock on the door. Abel Pearce waves me in.

"Back again, I see? This is not a very fair game of hide-and-seek we're playing, Miss Hoang."

"You always pick the same hiding spot," I tell him, simultaneously trying to pretend I'm not winded while gasping for breath between words.

Abel Pearce shakes his head and chuckles to himself. "What can I do for you now?"

I should have prepared a speech or something like last time. But all that's running through my head is *I am not Millie Dillmount. I am not Millie Dillmount. I am* not *Millie Dillmount.*

So I blurt: "I just saw the cast list. It says I'm Ching Ho."

Abel raises an eyebrow. "That's correct."

Clearly I'm doing great so far. A-plus, Everett. The sweat under my armpits trails down my sides. I try to wipe it with my elbows.

"Um," I say, "yes. Okay. I was just . . . I thought my audition . . . Well, is there anything I could have done differently?"

*To be Millie?* is what I want to add, though we both know I can't. I was so good in that audition. The best I'd ever been, to be honest. My high belt was clear and strong, and soared over Abel's head just like my voice teacher said it should. I saw his face. I saw all their faces. Did I imagine their awe? Did I stumble somehow?

Abel Pearce sits forward in his swivel chair, his checkered button-down creasing at the waist.

"Everett, you received the part you were right for." He says, "You should be pleased with the role."

He thinks I am right for the part of a henchman in a chintzy red jacket and conical hat, singing about the American dream in halfhearted English and pinyin Chinese. And then I remember the email he still hasn't responded to, the bullet points on Ching Ho and Bun Foo and Mrs. Meers I squished onto the page, subject header *thoughts on Asian American representation* like it was an essay instead of a letter to my summer camp theater director.

"Did you get my email?" I ask. "About my ideas? You know, the ones we talked about last time—"

"I remember."

I perk up. "Great. So with Mrs. Meers, and even with Ching Ho and Bun Foo and stuff, do you think—"

"Your ideas were solid, Miss Hoang. I appreciate your passion. But I would like to stick to the spirit of the story, which adheres most closely to what Dick Scanlan and Richard Morris have written."

"Oh," I say. It feels like a grand piano has just plummeted down my chest. "I see."

I should have listened to Ariel. When she picked up the phone for, like, ten minutes the other day (what a plot twist) she suggested I check in about the email I sent. She told me to write some eloquent explanation about why the show needed to change. She insisted I push even harder. But I never had to push before, not with Ms. Geringer when we did *Company*, or *Cabaret*, or even *Carousel*. What would Ariel do now?

I fight so hard to find the words. "It's just—Ching Ho is Chinese. And I don't speak any Mandarin or Cantonese or anything. You know, because I'm Vietnamese. And I just, well, I don't know how I'm really going to play this part."

At that, Abel Pearce stands up, his arms crossed. "Miss Hoang," he says, "would you like to be a member of the ensemble instead?"

I think I might break into a thousand pieces and shatter all over his office.

"Oh no, like, I'm very grateful for the part, really—thank you. I just—"

"Wonderful." He stands up, steps around me, and opens the door. The déjà vu practically smacks me in the face. "Then congratulations. Go celebrate with the rest of your cast."

With that, I'm back in the hallway, unable to move. It's like when our improv class plays the statue game, except I'm the only one playing.

I gulp it all down, little by little. I am not Millie. Instead in five weeks, I'll don a satin jacket with fake Chinese script from the costume shop and a mustache they probably recycled from last summer's production of *Newsies*. I'll pretend to speak another Asian language when I don't even know my own.

I replay Abel's response like I'm rewinding a scene from a movie—the crossed arms, the confusing speeches, the email likely dumped in his trash folder. It's clear to me now. Abel Pearce was never going to use my solutions. He was never going to change a thing.

And then a terrible realization sinks in. When I come home, I can't show Jia the taped performance and regale to her every single one of my theatrical choices. How would seeing her best friend pretend to be a Chinese henchman make her feel? What if we watched it at her house and her parents walked in and thought *Who on Earth is my daughter friends with*? I wouldn't blame them.

Tears nip the corners of my eyes and I swipe them away. I'm such a baby.

When I make it back to the list, everyone has left, which is honestly for the best. I want to be happy for Valerie, but right now I'd rather skip her squeals of joy as she and the hair-whip girls flounce around the courtyard. As much as I love acting, my role-playing only goes so far.

The heat closes in on me on the walk back to my dorm. Why did I come to Ohio? This is a place for gnats and corn, not for girls like Everett Hoang. I belong in Lincoln Center, where the ballerinas from Juilliard smile at you when they jaywalk at 66th, and the directors wear graphic eyeliner and funky earrings, and where old men with big empty words, and roommates from South Dakota that steal your part, don't exist.

*Oh Evie, my drama queen,* my mom used to say every time I screamed so loud I woke the neighbors or scribbled on the walls with crayon. What she meant was *Stop throwing a fit, suck it up, and be a big girl.*

I should be a big girl. I'm seventeen years old. When I climb the three flights up to my room, I try not think about how Valerie's voice cracked on her high note, how she'll be the one kissing Cheney instead of me, how I was so sure I'd get the part. I was *so sure.*

"You're here!" Valerie is running toward me before I even step into the room.

There are people everywhere. Sitting on my bed. Belting "Forget About the Boy" in the closet. The windows fog as drinks slosh from cup to cup.

"It's only, like, six o'clock," I shout as Valerie downs her drink. "The sun hasn't even set yet."

"Oh come on, Ev, we're celebrating!" She flashes a smile and shimmies in circles around me.

"How did you even get this stuff?"

"Ya know, bribed an RA." She winks while yanking Cheney toward her. "My leading man!"

Valerie collapses onto his chest, giggling. Cheney gently moves her to the side and picks up shots from the nightstand.

"I feel like you need one of these, Hoang."

"Do I?"

"Yes." He pulls me closer so his free hand is wrapped around my waist. "You do."

Valerie is now jumping on my bed in her sneakers, scream-singing, "Gimme, gimme."

I close my eyes and down the shot.

## *WORLDGAB GROUP CHAT*

**Everett:** Hiiiiiiii hav i told u guys how much I luv u

**Everett:** hehe dats a song

**Everett:** wait dats a song rite

**Everett:** oh NO its have I told u lately that i luv u!!! there we go

**Everett:** well anyway i dont love anyone BUT U

**Everett:** trulyyy

**Everett:** millie sucks men suck parents suck

**Everett:** U R THE ONLY ONES

**Everett:** who make me happpppppy when skies r hay

**Everett:** wait its not hay

**Everett:** it shud be hay that better lyric

**Everett:** GRAY

**Everett:** wow im a lyric qween

**Jia:** Hi, oh my gosh! Are you okay?

**Everett:** Wut are u talking abt im more than ok

**Ariel:** Everett, you're drunk. Do you want us to call you?

**Everett:** I PERFECT

**Ariel:** You are definitely not perfect right now.

**Everett:** ugh maybe im NOT thats why I didnt get MILLIE

**Jia:** You didn't get Millie??? Ugh, I'm so sorry, Everett

**Everett:** IM CHING HO

**Ariel:** Who is Ching Ho?

**Everett:** A PIECE OF

**Jia:** ??

**Everett:** CRAP

**Ariel:** Oh, I see.

**Jia:** Did Abel respond to your email?

**Everett:** HAHAHAHAHAHA

**Ariel:** I'll take that as a no. Ev, drink some water

**Everett:** vodka

**Jia:** Nope, no more vodka

**Ariel:** Yeah, I don't think that's a good idea.

**Jia:** Find an empty cup and fill it with water, Everett

**Ariel:** Yep I second that

**Jia:** Everett??

**Ariel:** You there?

# 15
# Ariel

Even through a grainy phone screen, I can still see Everett's vomit swirling in the toilet. She managed to prop us up against a skin cleanser bottle, so we get a shot of her blurry French braids and chunks of yellow in the toilet water. Jia does her best not to gag. Her comforter is curled up to her neck.

"That's it," she says, "just get it out of your system."

I want to check Everett's skin. Make sure it's not too blue or too pale. That she's not cold. That she doesn't need to go to the hospital. She looks okay through the screen, but that doesn't say too much. Someone at the party should be with her. Like Cheney, who can hand her five shots but apparently can't clean up the mess.

Everett flushes the toilet and face-plants on the seat.

"Ugh," she groans, "my head is killing me."

"There's a water bottle right next to you, Ev," Jia instructs. "To your left. No, your other left. That's it."

I shoot Jia a grateful glance. That girl has patience that bests even the kindest of kindergarten teachers.

We watch as Everett fiddles with the cap, twisting it back and forth before she pours the water into her half-open mouth. Liquid dribbles down her chin. She gulps and tries again.

Bea used to be like this. Slouched against the toilet. Tequila and mystery juice staining her top. Gurgling water and spit. When she was in high school, I had a whole routine. I waited until the front door clicked. Then I yanked back the covers, tiptoed down the hall, and dragged her into the bathroom, careful not to wake up Umma and Appa. After she was done puking, I pressed Advil onto her tongue like she was a dog, coaxing it back with a glass of sink water. I knew which of her facial towelettes were expensive, and which I could use to wipe the smudged mascara from her cheeks. When she finally crawled into bed, I couldn't resist the opportunity to lecture her, even though I knew she was falling asleep. I had to get the last word in. I had to remind her that she could be better, like me.

"Ariel, you okay?"

Jia's voice is soft yet tired. In the blue phone light, I watch her forehead wrinkle.

"Oh," I say, "yes. Sorry."

I flit my eyes toward Everett, who's yawning, her arms stretching toward the towel bar. I think her skin has more color.

"What were you thinking about?" Jia asks. "You kind of spaced out."

"Nothing," I say, and then, remembering my unsent email, their worried texts, I pause. "Well, Bea, actually."

Jia half smiles knowingly. "She had a lot of fun too, didn't she?"

She did. At least, I think she did. Ever since I scrolled through her Instagram the night of Bethany's party, I've kept returning to it. I used to look every week but now I find myself examining Bea's frozen face several times per day. I stare at that floral twist-tie top I've never seen in her closet before. I zoom in on Haejinloveslife's hand looped casually around my sister's waist. Bee's neck splayed out on Carl_Kisses's lap after a night of partying. Our last conversation burns in my brain. The knife in her voice, the way her eyes became slivers. *You don't know anything.* What don't I know, Bea? What were you hiding?

Everett clatters in the background, pulling herself up to her feet. She wavers a bit, clenching the water bottle, before straightening. She grabs her phone from the makeshift cleanser stand.

"I miss Bea," she declares, the first coherent thing she's said all night.

Stumbling out of the bathroom, she manages to lurch toward her dorm room. We watch her open the door and fall into bed. The sheets rustle as she rolls onto her back.

Now I hear only Jia's breath against the microphone. The crackle of darkness. The space where Bea belongs, the city she left behind. She had too much fun, but I wish she had more. I would give away all my awards and scholarships just to pick her up from the floor every day until we turned into visor-clad, wrinkly ajummas.

"Bee," Everett sighs in her sleep.

"Yeah," I whisper, "I miss her too."

# 16
# Jia

On the last day of June, Chinatown begins to overflow. The duck bao stand and Mr. Zhang's rolling cart have lines so long, they merge into each other. Main Street is wound with college students home for the summer, tourists sheepishly ordering in English, and locals with tote bags brimming with frozen dumplings. The mist blowing from the street vents pour over the city, coating my skin with a damp layer of condensation.

Mom and Dad don't mind any of it though. They herd in customers like pigs to the slaughter, pushing them into booths and makeshift tables sandwiched between the massive fans and the kitchen.

I'm still yawning after a sleepless night taking care of Everett over video-chat. When I sneak downstairs to wake myself up with coffee and egg tarts, Dad hands me a bunch of menus and points to a family with three screaming children.

"Pass these out," he instructs.

"But I have to go back up. I'm watching CeCe and Nai Nai," I protest, my head swimming as another party of five trips past me.

Dad is already weaving through the crowds to reach the kitchen. "Ten minutes." He turns to look at me. "So your restaurant will be successful."

I don't miss his slipup. *Your* restaurant. Not his, not Mom's.

Janice, one of the teen waiters roped into working because her uncle is a line cook, thwacks my elbow. "Your dad's in full boss mode today," she chuckles.

I groan. "Scale of one to five. Five being the worst."

"One hundred. And it's not even noon."

Janice swerves past a shumai cart while I press the menus against my sweatshirt and approach the yelling children. Their parents look like they've given up. The father is on his phone.

"Welcome to Lee's Dumpling House," I say in my smooth, professional waitress voice, passing out menus and pretending their toddlers aren't three screams short from breaking glass.

The father doesn't look up from his cell phone while his wife starts scanning her menu. Then someone in the back swears in Cantonese, and I hear a rush of panicked chatter followed by a high-pitched yelp. I know it's Mom before I glimpse her blouse whisking past the kitchen curtain.

"Excuse me," I say, weaving around sloshing teapots and dim sum trays.

I reach the curtain and pull one side back. Mom is pacing in front of crowd of waiters. Lizzie, the head chef, ushers me into the kitchen so our customers won't see. Before I can ask what's happened, she is standing beside me, her breath hot against my ear.

"It broke," she whispers.

"What broke?"

Then I see: Dad is lying under the commercial dim sum steamer, poking at its bottom with a chopstick. The stench of sour, leftover steam fills the air. Waiters and line cooks huddle around him.

I shake my head. "I don't understand," I say. "It was just working a minute ago. We have so much food out there. And so many customers. How can it just stop working?"

I am asking the obvious yet impossible-to-answer questions, I know, and am met with silence. Dad just keeps poking at the bottom of the steamer, as if he'll somehow find a button that will force it to work again. Then Mom stops pacing and starts yelling, switching so rapidly between Mandarin and Cantonese that I can barely understand her. I try to calm her down but she wildly points to her cell phone.

"Call repairman," she insists, her English harried, like someone's removed half the alphabet from her lips. She always does this when she's nervous.

"But what am I supposed to say?" I try to piece together Dad's futile chopstick method.

Mom shoves the phone farther into my face. *"Repair"*—she stabs the screen with her finger—*"man."*

Like any immigrant daughter and future restaurant owner, I obey. While Bing wipes vegetable oil onto his slacks and Janice races between the kitchen and our oblivious customers at the front end, I Google "Queens repairman" as fast as I can type. I soon realize that there is only one who fixes commercial appliances. When I dial the number, a man with a craggy, tired voice answers.

"Fusion Appliance Center," he says, "how can I help you?"

I remember how much I hate talking on the phone. But my parents are staring expectantly at me—Dad's crinkly eyes hopeful that he won't be stuck tinkering under the bottom of a broken steamer forever, Mom's arms folded over her rib cage as she silently prays for a low quote. I hide the dread in my voice.

"Our commercial dim sum steamer broke," I begin. "I'm not sure how but, um, I think the gas won't turn on."

The man from Fusion Appliance Center asks me a series of questions about water tanks and heating tubes. Dad responds in Cantonese, and I repeat it in English like I am a war correspondent. I listen as he prattles on about temperature control circuits, gas jets, and burners. And then, at last, I hear words I *do* know: *Unlikely. Seems unfixable. New steamer.*

"No," I hear myself say, "no, no, no. We can't afford it."

Mom jabs my elbow. She hates when I tell people that we can't afford things, even when it's true. Dad motions for me to keep going.

"How much would it cost?" I ask.

The man from the appliance center clears his throat. "Well, the good news is we have a sales department we can connect you with so you won't have to do more legwork. But if you're running a restaurant on that thing, about eight thousand dollars."

"Eight. Thousand. Dollars?"

Immediately, the small kitchen erupts with alarm, loafers squeaking against tile as a stew of Chinese spills across the floor.

"Yes," the man on the phone confirms. "Would you like me to connect you to the sales department?"

I stare at my parents, helpless. Eight thousand dollars is more than three months' rent. It's Nai Nai's doctor's appointments, and workers' salaries, and a lump of cash I haven't seen in seventeen years. But without a steamer, we barely have a restaurant. Dim sum is over half our menu. I can hear the cart wheels churning outside the kitchen walls. Soon, we will run out of egg tarts, and lo mai gai, and dumplings, and will have to turn away patrons.

Dad slips out from under the steamer, balancing himself with the chopsticks until he's on his feet. He motions for Mom and me to join him in the freezer.

"Can we have five minutes?" I ask the Fusion Appliance man. "I'll get back to you right away."

"Sure," he says, "I'll be here."

I put him on mute and follow my parents into the freezer. We never go in here, especially as a family. The freezer is for frozen ingredients and clandestine makeout sessions between teenage waiters. I can almost feel the staff's ears pressed against the door as it shuts behind us.

"The steamer is our lifeline," Dad whispers. "This place is nothing without it."

Mom agrees. They talk about bank accounts, and transfers, and things that seem too adult for me to hear. I wonder why they want me in the freezer, but then I realize: I am to inherit this restaurant. I need to be a part of the decision-making. Finally, they turn to me, their faces solemn.

"It will be a hard choice," Dad says, "but a necessary sacrifice."

"What?" I ask. "What will we have to sacrifice?"

Mom glances at me pitifully, like I am just beginning to learn how the world works. "Layoffs," she says. "We will have to fire some workers."

# July

# 17
# Everett

I'm texting Jia, who's telling Ariel and me about the restaurant's dim sum steamer debacle, when Rae bumps my shoulder.

"Well, well, well, if it isn't the shots queen herself." She giggles.

So I *may* have had a little too much to drink the other night. If I dig back into that super-fun carnival of memories, I vaguely recall puking in the trash can and dancing on the dresser while screaming, *Suck it, Abel Pearce!* Not my proudest moment. But hey, it's a brand-new morning and the first day of rehearsal, at that. A fresh start. Just going to totally ignore all the cute little whispers of *Well, Everett certainly knows how to par-tay* and *Oh my God, is that the shirt she wore on Friday? How did she even get the vomit out?* (News flash: it is not the same shirt—I own many similar fashion-forward tops.)

"You were *hilarious*," Rae emphasizes, like she's really trying to nail the part of Regina George in *Mean Girls*.

"Heard ya loud and clear."

I flip my ponytail over my shoulder and march down the steps until I find a seat right next to my favorite dimpled boy. Blessedly, he says nothing about my drunken escapades.

"Lookin' good there, Hoang," he whispers.

I smile triumphantly to myself. So he noticed. I *am* wearing my favorite lilac tube top and black leggings. In a few weeks, I'll have to dress like a Chinese man from 1922 as originally imagined by a white man from 1967, but for now, I can look *hot*. Which is one of my specialties.

My other specialties include having a positive attitude and never giving up hope. Both of which I am planning on nailing this morning. After my hangover wore off (bless you, dining hall tacos), I realized that I could still fix this. Sure, I'm not Millie Dillmount, and yes, that sucks, but I came here to be challenged and grow into a phenomenal actress—things I can still do. So Abel didn't want to read my email. But he's never seen my solutions in action. I can push my own boundaries as Ching Ho. I read through my notes last night, and made even more character choices for him that I hope Jia will be proud of. I decided that I'll be so stunning in this role, Abel will have no choice but to change his mind and be blown away. And then, one day, when I'm holding a Tony Award for Best Leading Actress in a Musical, Abel will squint at his quaint Ohio television and say, "She was always so talented and forward-thinking, that Everett Hoang!"

Abel Pearce and the woman from auditions step onto the stage—a glistening wood platform draped with curtains and a

series of black spotlights. My fingertips begin to tingle. This isn't
one of those makeshift, crumbling platforms in a dusty shack
(hello, middle school drama camp) or a boring high school auditorium stage complete with scuff marks and squeaky seats. This is
the big leagues.

Abel claps his hands together and surveys the rows of wannabe
Broadway stars.

"Welcome to 1920s New York City."

Everybody laughs and whispers excitedly to each other. It's
ridiculously ironic that I left the *real* New York City to be in
the fake one for an entire summer. As much as I love theater, I
miss the 7 train and the LIRR and Roosevelt Island picnics and
sleepovers in my living room. I miss hearing Ariel rant about psychology and watching Jia zone out as she sketches anime boys.
If I were home, I could sit with Ariel and find her an excellent
therapist or grief counselor or something. I could help Jia with the
restaurant now that she's basically juggling three jobs at once,
and of course, pick out her outfits for her dates with Akil (she
won't call them *dates* yet, but we all know what they are). But no.
I'm in Ohio. I'm at one of the best theater institutes in America.
A woman stands beside Abel in last-season designer sneakers. She
hoists a large cardboard box down the stage's steps and into the
aisle. I smooth down my top.

"This is your music director, Kayla," Abel Pearce explains.
"She's very sweet, but if you sing off-key, she *will* murder you."

Everyone laughs harder, but Cheney just smirks and shakes
his head. Knowing him, he probably has perfect pitch.

Kayla takes out a stack of glossy bound scripts. The tingling in my fingers crawls up my arms and tickles my neck. There's nothing as magical as a new script, just waiting for you to highlight and underline and write the all-important words *Enter downstage left, measure 25.*

"These are yours for the next several weeks," Abel says. "They're your babies. Your ruby slippers, so to speak. Lose them, and you'll never make it back to Kansas."

The cast isn't paying attention to his jokes and threats anymore. We are too busy watching Kayla give Valerie the very first script in the box. Of course, my roommate is sitting in the front row, surrounded by her posse of hair-whip girls. She takes out a pencil and starts immediately writing. I bet she's circling "Millie Dillmount" 335 times.

I swallow my snark and remind myself that women support other women, even when that woman happens to take the part you wanted and, frankly, deserved. Digging my nails into my leggings, I chant, *You're here to be challenged. You're here to be great.* When Kayla gives me my script, I smile with all my teeth and become the happiest Ching Ho in all the land.

Kayla announces that we're going to do a read-through, but we'll talk through the songs since we haven't learned them yet.

Valerie sighs loud enough for half the auditorium to hear her. "I can sing through mine," she stage-whispers. "I know them all."

*Come on.* Everyone knows Valerie's songs. Like, even the lighting crew up in the box know them. I shake out my ponytail and focus my attention on Cheney, who's flipping through his script and underlining "Jimmy" with a gentleness that implies he's *definitely* good with his hands. Our eyes meet.

"Too bad Jimmy and Ching Ho don't have any love scenes," he says.

My grin is bigger than Sweeney Todd's when Mrs. Lovett sells his first carnivorous meat pie. If there's anything that can cheer me up, it's Cheney and his beautiful, beautiful words.

The musical begins with a fresh-faced Millie running through the streets of New York, belting about the glamour of the city. Even though Valerie follows Kayla's instructions and speaks her lyrics, she rollercoasters through each line like she's rapping *Hamilton*. When she finishes her solo, we all join to shout, "Beat the drums." Cheney swings his arm to the back of my seat. The hair-whip girls chant, "Everything today is starting to go," and a chorus of voices echo through the auditorium. Maybe it's Cheney's hand on my bare skin, or the biting consonants vibrating through the room, but I feel a fire building in my belly. The world doesn't exist anymore. It's just us in this room, howling the lyrics together. I am so alive, I could burst through the ceiling. I love this feeling. I could *live* on this feeling. Finally, the song ends and everyone claps.

Abel clears his throat to quiet us. We continue with the rest of the script. As expected, Valerie proves to be a very peppy Millie, while Cheney is as suave and as charming as ever. I am totally *not at all* swooning as he effortlessly jokes, *Honey, you're my New York horror story.*

I'm scouring the pages, trying to see what page Ching Ho shows up when I hear a very loud, very sharp broken accent burst through the room. It's Sofia, crying Mrs. Meers's first line: "Sad to be all arrone in dis world." She sounds like she has marbles stuffed in her cheeks. Even though I know all about Mrs. Meers, watching Sofia stumble through her part makes me want to slash myself in two. She emphasizes (and butchers) "beeg warm famiries." The girls in the back giggle. But somehow I feel like they're not laughing at Sofia's incredibly bad acting. They're laughing because they think she's *good*. Because she's supposed to be *hilariously evil*. I listen to her gleeful broken accent again and again until her voice is just a metal fork scraping a plate against my ears.

"Everett? It's your line," Cheney says.

The auditorium is staring at me. *Shit.* I zoned out so much, I missed a scene. I skim the page. Ching Ho is supposed to be teaching Mandarin to Mrs. Meers. In a laundry room, of course. I breathe in the synthetic auditorium air. *You got this, Everett Hoang. Show them what you're made of.*

"Fōng," I say cheerfully.

"Fong," Sofia repeats.

"Mōūh."

"Mouh."

"Yūhn."

"Fong mouh yuhn for Miss Dorothy!" Sofia exclaims.

To the right, the text translates: *Room service for Miss Dorothy.* I am playing the part of a walking Google Translate for a white lady in yellowface. I breathe in deeply and remember the YouTube videos I watched this morning and the notes I reviewed. Time to give Ching Ho more agency, make him more real. I look up at Abel Pearce. He's stroking his beard and staring at me, totally undiscernible.

I channel my most disgusted voice. "I don't like that woman," I say.

Abel Pearce holds up a hand. "Wait," he interrupts, "read the left side of the page. Not the right. Say it in *Chinese*." He emphasizes the *s* so it sprays spittle down his chin.

"I know that's what's written," I reply, rushing through my words, "but I was thinking that realistically, Ching Ho likely speaks in a mixture of Chinese *and* English to Bun Foo. Because he's been here for a couple of years, so he's assimilated."

I mean, most people catch on to languages pretty quickly, especially if they're forced to speak them all the time. Jia's parents speak almost perfect English. I open my mouth to explain further but Abel Pearce's voice rings out before I can continue.

"Miss Hoang," he says again, this time louder, sharper, "while I appreciate the backstory you've given your character, you must read what's on the page."

"Well, I—"

"This is what Richard Morris and Dick Scanlan wrote. Are you going to question their choices?"

The entire room has pivoted toward me as if I'm under an invisible spotlight. Even Cheney is staring, and not in the way I want him to. My heart thrums louder than the boom of my director's voice. This is not how this conversation was supposed to go. In fact, this conversation was not supposed to happen at all. I was going to impress him. I was going to blow him away.

I find the strength to look up at Abel from my seat in the fourth row, his frame looming over mine. He looks just like he did in that small office, turning in his swivel chair, his threat sharp and clear: *Would you like to be a member of the ensemble instead?*

It would be easy for him, I see now, to make that decision, to push me aside and replace me, especially after the public spectacle I seem to be making. And that would be unthinkable. I don't know if I could ever show my face in this auditorium again.

"No," I whisper, "of course not. The writers know best."

"Exactly. So please *be* Ching Ho. The way he's written."

The guy playing Bun Foo, the other Chinese henchman, glares at me behind a pile of frizzy red hair and tortoiseshell glasses. He's clearly thrilled to be a supporting character. *Grateful*, like I should be.

I nod and look back at my script. I was so focused on understanding Ching Ho's personality that I never thought to ask Jia how to pronounce basic Mandarin words. Maybe I should have. That's what a good actress would have done. *Prepare.*

I close my eyes and begin. "Gooook. Daaak. Keeeuih. Hou Tou Yimmm."

Bun Foo responds with his line. *She's got a good head for business.*

"Ihhhhh. Haaaaak. Saaaahm," I reply.

Abel shakes his head. "With more conviction, Miss Hoang."

I can feel the words sink under my tongue. The room is completely silent.

"Come on, Ev," Cheney whispers, minty breath blowing against my ear. "Show 'em that Chinese grit."

*Vietnamese*, I want to say. *Don't you remember when you said I'd make a perfect Kim in* Miss Saigon?

But with Abel's eyes on me, and Kayla trying to melt into the carpet, and Valerie with a hand dramatically over her mouth, I know what I have to do.

"Yuh gwo meih gwok muhng haih gam ge, faat yuhn jo sin giu seng ngoh."

My mouth feels like molasses. I sound exactly like Sofia and red-haired Bun Foo—a perfectly imperfect Chinese peon.

"Exactly," Abel Pearce shouts, "there you go."

Cheney punches my shoulder like we are baseball buddies. To him, I just hit a home run. I lower my eyes to my script and reread the translation.

*If this is the American dream, wake me when it's over.*

# 18
# Jia

July Fourth in New York City is a series of mini explosions, block parties, and grilled hot dogs on corner stoops. It's the Lee family's favorite day of the summer. Not because of the parties, or because we particularly love America, but because we're the only restaurant open for miles. We don't close on holidays. Instead, we make triple the sales.

This Independence Day, my parents are hoping to make *quadruple* the sales. They've stretched our restaurant hours into the late night so tourists and still-drunk teenagers can stumble inside for a post-fireworks meal. With a quarter of our staff laid off to help pay the steamer bill, Mom and Dad are melting into the restaurant floor. There are no afternoon breaks, no feet dipped into hot water basins, no cheesy Chinese soap operas. And for me—no sketching at the park, no hours drifting through Mr. Kimura's comic book shop. No Akil. I find him only in quick texts under the table while reheating Nai Nai's soup, and in the silly TikToks he sends right before we both fall asleep.

Janice's face when she was fired keeps turning in my mind. It's not like she wanted to work here. But we all need to help our parents pay the rent. We are Chinatown girls; we know what's expected of us. Mom says that if we do well the next few weeks, we can rehire the laid-off staff. But for now, the bills seem to span lifetimes.

I text Everett and Ariel to see if they have July Fourth plans but only Everett responds. **Not really**, she says, **running lines. Call you later, okay?** Ariel is a tunnel of silence.

"Jie Jie, look, I'm the American flag!"

I untangle myself from the blankets on the couch to find CeCe bunny-hopping between the kitchen and the living room, her face stained with red and blue markers.

"Oh my God," I gasp as she catapults into my lap, squealing.

Nai Nai, her walker chair propped inches from the television screen, examines my little sister with great interest.

"Positively patriotic," she declares.

CeCe erupts into giggles, flopping off the couch and scream-singing "I'm the American flag" on loop. I slide off the couch and twist her body onto my lap like she's a massive croissant. Her multicolored cheeks are chunky and impossibly cute, even though she's the biggest menace.

"Mom and Dad are going to kill us," I tell her.

Standing up and tossing her over my shoulder, I haul her into the bathroom. CeCe cackles the entire way there. When she turns seven, I wonder if she'll be less annoying.

The sink water is rusty and coffee brown, which happens so often, the super has stopped coming to fix it. If you let it run for a few minutes, it sometimes turns clear. While we wait, CeCe crosses her legs on the toilet seat and starts reciting the presidents' names. I glance at her quizzically. No one taught her that at school. Maybe she really will be the genius my parents want her to be.

I pat wet toilet paper on her face and the blue ink smears across her nose. It reminds me of the aqua paint I'd love to trace my sketch of Konoha with, a wash of color bringing the hidden Naruto village to life. If I lived in Konoha, I wouldn't be spending July Fourth wiping marker off my sister's face. I wouldn't have to lie to Akil about where I am every day. I wouldn't eavesdrop on my parents' muffled fights behind the bedroom door, or worry about what my days will look like once I finished community college. Mr. Sa in his tank top, the stench of stale sesame oil—they would fade into faint dreams, memories of a distant and forgotten life.

"Sissy," CeCe interrupts, "someone's texting you."

I look down at my cell balanced on the sink's ledge. It lights up and at first I think it's Ariel, finally texting back. Instead, Akil's name flashes on my screen. Quickly, I open his message.

> Hey, you busy? If not, meet me at Citi Field!! Fireworks are AMAZING right now.

I shouldn't. I know I shouldn't. But then I remember Dad's words right before the dim sum steamer broke, when he forced me to waitress. *So your restaurant will be successful.* The broken steamer is only the beginning; the paint on the walls is cracked and peeling, the floor is yellowed and stained, the woks are on their last legs. Once I'm handed my community college diploma, the bills and dirty dishes will pile on and on until I'm suffocating under mountains of debt.

And the debt could start sooner than I think. If we don't make enough money tonight, Mom and Dad won't ever let me leave, and then I'll be stuck at home until school begins, when Akil's long given up on me. It's like I'm standing on the subway tracks with my future rushing toward me, crushing my body beneath its squealing wheels.

I put my phone in my pocket and examine my sister, exhausted after her marker extravaganza.

"Come on," I say, pulling her back into the living room.

She flops onto the couch with a heavy sigh, her eyes blinking shut. Nai Nai is still sitting in her walker chair, happily watching television fireworks explode into confetti pixels. My phone trembles in my hands.

"Nai Nai," I murmur, crouching down next to the walker, "if I leave for twenty minutes and come right back, you'll be okay, right?"

My grandmother smiles. "Of course, Jia. I'll be just fine." She wraps her fingers around mine. "See you soon."

I hug her as hard as her bony shoulders can take. "See you soon."

I text Akil, tell CeCe to behave, and run down the steps so I can't worry about my decision.

The wind howls against my back as I pump my bike wheels down the street. The night is aglow with sparklers and boom boxes pounding rap in front of the herbal medicine store and the mall. Even Mr. Zhang, whose food cart has long closed for the night, peels an orange from his balcony and bops along to the music. Flushing is a neighborhood of immigrants celebrating the America they are so desperately trying to sink their teeth into.

I roll down Roosevelt Avenue on the pedestrian walkway because the road is too busy with speeding cars and taxicabs. A few people yell at me for zipping around them, but I don't mind. I'm too busy thinking about what's on the other side of the bridge— about *who's* on the other side of the bridge.

When I arrive at Citi Field, the stadium's rim is covered in lawn chairs and picnic blankets. After the Mets game, the team always has a gigantic fireworks show. If you stand right outside the stadium and crane your neck all the way up, you can see them perfectly. I've never gone before—usually, Everett, Ariel, and I fill up on popcorn in her room and watch the Macy's fireworks explode over the East River on television.

But tonight is different. Everett and Ariel aren't here. Instead, Akil waves to me in a baseball cap and neon sneakers. As I chain my bike to a streetlamp, I realize I'm still in my ratty jean shorts and pajama shirt. My bangs are all askew and I likely have a serious case of helmet hair. But Akil doesn't seem to notice. When I reach him, he pulls me into a hug. I am forgetting my future, little by little.

"You made it!" he shouts, releasing me as the roar of the crowd and the fireworks settle between us.

Golden sparks glitter in the air and blue and red streams erupt over our heads. I glance at his profile, full and gentle. He is an open book. My palms are sweating.

"You know," I begin, "I almost *didn't* make it here."

"Yeah?"

"Yeah, I mean, Roosevelt is so packed I could have gotten trampled." I smile at my own exaggeration. "I could have died."

Akil takes a step toward me. His shirt brushes against my rib cage.

Softly, he says, "Well, I'm really, really glad you didn't die."

My heart is hammering louder than the fireworks above our heads. I can feel his racing too. This is the moment, I know, in this small bubble of time that is barely real, with his face shadowed in the stadium lights, so close to mine. Tenderly, tentatively, he presses a hand to the small of my back.

"Because I like you, Jia Lee." His face is flushed, eyes wide and nervous. We might both throw up.

*Be brave*, Winry Rockbell whispers. I think of our late-night texts, his arm curving around my waist, the bees buzzing around my insides. I think of all the things I want to be—fire escape dreams and glass tower fantasies. So I do what I promised Winry and myself.

When I lean toward him, I can see every freckle speckling his cheeks. And then, he closes the gap.

His lips taste like Popsicles. I can barely think. I can barely breathe. We come apart, and I stare at his long, perfect eyelashes. Akil rests his forehead against mine.

And then, for the second time tonight, my phone glows in my pocket. At first, I don't dare move, but it flashes again and again, so bright even he notices.

"Sorry," I croak out, hurriedly pulling my phone from my shorts.

That's when I see Dad's texts. Then Mom's. Then Dad's again.

Jia where are you

Jia come home

I don't know where you went but you need to come home now

Your Nai Nai fell. The ambulance is on its way.

# 19
# Ariel

Bea is everywhere. She is sitting in the empty spot in the back of the auditorium, smacking her gum. She is jamming out in the courtyard. She is shaking her head at me when I avoid Simi and Sarah in the cafeteria. She is stalking me. Or, I am stalking her. I can't decide which.

Hallucinations are creations in your brain that are separate from reality. They are sometimes brought on by the death of a loved one. One third to one half of widows hallucinate their dead spouses. But I am not hallucinating my sister. She is not standing in front of me. She is consuming me. She is flailing beneath the flipped pontoon. She is dragged onto the beach, bikini bottoms sliding down her hips. She is lying there as we all shout, *Reckless.*

"Are you going to finish those mashed potatoes?"

Eric, one of the Ultimate Frisbee bros, is staring at my full plate of food. It's American Day in the cafeteria to celebrate the Fourth.

Hot dogs. Hamburgers. Macaroni salad. Watery mashed potatoes.
I slide over the entire tray.

"All yours."

"Niiiice." Eric stacks my tray on his and scoots back to his
friends.

I fiddle with the napkin holder. When she was thirteen, Bea
begged my parents to buy sparklers. They were terrified she was
going to burn her hand off. But if there was one thing Bea was good
at, it was begging. She was extremely persistent. So they gave in. We
had the best time waving around sparklers on the front stoop. Later,
Jia's and Everett's parents dropped them off. We danced down the
sidewalk like fireflies. For once, Bea and my parents were happy. It
was a July Fourth miracle.

Tonight, the school is taking all the precollege students down to
Fisherman's Wharf to watch the fireworks. They heard about the
last party, so they're going to check bags before boarding the bus.
No drinking allowed. Surprisingly, no one seems to care. They are
too excited. I can hear Bethany telling the girls that there's going
to be a live band and a dance party. Bea would love that. She was
always the first one on the dance floor. The queen of body rolls and
TikTok choreography.

Bea is sitting by the stained-glass windows, shaking her head
and wolfing down a juicy hamburger.

*You don't belong here.*

*Where, then? Where do I belong?*

My sister's body changes into a collection of poses I've memorized. Her breasts spilling out of a skintight off-the-shoulder party

dress. Her puckered lips as she blows a kiss to Haejinloveslife. Her thin hands as she slides that wallet across the kitchen counter. Like a video game character choosing an outfit, she settles into the final frame. Her sneer over video-chat morphing into hurt. Into pain.

*You don't know anything.*

I bolt up from the table. It shudders loudly and all the Ultimate Frisbee bros turn and stare. But I'm not thinking about them. I grab my backpack and run out of the room.

Perhaps my frontal lobe is broken. I've lost all my critical thinking skills. I can already hear Umma and Appa yelling, *Ari-ya, don't be so irresponsible.* Bea says, *Come find me.*

In the courtyard, I start running. The sky is heavy and gray. I pause by my dorm and open WorldGab and find Imo in my contacts. The phone rings and rings. Finally, she picks up. She always picks up.

"Ariel, I'm not at home right now. I can't show you the ocean."

Imo is in a coffee shop filled with trendy Monstera plants and marble tables. It's ten a.m. in Busan. This is where she does most of her work.

"That's not why I called."

Behind her, people start forming a line at the counter. I can hear them gabbing in Korean. They seem so cheerful. They seem like they're on another planet.

Imo frowns. "Are you okay? Are your parents okay? Is there an emergency?"

"No, everyone's fine." I pause. "But there *is* an emergency."

Imo sits forward, brows knitted. "What?"

"You still have a spare bedroom, right? You didn't get rid of it or anything?"

Imo owns an all-female tech startup. She works from the coffee shop and her home office, but she's always looking for more space in case she hires additional employees. She thought about converting the spare room when Bea left. But then, of course, she left forever.

"Yes, I still have it." Imo squints her freshly mascaraed eyelashes. "What's this all about? Ariel, you're not going to do something bad, are you?"

I march toward my dorm room. Imo's concerned face jiggles in front of me.

"Not bad. Necessary."

"Oh, Ariel—"

I halt at the dormitory entrance. I hold Imo up so she can see me clearly. So she can see how serious I am. How desperate I am.

"Please," I say, "just tell me it's okay."

Imo rubs her temples. "You put me in such a difficult position. Your mother is already upset with me."

"It's not your fault."

"I know it's not, but she's my sister and I can't just have another daughter of hers—"

"Please," I repeat, "*please*. I'm begging you."

*Come find me. Come find me. Come find me.*

Tears well up in my eyes. Imo looks stricken. She's never seen me cry.

"I need this," I say.

Imo bites her lip. She looks around the coffee shop.

Finally, she whispers: "Okay. Text me the details."

With that, she hangs up. For the first time all summer, I feel like I'm in control.

In the dorm room, I email Jia and Everett what I wanted to write weeks ago. What I didn't have the courage to say. They are both too busy to answer right now, which is how I want it. They should enjoy their nights. Everett is knee-deep in her musical. And Jia's with CeCe and Nai Nai. They can look at their emails tomorrow, when I'm in the air and there's nothing they can do. My fingers hover over Umma and Appa's contacts in my phone. *Ari-ya*, I hear their voices echo in my ears, *what about Briston? We're so disappointed. Don't be rash.* But Bea's voice is louder than theirs. She is screaming now. *Come find me.* I shut off my phone and throw my suitcase on the bed.

Here is what I know:

Bea drowned in Busan, South Korea, ten months ago.

Her secrets died with her.

I have exactly $2,300 in my bank account from tutoring all those Upper East Side kids last year.

I am flying to Busan tonight.

I am going to figure out what happened to my sister.

From: arielunderthesea_29@gmail.com

To: jialee@leedumplinghouse.com; everetthoang24601@gmail.com

6:33 PM

Subject: Important

J and E,

Sometimes I feel so lost, I'm not even sure where I am. It's like this. I wake up every morning. I see the palm trees. And my crappy dorm furniture. The old important buildings out my window. But I'm not really there. I don't process any of it. I have felt like this for so long. Too long. I think even when I was home with you, making dumplings, and going on bike rides, and eating pizza, I wasn't really there either. It's like I clocked out of the present. Am I making any sense?

But I found a solution. Well maybe not a solution, but a way out. Or in. I keep replaying my last conversation with Bee. She said she had *business deals*. Secrets. I don't know, she was never at Imo's and I don't think she was just clubbing all the time. Or maybe she was. That's what infuriates me. I know nothing. My sister is a stranger. I barely even know how she died.

So I'm going to figure it out. All of it. I'm flying to South Korea tomorrow morning. Busan, specifically. I'm staying with Imo. It's all arranged. I know this is the most batshit thing you've ever heard and I know that my parents will chop my head off, but you have to trust me. This is something I need to do.

I love you guys so much and being this real with you is honestly terrifying. But even if you don't understand what I'm doing right this minute, I promise you will someday. I'll text you when I land.

XO,
Ariel

# 20
# Jia

The medical ward of New York-Presbyterian is sterile and beige, but it has a nice view. You can spot a row of neat townhouses behind a pocket of trees, a rare sight in Queens. If the people in those townhouses looked through the window on the tenth floor, they'd see a peaceful, sleeping old lady. What they wouldn't see is Mom and Dad, yelling at me.

Last night, they were too worried about Nai Nai to shout. We were all too tired to do anything but stare at her frail body in the hospital bed, tucked under scratchy blankets and the knit afghan I brought from home. In the twenty minutes that I was watching fireworks with Akil, Nai Nai went to reheat leftover doufu in the microwave. As she teetered from the living room to the kitchen, she slipped on the tile and crashed onto her hipbone. Thankfully, she didn't fracture anything. Still, she needs medication to lessen the pain and at least a few weeks of inpatient rehab. When she's not asleep, the nurses feed her applesauce until she's dazed and groggy. Dad makes hushed calls to her insurance, and I overhear Mom tell Lizzie that we'll need to hold the layoffs for one more week. And it's all my fault.

"This is all your fault," my mother echoes, towering above me as I cower in the hospital chair.

"I know," I say, "I'm sorry."

But Mom doesn't care about my apologies. "Things are hard enough," she continues, "and you've made them harder. We trusted you. And you left without even calling, or texting. I thought you were all grown up. A young lady. But you are a child. Putting your grandmother in harm's way and—"

"Okay," Dad interrupts, placing his hand on Mom's back, "she made a mistake."

My mother looks at her husband like she has no idea who he is. The dark circles under her eyes seem to pour down her cheeks.

"This is *your* māma," she tells him, "and she was Jia's responsibility."

"She's *our* responsibility. As a family."

My father crouches down so we are face-to-face, like I am eight years old again and he's teaching me how to hold a paring knife. His shirt is wrinkled, evidence that he hasn't changed or moved in hours. While Mom and I took turns sleeping in the chairs last night, Dad just stood by his mother, watching her hospital gown rise and collapse with every breath.

"What you did was wrong," he murmurs, "but it was an accident. Nai Nai is not upset with you. She loves you."

My mother scoffs. "Of course she does. We all do. But that is not the point."

"It could have happened any time," Dad gently argues. "We aren't able to watch your grandmother every second."

Nai Nai's eyelids flicker like she's in the middle of a terrible dream. Mom ignores Dad's remark and crosses her arms.

"So tell us," she says, "where were you last night?"

I've been waiting for this question since the moment I left Citi Field, speeding away from the kiss, the fireworks, and the butterflies in a desperate attempt to turn back time. I have done all the mental calculations on how this very conversation could go, and I have come to a decision: the truth is worse. Smothering my parents with lies seems like the only viable option, and the only choice that prevents me from saying the name *Akil* out loud. As much as I like him—and I do, I really do—the image of his crinkled, confused eyes, his unanswered calls, the squeal of my bike wheels as I whizzed away from him, makes me want to dive into my stomach's black, empty pit. I won't touch my phone even though I know there are at least half a dozen messages from him, questions I can't answer.

"Meera Mehta called," I blurt. "She needed help on our summer project."

"Mehta? You mean like the Mehtas that come to the restaurant?"

Yes, the Mehtas my parents like. Meera and her family come for dim sum every Sunday. Sometimes she waves and smiles like we are friends, even though the only time she talks to me is when she forgets her pencil in English class. I tell my parents that Meera and I are partners for our biology summer assignment, and that she had a disaster with the lung diorama and needed my immediate help. I promised to go for twenty minutes and come right back. Part of it is true: We do have to make a diorama for biology, although I haven't started, and was planning on getting Ariel to help me. Meera is probably partnered with Brad Armstrong, who plays soccer and always jokes that he's going to be as rich as David Beckham and buy her a Lamborghini one day.

Mom responds to my elaborate story with a sigh, which is as close to forgiveness as I'll get today. "I understand what happened," she says, "but next time, if Meera—or anyone—needs your help, you tell them to come to the restaurant. Or at least let us know and see if Dad or I can come up for a few minutes."

I nod, tears splashing my shirt. "I'm sorry," I say again. I wish I could apologize to Nai Nai too, but I can't bear to look at her in that hospital bed.

My mother softens. "It's been a long day. Go home. Wash up. Dad and I will meet you there."

I wipe the tear stains from my chin and pick up my jacket and phone from the windowsill. The halls feel larger than they did last night, when the nurses and the night sky seemed to close in on us. A doctor in long, pinstriped pants and a Crest-white lab coat smiles at me when she walks by. She makes me think of Akil's mother, who I haven't met and now will likely never meet. The taste of his kiss still lingers on my lips.

For the first time in several hours, I look down at my phone, scared of what I'll see. But Akil's name doesn't fill my screen.

Instead, Everett's does. There are at least ten missed phone calls and voicemails from her. When I scroll down, I see an email notification from Ariel. I rapidly start skimming, but my phone rings before I get very far.

"Hello?"

Everett's voice cuts through the line, sharp and restless. "Ariel, code red," she chokes out. "She needs us."

## *WORLDGAB GROUP CHAT*

**Everett:** Oh my God Ariel you're online!!! How are you? Are you okay? Did you land safely?

**Ariel:** Hey guys. Yeah I'm okay. I'm sorry for making you worry. Again.

**Jia:** Don't apologize. We're just glad to hear from you! Where are you?

**Ariel:** I'm on a layover in Seoul. I just wanted to say that I know that email was a lot last night. I hope I didn't freak you out. I just wanted to tell you the truth.

**Jia:** Ariel, you don't have to explain! Not even a little bit. Really, we're just so glad you felt comfortable telling us all that

**Everett:** Yeah like to be honest we know it's been super hard for you and we've been so worried but like not sure what to do so thank you for opening up and we'll try to do everything we can to support you 🖤 🖤

**Jia:** What Everett said. We love you so much

**Ariel:** Ugh you're going to make me cry in an airport.

**Everett:** Girl flees to Korea, cries in airport over amazing friendship, I mean you're basically in a movie at this point

**Ariel:** Haha straight from Queens to Netflix

**Everett:** You know it 😊

**Jia:** So do your parents know? And Briston?

**Ariel:** Yes, unfortunately

**Everett:** Uh oh, was it bad???

**Ariel:** I mean, Briston is an institution so they don't *really* care at the end of the day. Umma and Appa are another story.

**Everett:** Oh noooo

**Jia:** Well, if it makes you feel better, I am also in club Bad Daughter 🙁

**Everett:** JIA??? A BAD DAUGHTER? Impossible. What happened?

**Jia:** I did something horrible. Akil asked me to watch the fireworks with him and I thought it'd be ok if I left Nai Nai and CeCe for twenty minutes. But then Nai Nai went to get some food from the kitchen and she fell.

**Ariel:** Oh my God. I'm so sorry, Jia. Is she okay?

**Jia:** She's okay. No fractures. She's going to need a few weeks of rehab though.

**Everett:** Thank goodness. But also don't beat yourself up too much!!! You couldn't have guessed that would happen ☹

**Ariel:** She's right, Jia.

**Jia:** Yeah. Ugh. I just feel terrible. And mom and dad aren't too happy with me, of course

**Ariel:** Well, Ev, looks like it's up to you to get the parentals to forgive us delinquent children

**Everett:** UHHHH you're the star debater, Ariel

**Ariel:** yikes

**Jia:** Don't worry about me. Anyway, Ariel, regardless of what your parents say, I think this trip is going to be really good for you 🖤

**Everett:** Completely agree! AND you are hereby the rebel of our friend group which makes you the coolest one of all. We bow down

**Jia:** Our queen 😊

**Ariel:** I love you both beyond measure

**Everett:** And we love you!!!

**Jia:** 🖤

# 21
# Everett

"Let's take it from the top!" Our choreographer, sporting a neon headband and aqua nail polish, stands in front of the wall-to-wall mirror and tries not to strangle the extremely terrible dancers behind him.

I wouldn't blame him if he did. The six ensemble boys only have forty-five seconds of solo dancing before the girls come onstage. Yet they can't seem to box step to save their lives. In our Lucius Brown acceptance letters, Abel Pearce said that the program was *so* competitive, they could only accept "triple threats"—those who could sing, dance, and act. Well, these boys? They're, like, zero threats. Ian Elmstead has tripped over his feet so many times, I'm concerned he's about to face-plant and break his teeth. The dance room reeks of toe sweat and humiliation.

Garfield, our choreographer, blessedly let me be in the opening number after considerable begging and excessive compliments on his athleisure wear. I told him that Ching Ho doesn't come on stage until scene 3, so I have tons of time in between. What I *didn't* say is that if I'm forced to play an awful part that doesn't even get to tap dance, at least I should be able to utilize my skills elsewhere. I think he caught my drift. I sit crisscrossed against the wall and lay out my script next to my dance shoes. Above me, Garfield groans.

"It's not that complicated," he sighs as the boys stumble across the floor. "Literally just two chassés and a ball change. Basic stuff."

Ian wipes snot on his tank top. "Basic to you," he mutters.

Across the room, Valerie meets my gaze and gestures to the boys, rolling her eyes. I smile, but my face is Botox stiff. We haven't really talked in days. Valerie's been too caught up rehearsing Millie scenes and sipping milkshakes in the quad with the hair-whip girls to notice that I've been cooped up in my dorm room poring over the script and trying to say *O lafola, daaling!* with as much gratefulness as possible. There's no way in hell I want to relive Abel Pearce's very public wrath again. I've been humiliated enough times in one week, thanks.

Besides, I *want* to understand the choices these writers made. I *want* to understand Ching Ho better. Sure, I don't love his heavy Chinese accent, or the way he prances around stage, but I sort of get his dreams. He wants to escape Mrs. Meers's trafficking scheme and . . . marry some white lady he's barely spoken one word to. Okay, fine, I don't get that. But I have dreams too. I have to believe that this role is an important part of my journey. That there's some valuable tool here for my future Broadway career.

I look back at the script and sigh. Every time I think I've

finally figured Ching Ho out, the writers turn his lines on their heads—making a joke out of his crush on Miss Dorothy and his bite-sized English. It makes me wonder how people have been putting on this show for decades. Which Asian actors and actresses have donned the conical hat and the sugary, fake accent? Worse yet, which *white* actors have done this? I trace my nail along the edge of my highlighted character name: *Ching Ho.* If Ariel were here, she'd relay, like, the history of stereotypes in theater to me, because she literally knows everything.

I hope she knows what she's doing now, on the other side of the world. I keep thinking about what she wrote in her email: *I clocked out of the present.* I guess that's what she did every time she disappeared midconversation or stopped answering her texts or drifted into a place we couldn't reach. I was just so frustrated by it. I wanted her to be okay. I wanted her to be happy. Jia says that maybe we can't expect Ariel to be okay right now, much less happy, and that's fine, that's normal, and Ariel recognizing that and working to learn the truth about Bee are good things. She's right, as always. I don't know how she honestly has time to be so wise. With the restaurant, and Nai Nai, and Akil, who she apparently KISSED but refuses to talk about, she certainly has her hands full. I want to tell Abel Pearce that she's the *real* immigrant story. My best friend's family and her history aren't just cheap shots or henchmen plot devices. I slam the script shut. I understand Ching Ho well enough.

Finally, Garfield calls for the girls. Sitting up, I decide I will enjoy my slice of freedom. I tighten the buckles on my character shoes and zip to the front of the room. He's placed me in the first row, which is probably because I'm short, but I view it as an opportunity to show him what I got. To show *everyone* what I'm made of.

"We're going to skip to the dance break. I know y'all just learned it, so no worries if you mess up. Just try your best, and remember, HANDS. Strong hands make the dance! All right: five, six, seven, eight . . ."

I ready myself. And then the music starts flying. My reflection moves in the mirror, in time with the piano and the brass band and the hard clack of heels on the floor. No one exists here. Not Abel. Not the hair-whip girls. Not even Cheney. As the song crescendos, I twirl with it, every pirouette and kick dragging my body down the dance floor like a river current. I stop only when Valerie is center stage, poised to belt her final solo in the opening number.

"Okay, cut!" Garrett shouts, and we all pause, bellies heaving.

He surveys the room and I can't tell if he's about to ream us out or kiss our cheeks.

"Everett," he says, and the room snaps toward me.

Oh God, what now?

"Excellent. Just excellent. Everyone, follow her lead, okay?"

Are you serious? I am doing my absolute best not to victory scream *I told you so* at the top of my lungs. I think I could do six hundred cartwheels. And I may just be imagining it, but I swear someone's clapping for me. Then Garfield says we can take a break, and the guys immediately jet to the water fountain, and everyone moves on to midday gossip. But I stay still, staring at my reflection. I glimpse tan character shoes in the mirror, and see Valerie moving from her spot to pinch my arm.

"Congrats, girl," she whispers, "you were awesome."

For a moment, it's just like we're in the bathroom again, meeting for the first time, instant best friends.

"Thanks," I say.

Maybe Garfield will report back to Abel and tell him how great I was in rehearsal today. And then Abel will be so impressed that he'll let me sneak into other songs, like "Forget About the Boy," which would be amazing because that's the ultimate tap number. Or better yet, Garfield can make me dance captain. I know it's a little late, but I could slide into that role so easily, so—

"Everett?" Garfield's voice is cool, hesitant.

I move away from the mirror.

"Abel needs you and Bun Foo," he says, jutting out his head toward Ryan, "in the theater."

"But we haven't finished this number," I protest. "We still have the end to cover."

Garfield shrugs. He takes a swig from his water bottle. Droplets dribble past his bottom lip and onto his shirt.

"Duty calls."

Ryan is already speed-walking toward the door, eager to leave chassés and box steps behind. Valerie is back with Rae and Sofia, their legs entangled on the floor as they giggle at something I can't hear.

I grab my tote bag and trail after Ryan, ready to stumble through pinyin Mandarin and tell Miss Dorothy I love her—one of the only English sentences I say in the entire show. Duty calls, indeed.

# 22
# Ariel

The first thing I smell is fish. Eel in crowded strips on the outdoor display. Mackerel dangling from the tarp, their mouths permanently hooked. Carp deep in the ocean. And then I hear the boats whirring their engines. From a distance, girls like Bea in rash guards and sunglasses, laughing from pontoon decks. The maritime ships, blasting their horns, cruising to shore as waves pile high. *Is this what you want?* Mom screeched over the phone. *To destroy yourself?* I was standing in the middle of Gimhae International Airport, trying to get a new SIM card. Except Mom wouldn't stop shouting, and the teller wanted my phone. So I told her she was being dramatic. And then I hung up.

But now, flanked by the motors that killed my sister, I muse that maybe I do want to destroy myself. It's not such a terrible thought after all.

My taxi driver is long gone. It's just me and my suitcases outside

Imo's high-rise. I look up at the glass building. Just like my aunt—tall, ostentatious. The opposite of my mother in every way.

The last time we were here was for my grandpa's funeral. I was six. Bea was eight. I barely knew him. He was reserved and methodical, and he never traveled to the States. He used to sail cargo ships. And he made lots of money doing it. Sent both Mom and Imo to college in America. Except Imo came back. And then Bea came back. And now, it seems, I'm back too.

*Come find me.*

I ring the buzzer. I can tell Imo has been hovering by the door because she lets me in immediately.

When I enter the lobby, I remember how clean Imo's building is. The floors look like they belong in a model home. There are no black trash bags, or rats, or vague smells of urine outside. I am a dirty Queens girl in a sparkly new world. I smell like airport and stale cheese.

In the elevator, I think about all my sins. Pastor Kwan would say I have many. Briston, too. They were none too thrilled when I upped and left. *You are aware that you have a full merit scholarship, correct?* Yes, I am very aware. I told them I was having a long-term medical emergency. And Mom and Dad confirmed as much over the phone. We may be Christian, but when it comes to preserving our reputation, we are excellent liars. Mom and Dad's last hope is that I'll be back in California in the fall. Back to proper, star student Ariel Kim.

The elevator dings and Imo flings open her apartment door. It is eight thirty in the morning, and her red lipstick is already immaculate.

"Oh, my Ariel," she says. Then she hugs me.

We enter the foyer. There are so many things I want to say. *I'm sorry. Thank you. I know this is a lot for you to handle. Am I as reckless as Bea? More or less reckless?*

Instead, I say: "Your place is unreal."

Imo smiles triumphantly. "Welcome to paradise."

Her apartment is spotless. All white and peach tones. Plants hanging from the ceiling. Marble countertops and designer soap bottles. But that's not what makes it paradise. It's the ocean—filling every window and wall. Gray blue and endless.

Imo rolls my suitcases into the bedroom at the end of the hall. The ocean towers high over the bed. The edge of the island peeks out from the corner.

"Your room," she says. But what I see is Bea's room. The place she spent one whole year. I am going to sleep on the same mattress. I am going to put my clothes in the same drawers. And I am going to follow in her footsteps. I am going to figure out the truth.

"Imo," I say, "do you know Bea's friends? Do you have their numbers?"

Imo purses her lips and starts unzipping my suitcases for me like I am a child. "Ariel, you just got here. Why don't you rest? Or eat? I made ramyun."

I rest my hands on hers and they still over the zipper. "Thanks, Imo," I say. "Maybe I'll take a nap."

Imo pauses like she wants to say something but simply walks back to the kitchen. I close the door. I am exhausted, but lighter. If I touch the glass, I can almost feel the ocean's current. I can imagine Bea's perfume on the sheets and the pillows. I open my phone and WorldGab Everett and Jia to let them know I'm here. Jia immediately texts back a series of smiley faces. **Stay safe**, she says. It's a flippant turn of phrase but we both know what she's really saying. *Don't die like Bea. Don't lose yourself.*

My phone starts buzzing. It's Umma, calling for the eighth time in the past twenty-six hours.

"Hello?"

"I assume you made it to your aunt's," she says. No introduction. No pleasantries. Her words are clipped and hollow.

"Yes."

I can hear Umma pacing in the echo-chambered bathroom, the only place she's allowed to take calls. Which she rarely does. *I need to be professional, and personal calls are unprofessional,* she used to tell me whenever I complained that she never picked up the phone. The last time she answered her cell at work was when I told her my SAT results. I got a perfect score. We were both so happy.

Now her pacing is frantic. So I say, "I'm sorry. I really am."

Umma scoffs so loudly, her breath echoes against the receiver. "Oh, you're sorry? Are you going to go back to California then?"

I know my answer will not be what she wants to hear.

"That's what I thought."

The receiver is silent for a moment, which never happens. Umma is always talking—always asking questions, always digging deeper: *Are you dating that boy from science research? Is Everett taking you to wild parties? Do I need to call her mother? Are Jia's parents going to get mad at you for eating all that free food? We should cook for them.*

*Although your Appa is not nearly as good of a chef. We might embarrass ourselves. Ariel, are you listening to me?*

I feel her anger in the phone's static, in her sniffle. And then:

"I'm so disappointed in you, Ari-ya."

My mother is a boxer and I am her punching bag. She wails as I swing against the concrete.

"I don't think that's fair. I'm here for Bea. I'm here to—"

"Your sister is gone. What are you going to learn in Busan, huh? Nothing. Case closed."

"Case closed? How could you say that?"

What about all the dinners where I begged my parents to tell me exactly what happened—how Bea fell in the water, how the water churned, how the girls on the boat floated farther and farther away? What about the funeral buffet, when Imo tried to sit with us but they put her with the senile ajummas from church like we were in middle school cliques? What about the fact that Umma hasn't said one good thing about Bea since she died?

"You're supposed to be a smart girl, Ariel. You're going to Briston a year early. You graduated top of your class. You have a bright future ahead of you." She says it like she's reminding herself, not me.

"I know, but I—"

"News at church travels fast. Did you ever think of that? Your Appa and I are this summer's hot gossip. One child dead, the other clearly insane."

"I'm not insane. And that's not accurate, anyway. Insanity and mental illness—"

"Oh, you're going to lecture me about psychology now, are you? Well, what do you know? You quit precollege. You know zilch."

My mother is exploding. The shrapnel pierces my lungs.

"Umma," I say, "just stop."

But she refuses. She is just beginning. Her voice comes out in a clenched whisper.

"You are just as thoughtless as your sister," she says, "and if you end up dead in the ocean, you have only yourself to blame."

And then the line cuts off. I drown in her words. My phone pings. WorldGab asks in cheery letters: **How would you rate your cellular connection?** It offers a series of five stars. I press all five. Excellent reception. Message heard loud and clear.

# 23
# Jia

"Your grandmother is improving marvelously," Naomi the physical therapist says, pulling back an invisible curtain to present Nai Nai's strut down the hospital floor.

CeCe claps like a dutiful audience member. Normally, my sister and I sit outside Nai Nai's physical therapy sessions, squished onto stiff hallway chairs, listening for our grandmother's footsteps while CeCe plays games on my cell phone. But today Naomi wants to show us Nai Nai's progress.

We've been coming here every day for a week. Mom and Dad can't make it to rehab in the afternoons, so I am the fake adult—taking notes, making sure CeCe doesn't break anything, and trying not to cry every time Nai Nai hobbles home on her strained hip. Not that Nai Nai is anything but cheerful and serene.

She particularly loves Naomi, grinning at the word *marvelously* and patting her cheeks like she is the third granddaughter.

"This is my runway," she gloats as she pushes her walker from the treadmill to the rubber therapy balls.

Her baggy pants tremble with every step. I hold my breath, worried she will crash and I'll see it this time—my Nai Nai crumpled on the floor, knees twisted in some awful direction, flailing as she searches for balance. But then I remember that Naomi is just a hairsbreath away. Her eyes never stray from Nai Nai's wrinkly fists curled around the handles. When my grandmother makes it to the halfway point, I notice that her steps are steadier, more confident. She is not as hunched and lopsided as she was a few days ago. Her back is nearly straight.

She reaches the finish line and lightly taps the ball with her toes. "Catwalk complete!" she exclaims.

I laugh. Naomi must have taught her that word.

"Fabulous. Just a few more sessions, and you'll be as good as new. Your pre-accident self."

*Pre-accident.* It's a thing the hospital staff has been saying lately, a reminder that there was a time before this, when Nai Nai was getting around okay and we didn't have to worry about bruises, muscle strains, and bills. Now, my grandmother must work for every footstep. And not because of an "accident," but because of me, because of her granddaughter.

A lump runs up my throat. I stare at my phone and will myself not to cry. But, of course, looking at my notifications is a terrible decision. Akil's name fills every crevice of my screen. At first, his texts were polite, unsure. **Hey, I had a really good time the other night; hiya, how are you?**; and then **I'm going to the park soon,**

**do you want to come?** Yesterday, he escalated to **Is everything all right?**

I think about answering sometimes. In the middle of the night, when Queens is cloaked in murky black sky and headlights, my fingers float over the keyboard. I imagine us reuniting in the park, or the comic book store, or that café Akil really likes—Paulina's—with the kitschy French music and red velvet chairs that remind him of Paris. But then I remember Nai Nai, who is struggling to sit comfortably in her wheelchair, her legs spent after fifteen minutes of walking. I think of my parents, who text me every twenty minutes, just to make sure I am where I say I am. I look at these sterile hospital walls, and my sister half asleep, trained to pass out in any hospital chair. I remember my future. The chopsticks and the apron are waiting for me. I belong to them now.

My screen flashes once more. Akil again:

Are you mad at me?

I can't help it. The tears I am trying to force down my throat pinprick my bottom eyelashes. My whole body constricts. Naomi looks up from the bouncy ball, her forehead creased. A shadow where the sunlight can't reach canvases her face.

"Jia," she says quietly, "why don't you go and get some fresh air? Take a moment?"

Nai Nai is resting in her wheelchair, still catching her breath. CeCe is fully conked out, her miniature sparkly sneakers wedged

between the armrest and seat cushion. I'm not supposed to let
them out of my sight. I can't let anything happen to them again.

"Don't worry." Naomi smiles. "I'll be here. Just take five minutes. You need the break."

Her voice is so soothing, so persuasive. Before I know it, my feet
are lugging me down the hall and into the elevator. In the lobby,
the automatic doors spring left and right, opening to humid July
air and an imposing metal overhang. There are no benches here, so
I just stand, inhaling car exhaust from the makeshift parking lot
and the lingering antiseptic sting of the hospital.

A woman in a doctor's coat and fitted trousers lingers nearby,
her phone squeezed between her shoulder and her ear as she snacks
on a granola bar. She is telling the person on the other line that she
only has five minutes, so the details of the charity gala need to be
finalized immediately. Words like *silent auction* and *begonias* fill
the overhang. They remind me of things that Everett's parents talk
about when I sleep over and hear them chatting in the kitchen.
I glance at the ID tag clipped to her coat. First line: *Dr. Amelia.*
Second line: *Abboud.* My tears taste salty on my tongue. When I
examine her more closely, I realize the bridge of her nose resembles
Akil's. Even the freckles on her cheeks match the pattern speckled
under Akil's eyes.

This is his mother, the new chief of surgery, the one Akil's family moved here for. She is the woman I thought I'd never meet. I
am so close to her, and so close to him, holding Akil's texts in my
palms. If Everett and Ariel were here, they would tell me to wipe
my tears and introduce myself to Dr. Abboud. She looks kind.

Maybe she would invite me to dinner, and I'd eat pastries with her family, and dig my toes into fluffy Persian carpets, and talk about art and surgical research. If she asked where I lived, maybe I would tell her the truth.

"Perfect," Akil's mother says to the person on the other line. "I'll see you tomorrow at eight. Yes, okay. Okay, bye." She hangs up, crumpling the granola bar wrapper and tossing it into the recycle bin.

I wait for her to go back inside, but she doesn't move. She doesn't notice me either. If I talked to her, how would I begin? *Hi, you don't know me, but I like your son—in fact, I kissed your son.* Did he tell you that? Did he describe the stadium, the night sky, the fireworks ricocheting through the air? Did he mention that I upped and disappeared? I'm sorry that I hurt him. But if he knew why, if he knew about all the lies I've been hiding, he wouldn't like the girl he kissed. He wouldn't want to waste his summer.

Dr. Abboud rolls her shoulders back and forth. I've changed my mind: I don't think she'd invite me to dinner. I don't think she'd like me at all.

I return to the double doors and step into the lobby. Upstairs, Nai Nai and CeCe are probably wondering where I am. I have to get back.

From: everetthoang24601@gmail.com

To: jialee@leedumplinghouse.com; arielunderthesea_29@gmail.com

11:55 AM

Subject: I miss you and I want taiyaki


Dearest Ariel and Jia,

It's been a minute since we video-chatted or texted so I thought I'd go old-school and email ya. Anyway, I miss you both. Ariel, that picture of the ocean was beautiful, but not enough of a real tour! You'll have to send us more pics once you explore the area. And Jia, I'm so glad to hear that your grandma's doing better. Also, how's Akil? I know things were rough after the fireworks, but I'm sure you lovebirds can work it out!

I wish I was with you guys. Maybe Ariel's aunt has room in her apartment? Haha. In all seriousness, I know I'm lucky to be here, but like, every time I read one of Ching Ho's lines or watch Sofia or Ryan butcher a Chinese accent, it low-key makes me want to gag. Also, the weirdest thing keeps happening where sometimes, I'll be onstage saying my lines but I don't think I'm really there you know? I mean I can hear myself speaking the words but nothing is going through my brain. It's not that I'm unfocused and thinking of something else, just that my mind is complete static. Like the sound of an air conditioner on blast.

At least Abel isn't criticizing me anymore, thank God. Maybe I can still get a good recommendation out of him when I apply to college theater programs in the fall. And I still have Cheney to keep me entertained. Last night, he pulled me from my table and asked me to get ice cream with him right before the dining hall closed. It was pretty crappy ice cream, but STILL. It was cute.

Ugh, now I'm hungry. When we're all back in Queens, we must go to Taiyaki and get those little fish-shaped waffle cones. And matcha. Yum.

Let's video-chat soon, okay?


Love youuuu,

Everett

# 24
# Ariel

Meokja is a hole-in-the-wall tteokbokki restaurant on a cliff. It towers over the rocky coastline. You can hear the ocean from the plastic seats. It was Bea's favorite place and her favorite food. When we video-chatted, she would squish the silky rice cakes between her chopsticks and hold them up to the camera.

"This," she declared, "is the best tteokbokki I've ever eaten."

Now, I am inanely following in her footsteps. Hoping to find clues about her life here. I've been to Gukje Market, where Bea used to buy funky handbags and keychains she always promised to mail me but never did. I trekked across Namhang Bridge and landed in Amnam-dong. I stood on the beach with my toes in the sand and pretended I could hear her laughing. Meokja is my last stop. There is nowhere else for me to go. Yeongdo is a tiny gu on the southern tip of Busan—it is not made for tourists and girls trudging after their dead sisters. It is made for the fish and the docks. For mountains and riptides so strong, they can hurl a teenager five feet underwater.

I've tried to find Haejinloveslife and Carl_Kisses too. I DMed them on Instagram but because their accounts are private, my messages went straight to their requests. I pressed Imo for their numbers, but she said she doesn't have them. And Umma and Appa are certainly not going to hand out Bea's friends' numbers now. Not after Umma has iced me out and Appa has threatened to drain my bank account.

So I am stuck standing in front of a bored middle-aged woman who smells like boiled eggs and noodles. She asks for my order in huffy Korean.

My mother insisted on Korean classes right after church service every Sunday. Bea and I went from second to eighth grade. Bea became fluent. It was the one thing my parents were proud of. Her worksheets were always perfect. Because Korean school never gave us grades, Umma would write her own: *100%* in red Sharpie. She put them on the fridge, lodged between my science tests and honor roll ribbons.

But language is not my specialty. While I understand what the cashier is saying, my own voice comes out like a garbled whale spitting up salt. The woman blinks.

"Say it in English," she instructs, clearly irritated by the disparity between my Korean face and my American accent.

Embarrassed, I obey. She motions for me to sit, and even though the restaurant is empty, I choose a table by the corner window. My tteokbokki arrives in a tinfoil bowl. The rice cakes are flooded with scallions and spicy red sauce. I pick one up and pretend like I'm holding it to the camera, just like Bea. It rushes down my throat like sweet fire. This is different from the kind we get in New York. Different, even, from the one Appa used to make when we were kids. He could never get the sauce right. My tongue starts to burn. Is this why Bea loved it so much? Did it make her feel more alive?

The front door opens. My hands freeze around my chopsticks. The girl walking in looks just like Bea. Dyed auburn highlights. Coral bathing suit. Dewy cheekbones because she's probably following a ten-step skincare routine like a good Korean. The rips in her shorts swing when she walks.

Freezing in place is a neurobiological impulse. The parasympathetic branch takes control. But with just a few deep breaths, you can release yourself. I swallow hot, fishy air. My body returns to me. When I look back at the girl, I realize that she doesn't look like Bea at all. Her cheekbones are higher and her nose is thinner. She also has on pale pink lip tint—something Bea would never wear. My sister was always experimenting with bold colors and big earrings. She relished when strangers would turn and stare.

And then I realize something else, something far more important. I know this stranger. I've seen her on Bea's camera roll, partying in Haeundae under flashing neon lights. I've seen her in Korean news articles, stone-faced on the beach.

Maybe Pastor Kwan was right about miracles. Because standing in front of me is Haejinloveslife. Real. In the flesh.

I watch her lean over the counter and order in perfect Korean.

She doesn't look like someone who'd leave her best friend to drown in the middle of the ocean. Who'd refuse to call or even text *I'm sorry*. But appearances are deceiving. In Bible study, Mrs. Jung always told us that the devil doesn't have red horns and a beard. Satan has changing faces.

Jia and Everett would argue that imagining Haejin as the devil is probably not the best tactic. If I scare her away, she will never talk to me. She will retreat into her hard shell like a turtle. And then I will have traveled 5,627 miles for nothing.

I try to channel Jia and lightly tap Haejin's back when she's grabbing a napkin. She is so tall, I have to stand on my tiptoes. She whips around. Up close, I can see water droplets stuck to her eyelashes.

"Hi," I say, "are you Haejin?"

"Who's asking?"

She's British. And from a posh part of England too.

"I'm Ariel Kim." I hesitate. "I'm Bea's sister."

Haejin drops her napkin on the floor. "Wow," she says. "Well, shit."

We stare at each other. And then I find myself blabbering. I tell her that I left California to come here. That I'm supposed to be at a precollege program. That my parents will likely murder me when I get back to New York. The cashier shoots Haejin a look from behind the register, one that says *The American girl has lost her mind.*

Haejin holds up a hand like she is the judge and I the defendant. I stop midsentence.

"You're going to give yourself an aneurysm," she says.

I want to tell her no, I know how aneurysms work, and you can't get them from talking too much to a stranger. That's scientifically impossible. But Haejin has turned back to the counter. She scoops up her tteokbokki and motions to my seat, the only one with a tote bag dangling from the chair. When she sits, I realize a one-piece clings to her skin and a wetsuit spills out from her backpack. In San Francisco, Everett was desperate for me to meet a cute surfer boy. Well, I've met a different kind of a surfer.

"I can't believe you're here," she says, and then: "I can't believe you found me."

Her sins come rushing back. So she wanted to stay hidden. She didn't want to call my family, or check in, or offer her condolences. I want to ask: *Was Bea really your friend if you never gave a damn?* I sit on my hands to stop them from clenching. If I can't be calm and pleasant like Jia, I must pretend. I must perform, like Everett. I must make nice.

"It was a coincidence," I admit. "Bea told me she used to come here all the time."

"Yeah." Haejin cracks a smile. "It's where we met."

She slurps her sauce. "You know, you kind of look like her. Except she was much more—"

"Exciting."

Haejin shakes her head. "No, not exciting." She's careful not to insult her dead friend's sister who she just met.

"Flamboyant," I offer.

Haejin smiles. "Yeah, flamboyant."

I push the scallions around my bowl. I am not hungry any-more. The rice cakes flop to the bottom of the tinfoil. I should have prepared questions. I can't very well start with *Was my sister hiding anything? Because it sure seemed like it. And why did you let her die?*

Before debates, I made notecards. Hundreds and hundreds of them. I memorized them. I practiced my speech in the mirror. By the time I reached the microphone, I was transformed. I was proud, assertive Ariel. I had an arsenal of arrows in my back pocket, ready to shoot when my opponents least expected it. But now I have nothing.

Haejin sits up. "So," she says, "in your whole little speech, you never told me why you're here exactly." She flips her still damp hair over her shoulder.

When I don't answer immediately, she scoots forward. "It's not your Imo, right? She's not sick or anything?"

Why would she care about Imo when she doesn't care about Bea? *Play nice*, I remind myself.

"No," I assure her, "Imo is fine."

"Phew." Haejin relaxes in her seat. "That would have been shit."

"I'm here because . . ." The words are still stuck in my throat. If this were a real debate, I'd have negative points.

Haejin is hanging on to every word I say.

"Because I just feel like I need to be. For Bee. And for Imo and stuff."

It's a flimsy excuse. But Haejin's face softens.

"Yeah," she whispers, "I get that."

She stands up and loops her backpack over her shoulder. I look down at her bowl. It's somehow already empty. Mine is drowning in sauce.

"I have to hit the waves before they get rough," she says.

*Wait*, I want to shout. *How can you leave? You just got here. I just found you.* But her feet are already moving toward the door. And then she turns around.

"Gimme your phone."

"What?"

She shakes her head like she's done with my questions.

"Just give it."

I dig around in my backpack and hand it to her. She swipes up so that the screen reads *Make an emergency call* and then sticks her number in the empty box.

"Screenshot that," she tells me, "and then text me your name."

She hands me back my phone.

"We're not friends," I blurt.

Haejin's eyes narrow. I was doing so well and now I've ruined everything. But then she smiles.

"Okay," she says, "we're not friends. But you're new. You'll need a tour guide."

With that, she is off. I watch as she disappears down the mural-covered stairs. I may look like Bea, but Haejin is just like her. Always in a rush. Always full of secrets. Always inviting you to walk just a step farther, just a little more, if you dare.

# 25
# Everett

Valerie has food poisoning. I know because I woke up this morning to the sound of her vomiting in the garbage can. Apparently, her bile came up so quickly that she didn't have time to make it to the communal bathroom, which is really such a joy considering our garbage can is one of those plastic nine-by-twelve-inch things. She stank up the whole room, got regurgitated hamburger on the carpet, and cried her way through the morning. I brought her some chicken noodle soup from the cafeteria, but it was just as processed and as questionable as the bad hamburger she ate last night. She barely touched it. Since we're in the middle of nowhere, there are really no other food options. I could theoretically pull some corn from the fields but I don't think the Ohio farmers or Valerie would appreciate that too much.

At rehearsal, everyone keeps asking about her. I tell them that she's the only patient in the nurse's office so she's getting VIP services, but they don't find my humor very funny. In fact, Rae genuinely starts sniffling but then Kayla tells her to stop being a drama queen and go back to her seat. Turns out our music director has more of a backbone than I thought.

Meanwhile, Abel Pearce hasn't even noticed that Valerie's missing. He's too busy whispering to Garfield by the stairs. We're supposed to block act 2, scenes 2, 3, and 4. The first one is where Jimmy and Millie finally confess their love for each other and sing an adorable duet. The second is another terrible Ching Ho scene where he and Bun Foo cry for their *mammy*. And the last is an ensemble scene in a twenties jazz club. Yesterday, Abel said he wants everyone in the auditorium this morning, because if we work hard and focus, we can "whizz through this in two hours" and leave for lunch early. Also, he noted that we "should learn from our fellow cast members' performances." Considering that he and Garfield seem to be having a never-ending conversation, Valerie is throwing up, and Rae is near tears, I'm skeptical that an early lunch is going to happen.

I slink down in the lumpy auditorium chair and overhear Sofia, four rows back, running lines with one of the chorus girls.

"Sad to be all arrone in da world!" she cries. "Ugh, my accent isn't right. It needs to be more pronounced, ya know?"

The chorus girl hums in agreement. I bury my face in my script so no one can see me rolling my eyes. But when Sofia slaughters yet another line, I give in and twist around to watch her faraway lips pucker and curl. At this point, I might just pull a Valerie and throw up everywhere too.

Abel Pearce is still muttering by the stairs. He's wearing an ironed tartan shirt and tailored pants as per usual, but he doesn't seem so cool and professional anymore. In fact, he kind of looks like a knockoff Santa. My director's threat still echoes in my head: *Would you like to be a member of the ensemble instead?* After weeks of bumbling through poorly written lines and forcing fake smiles, that option honestly doesn't seem so bad anymore. Maybe I'd have more fun in the background, dancing my feet off, not a care in the world. But then who would take my part? Rae? Another sun-kissed white girl who wouldn't be ashamed to cry in a mess of Chinese and lurk in the laundry room? No, I couldn't do that. Somehow, watching someone else ruin this role would be much worse.

And then, at last, Abel Pearce claps Garfield on the back and steps on stage to turn to his cast.

"All right, everyone, let's get started."

Isn't that what we all wanted fifteen minutes ago?

"We'll block act two, scene two first," he says, "so Millie and Jimmy, I'll need you on stage."

"Um," Rae calls out, her fingers wiggling in the air, "we don't have a Millie. Valerie's got food poisoning."

You know, that might be the smartest thing Rae's ever said. Before I know what I'm doing, I shoot up, my seat banging against the headrest.

"I'll do it!" I shout a little too eagerly. "I can fill in for Valerie. We're roommates, so I can take notes to show her when she's better."

I'm surprised at the fierceness in my voice, and Abel must be too, because he spends a considerable amount of time stroking his beard in silence. Come on, knockoff Santa, give me this one gift. And then I'll go back where I belong.

"All right," he says, "fine."

"Really?" I can barely believe it.

"Yes, really." He gestures toward Cheney, who's probably chuckling as he watches this scene unfold from the empty back row. "Both of you come up. We'll make this quick."

My feet feel like they're floating to center stage. I don't even look at the other girls, who are probably pouting that I got to Millie first. Instead, I watch Cheney's beautiful body swagger down the aisle until he finds his place next to me. He smirks, showcasing those signature dimples. A stream of Axe cologne waterfalls down my lungs.

"Well, well, well," he says, "we finally get our love scene."

"They don't even kiss," I remind him.

Cheney sighs dramatically. "Touché."

Abel puts on his spectacles from the lanyard around his neck and stands behind us. He starts with a series of stage directions that I dutifully scribble down. Then he explains our character motivations.

"So at this point, Millie is miffed because she realizes she likes Jimmy, but thinks he's in a relationship with Dorothy. When he climbs up to her office window, she acts annoyed, but that's only because she's jealous. Got it?"

"Got it," I say.

"And Jimmy's just realized that he's in love with Millie. He prides himself on being a jaded New Yorker, but now he's head over heels. He's trying to understand this strange new feeling."

"Great," Cheney says. "With Ev, that should be a piece of cake."

Have I mentioned that Cheney Whittaker Aldrich is the most charming guy on the planet? Bless him for keeping me sane these past few weeks.

Abel pinches the bridge of his nose like he's already exasperated by the existence of teenagers.

"Go to your places and we'll run it once."

I walk over to Cheney on the fake window, pretending to be upset and fed up by my dismal love life and failure of a job. Then I get angrier, confronting him about his rendezvous with Dorothy in her room the other night, confused when he reveals how mixed up he is. Cheney furrows his eyebrows and looks off into the distance as he confesses how much he likes me. I mean *Millie*. He's so cute when he's vulnerable, even if it's just for show. Then he starts singing the beginning of our duet.

"Hold it," Abel interrupts, "no singing. Kayla hasn't gone over it with you yet. Let's just speak the lyrics."

Cheney frowns, disappointed that he didn't get to show off his skills. I mean, I don't blame him. He sounded magnificent.

"Now," Abel says, "as you move through the song, I want Jimmy to step off the ledge and walk into Millie's office. And Everett, keep backing up as Cheney walks toward you. And remember, you two are finally confessing your feelings for each other, so your lyrics should start to crescendo. By the end, you should be an inch from each other's faces. You're about to kiss just before Mr. Graydon cuts in."

I know knockoff Santa is just trying to give his characters

sexual tension, but man, if I didn't know any better, I'd think he secretly ships us as a real-life couple. Maybe I should give us a fandom name. Cheverett. Eveney. Hoangitch. Whithoang. Cheney has too many names to make this work.

"Miss Hoang? You ready?" Abel Pearce adjusts his collar and gives me one of those *You better nail this* looks.

I nod, preparing to look as in love as ever. I thought it might be weird speaking the lyrics to a song, but with Cheney, it isn't. His words are heavy with adoration as he emphasizes *when I met you*. I respond in kind, echoing his lyrics with innocent, breathtaking revelation. Before I know it, he's so close I can see the outlines of his dimples.

"All right," Abel says as the ensemble girls titter in the audience. I had forgotten they were there.

I turn away from Cheney and glance at Abel, worried he's going to say we took it too far. He'll probably chastise me *again* in front of everyone. But instead he starts clapping. Like, so loudly that the cast feels compelled to join him. I almost want to curtsy.

"Great job, you two. Nice chemistry. And Miss Hoang, you make a lovely understudy."

Did I hear him right? Did he say *understudy*?

"Don't forget to teach Valerie the blocking," Abel reminds me.

"I won't," I reply, but the brass band thrumming in my bones is out of control. I barely hear him when he turns to the rest of the cast and tells everyone to take ten.

The auditorium seats are suddenly empty as the cast races to the first-floor vending machines. It's the only food that's not from the dining hall, and honestly, sometimes it's better. But I don't care about stale Cheetos. A saxophone is riffing in my lungs. Abel Pearce may suck sometimes but he just said I was *lovely*. The lovely understudy. And the whole cast saw—I bet they're talking about it right now. I see it so clearly: Rae and Sofia gossiping with the other girls over a bag of Lay's potato chips, Ryan shocked that there's more to his scene partner than meets the eye. *Impossibly talented, that Everett Hoang. We underestimated her. We never saw her coming. But she was born to be a Broadway star.* I whirl around and realize Cheney is still beside me. He steps forward, his hand grazing my hip.

"Did you know that you are the most dazzling Millie on earth?"

I step even closer so that we are in the same position as minutes earlier.

"Yes," I say, "I did know that."

"It's too bad you're not her for real. Because then we would *actually* get to kiss."

He moves his hand to my cheek. I'm pretty sure I'm not breathing. The last time he touched my face was at auditions, when we barely knew each other. But this touch lingers. This touch *means* something. Holy crap. This could be better than the time Richie pounced on me on the upper level of Starbucks. It was during seventh period study hall—the only time we were allowed to leave school—and I remember feeling so mature then, so alive.

Cheney looks around the room to make sure everyone has left. When he realizes we are being watched only by hundreds of empty seats, he returns his focus to my lips.

"Maybe you can't kiss me in the show," I say, "but you *can* kiss me now."

Cheney laughs. "Well, you're certainly a girl who knows what she wants."

"That I am."

And then, finally, he does what I ask. He kisses me.

## WORLDGAB GROUP CHAT

**Jia:** Hi friends 🙂 Everett, I'm so sorry I never responded to your email. How are you doing? Is Millie going any better?

**Ariel:** Yeah, things sound really shitty over there. Are you okay? Let us know if we need to punch anyone.

**Jia:** For sure. Except I can't throw a punch to save my life but maybe Ariel can?

**Ariel:** Uh, TBD on that front

**Everett:** Hi ladies!! Don't worry. I'm actually doing great today 🙂 🙂 🙂

**Ariel:** Wow, that's a lot of smiley faces

**Everett:** VERY happy smiley faces! Because long story short Valerie has food poisoning so she couldn't come to rehearsal, so guess who filled in for Millie?

**Ariel:** Idina Menzel?

**Jia:** Honestly impressed that you pulled a Broadway name out of a hat like that

**Everett:** Haha, very funny. No. ME. And I was so good that even the most annoying director in the world thought I was great! In fact, Abel made me Millie's understudy!!!

**Jia:** Oh my gosh, that's fantastic. Congratulations, Everett!!

**Everett:** Thank youuuuuu! And that's not even the best part. After rehearsal, Cheney and I kissed!!!! It was perfect. And magical. And then he walked me back to the dorm and kissed me again and it was even more perfect and more magical

**Jia:** About time!

**Ariel:** Who could have seen that coming?! Haha. I'm happy for you

**Everett:** Yeah! Today was just so GOOD. It felt like everyone was finally seeing me, you know? For what I'm worth. I've been thinking, maybe that's the whole point of this experience. So I can figure out how to show my value, even in a crappy show lol

**Jia:** I mean, you are very worthy, in all things. But also, I don't know. You shouldn't have to prove that?

**Ariel:** Yeah, I agree. You're amazing and a theater shouldn't be making you feel crappy or lesser than in the first place.

**Everett:** Aww thanks guys 🖤 I hear what you're saying, but I also just really think everything is gonna be different from here on out! I have a good feeling after that rehearsal

**Ariel:** All right, if you say so

**Everett:** Anyway, Jia, SPEAKING of boys, how is my favorite Flushing couple?

**Jia:** Erm. Nonexistent.

**Everett:** What??? I thought you were gonna talk to Akil

**Jia:** I was. But I just can't.

**Everett:** JIA he's like PINING after you, you can't just leave him hanging

**Ariel:** I second that opinion

**Jia:** I know, but like there's just too much to explain 🙁 And honestly, I have to focus on Nai Nai. She's leaving rehab tomorrow so I'm back to watching her full-time

**Everett:** Aw girl 🙁

**Jia:** It's fine! I'm excited for her to come home.

**Ariel:** Well give her a hug for us

**Jia:** I will! Also, Ariel, I just realized, isn't it like 6 am in Korea? Did we wake you up?

**Ariel:** Oh haha no don't worry. I'm always up early coz I'm still jet lagged. I think my sleep schedule is permanently screwed.

**Everett:** Well in THAT CASE, we should take this truly rare opportunity to video-chat

**Jia:** Okay!

**Ariel:** Calling now 🖤

# 26
# Ariel

"Welcome," Haejin says, "to the most touristy spot in Busan."

She steps back and fans out her arms like we're standing in front of a painting. In reality, a steep trail overlooks stacks of pastel houses joined by cable wire. Old women in brimmed straw hats and girls taking photos for social media spill over the streets like leftover toothpaste.

"Wow," I say, "it's beautiful."

Haejin smiles triumphantly. This morning, she texted me: **Okay so we're not friends, but you must let me show you around town. Pick you up at 12?** I waited twenty minutes before pretending to reluctantly agree. It was like she fell right into my trap.

Haejin came to the lobby of Imo's apartment in coral coveralls. No bathing suit to be found this time. As we walked to the metro, I decided that she was only being nice because she felt guilty. She probably wanted to atone for her sins. But she didn't act guilty at all. On the train, she chattered endlessly about the summer courses she was taking. They sounded far more interesting than the ones at Briston. Haejin studies marine biology apparently, a fact Bea never mentioned. She only talked about the parties they went to and the boys they texted.

At Toseong Station, I met the last part of the trio: Carl_Kisses. His real name is Carl Adebayo, and he is a half-Korean, half-Nigerian boy who jet-sets around the world as a teen model. When he saw us, he gave me the biggest hug like we were best friends. He looked as perfect as his Instagram pictures. I contorted my face into a serene blank canvas so he couldn't tell that I'd been cyberstalking him for months. We hopped on the minibus and he told me the story of how they all met.

"The old-fashioned way," Haejin said.

Carl flipped his cross-bag over his chest. "The magical way."

He talked about a pink flyer in Jagalchi Market, advertising a get-together for expats new to Busan. He was worried it was a ploy to lure him into a sex-trafficking ring, but he went anyway. There, he met Haejin at the same trendy café Imo goes to for work. Haejin said she made the flyer because "despite the fact that you're supposed to meet your lifelong friends at uni, no one likes a random Brit." And then she met Bea at Meokja. The rest was history.

"It was fate!" Carl declared as we piled into Gamcheon Culture Village.

I always imagined that Bea and her friends found each other under a disco ball, drunk on Dua Lipa and vodka cranberries.

But no. Bea had her own adventures beyond the late nights and clipped calls home.

Looming over the colorful village, I watch Haejin steal Carl's sunglasses and pretend to throw them off the ledge. Carl yells and wrestles her to victory. He was on that boat with Bea when she died. Like with Haejin at Meokja, I try to imagine him leaving her behind. Not waiting at the hospital. Not calling the day we buried her in Queens. The two friends embrace after their mock fight. They look like harmless swans.

The ledge gets crowded, so we walk back down the stairs. Now we are ground level with the mint-green houses and tented food stalls.

"M'lady," Haejin says, grabbing my hand as we weave through the village, "'tis time for your grand tour. Carl, will you do the honors?"

Carl bows and kisses my knuckles. "Gladly. First," he says, pointing to sweet shrimp fritter smoking on the grill, "we need the goods."

He orders three. After wrapping the flaky half-moon in a napkin, Carl places it in my palms.

"Eat, dear," he instructs, and I do.

It tastes like the heaven Pastor Kwan talks so much about at church. I wonder if Bea thought they were just as delicious. If the salty crunch kept her close to the sea. I want to buy more, but Carl and Haejin are already dragging me through a series of murals. Spotted fish placards that make up a larger, patterned fish. Crooked steps painted like book spines. I think of Jia sketching in one of these corners, lost in the contours of Itachi Uchiha's cheekbones. I'll have to take her here one day.

Carl tells me that the village used to house refugees after the Korean War. It wasn't a nice place. But in 2007 (*2009*, Haejin corrects), the government decided to transform the neighborhood into a creative community.

"Now it's an artist's haven," Haejin explains.

I am surprised that she knows so much. I watch her sandals twist expertly through American tour groups.

"For dream makers and do-gooders!" Carl shouts.

In my head, hundreds of townspeople transform into women with paint palettes and fringed shawls. Haejin's feet pause.

"For your sister, too."

I look up. We've stopped at the doorway of a small boutique. Inside, women peruse shelves of patchwork handbags.

"My sister?" I croak.

My voice is muffled by the clink of sea glass and the shuffle of hangers. Haejin gnaws at her fingernail. I didn't expect Bea's friends to reveal her secrets so soon. I hold my breath as Haejin's eyes dart to Carl's.

"It's why I brought you here," she says, knotting her forefinger and pinky like she's making a promise with herself. "Bea was working on something. She wanted it to be a surprise. But since she . . ."

"Since she can't tell you, we might as well," Carl finishes.

I nearly topple into a couple leaving the store. *This is what you wanted*, I remind myself. *This is what you came for.* But now it all feels too soon, too much. What kind of surprise could my sister have? What if she was involved with bad people? I plunge into inconceivable scenarios: Bea was selling drugs, she was a closet alcoholic working on her recovery, she had a secret boyfriend and wanted to run away with him to some other distant country. I would have to follow her to Siberia now.

We move from the boutique and drift into an alley. Wet underwear hangs on a clothesline pinned between two roofs.

"Bee was inspired by this place," Haejin says, gesturing to the walls around us, "by Gamcheon and by your grandfather. He was a sailor, right?"

I find myself nodding as I string together Haejin's sentences into a story I can understand. Our last trip to Busan was for my grandfather's funeral. I remember Bea, ankle-deep in ocean water, refusing to turn around, even when Mom and Dad begged. She couldn't leave him behind, she said.

"She loved the sea here," Haejin continues, "and the colors of the Gamcheon homes. So she decided to start a jewelry line. Environmentally friendly, glass-blown stuff—mostly pastels."

Carl smooths out the wrinkles on his T-shirt. "She did a lot of research. Got some tips and bought supplies from the locals. Very nifty, that girl."

Haejin laughs. "She could make a wall fall in love with her. People in this village were very charmed."

I reconfigure Bea into a girl gallivanting around Gamcheon with a little notebook and a fuzzy pen, giggling with the handbag lady and tearing up as the watchmaker relayed his life story. She

was always a whole box of front stoop sparklers, igniting everywhere she went. She still is. Even in death. I can see the memories
exploding in Haejin's faraway eyes. She fiddles with her friendship
bracelet.

"How far did she get?" I whisper.

"A couple of prototypes. And she struck a deal with one of the
stall owners here." Haejin smiles. "She had plans. Wanted to start
a website. Buy ads, expand to New York. You know, the whole
shebang."

So my sister wasn't a drug dealer. She didn't have a secret boyfriend. When she said she had *business deals* over video-chat, that's
truly what she meant. It all makes sense now.

A week before she left for Korea, Bea and Umma got into a
giant fight. I was sitting in the living room eating Doritos, pretending I couldn't hear them screaming in the kitchen. *I'm going
to do big things*, Bea spat, *college or no college*. Even though I was
staring into a bag of orange dust, I could see Umma's eyeroll. I
could hear her sneer. Our mother's words were sharp, meant to
draw blood. *The only thing you'll be doing is wasting your life.*

Bea stormed out after that. She revved the engine and peeled
off into the lonely enclaves of Queens. I didn't go after her. I didn't
call. At dinner, Mom and Dad complained about how difficult she
was, and I sat there and said *Yes, so difficult* before moving on to
other topics, like my research projects and debate competitions.
Bea came back in the early morning, in time for Appa to drive the
car to work. She refused to talk to Umma until she left for Busan.
Now I see that she was trying to show what she could do without

Umma's expectations. She could prove our mother wrong. Except the next time Bea reunited with Umma in person, she was in a body bag.

I want to ask: If my sister had such big plans, if she was going to make a jewelry line, why didn't she tell me? Why didn't she proudly announce her deals like my parents did every time I won some ridiculous award? I called her every week. I stared at her blurry, laughing face on video-chat.

But then I remember all the questions I didn't ask. All the conversations I blew off, assuming they were drunken escapades. I didn't think my sister was capable. I didn't believe in her.

I clutch the side of the alleyway. Bea probably thought that if she built up her business, got a storefront on the Lower East Side, toted my parents around as they admired her streams of customers and wads of cash, she'd give her little sister a reason to brag. *I'm going to do big things.*

"Where are the prototypes?" I ask. "Can I see them?"

There's a hand on my arm. I realize it's Carl's.

"Yeah. They're in my apartment. Wanna head over and take a look?"

His voice is gentle. I can tell they've prepared for this. I eye Carl in his artsy melted ice cream top and aviator sunglasses resting on the crown of his head. Haejin is biting her lip. They are nervous. They want to please me. They want to please Bea.

*Come find me.*

"Okay," I say, "yes, I'd like that."

Suddenly, we are schoolchildren filing out of the alley one by one. The Crayola-pink houses seem larger. There is nothing but silence amid the clang of butcher knives and the dense stew of Korean and English. Did Bea fall in love with this sound? Did she stand in awe at the pastel houses? Did the dizzy murals make her weep?

We make it back to the minibus stop. Haejin lets out a gust of air. Carl stretches his shoulder blades. It's like we were all under Bea's spell, down the rabbit hole of her tiny world. Now we are free.

"Well," Carl says, looping his elbow with mine, "I'd say I was a pretty stellar tour guide, don't ya think?"

Haejin flicks fritter crumbs off his shirt. "Brilliant. Right, Ariel?"

The bus pulls into the parking spot. Its doors belch open. Haejin and Carl walk up the steps. I know what they did. Their revelations do not counteract their guilt. But my sister stands before me—her plans, her endless, ended future. I follow them onto the bus.

"Right," I say, "brilliant."

# 27
# Jia

Our trip to the Queens Botanical Garden is the first outing my family has been on in ages. Dad has traded in his cheery owner smile and slacks for a New York Yankees baseball cap and a loose T-shirt. Mom pulls down her straw visor to protect her face from the sun, jogging to catch up with CeCe. And I walk with Nai Nai, fresh from rehab, her short steps on the cobblestone timid but steady. *We should take a day off,* Dad declared on our drive home from the hospital the other day. We hadn't taken one since Christmas. In the backseat, I waited for Mom to start berating him in Cantonese, shouting that was no way we could leave the restaurant—not when we just rehired the laid-off staff and the steamer was still so new, you could see your reflection in the steel walls. But my mother simply leaned her head against the car window, her eyes heavy as she murmured in agreement. Even CeCe didn't say anything, too fixated on humming her favorite cartoon's obnoxious theme song for the fiftieth time. No response seemed like the most resounding *yes* we would ever receive. So Dad cleared his calendar today, put Lizzie in charge of the restaurant, and carted us out to the gardens by midmorning.

Now CeCe races down the flowered lane, following the path of lilacs bursting from the perimeter. Dad tackles her, swinging her torso over his shoulder as she laughs uncontrollably.

"My little monkey," he says. He hasn't called her that since she was a toddler.

When I was six—before CeCe was born, before Yeye died, before Nai Nai got sick—I went to the botanical gardens all the time. Business was booming then—money rained down like confetti, so heavy we needed two cash registers. On breezy spring afternoons, we played hopscotch in Cherry Circle, stopping only to look up at the pink and white blossoms sprinkling the sky. Nai Nai always brought an extra wool sweater and would stuff me in it even though it was 65 degrees outside and I was hot from running. After we visited the gardens, my grandparents took me back to eat lunch at the restaurant, where Yeye escaped to smoke a cigarette with the chefs on the back stoop, and Nai Nai slurped her noodles while muttering about his hacking into the night and the smell of nicotine on their clothes.

Life seemed simple then. There was no talk of who would run the dumpling house when my parents were too old, or what I'd be when I grew up. There were no boys to fall for and lie to and ignore. It was ten years of bliss.

Nai Nai pats my leg. "Come on, girl," she says, rushing to catch up to the rest of our family. But it is too late: CeCe is nothing but a faraway cackling dot.

I smooth down a strand of windswept hair on my grandmother's head. "Don't walk too fast," I remind her. "You're supposed to take it easy."

"Yeah, yeah," she says. We pause on a bench, setting the walker to the side. Nai Nai has gained a few much-needed pounds, and the color has returned to her cheeks, but she still wears three layers of clothing and shivers when the wind picks up. I take off my jean jacket and lay it over her lap to keep her warm.

"My sweet granddaughter," she says.

It's not true, not really. But there's no point in fighting with a seventy-eight-year-old woman on our day off. Instead, I take in the silence and the scenery. The trees are tall and impossibly green, like warriors protecting the baby flowers. In the fall, they'll turn crispy yellow, and I'll traipse through the leaves on my way back from school. Everett will come by the restaurant in her knee-high socks and plaid uniform skirt, and we'll eat dumplings, and video-chat Ariel in San Francisco. And then Ev will apply to college, and likely get into some prestigious theater program. I hope she doesn't go too far away. Nai Nai pokes my arm.

"Where'd you get that from?" she asks, inspecting my shirt.

I forgot I was wearing this today. All my tops were in the laundry pail, so I threw it on. It's my rumpled *City College of New York* T-shirt I got from the college fair in May. I had skipped lunch to attend. In the gym, the principal set up rows of tables blanketed with starched white tablecloths and signs that welcomed all the recruiters. My classmates clumped around each booth, collecting keychains and flyers and branded plastic water bottles. I made a beeline for the community colleges like I was supposed to. But there were only three tables dedicated to two-year schools, and they didn't have any goodies or trinkets—just sign-up sheets to be on their listservs. So I walked to the Hunter table, and then the CCNY one, lingering behind a row of people and backpacks as admissions staff talked about GPAs and personal statements. When I somehow found myself at the front of the line, a woman in a pantsuit asked me what subjects I was interested in. *Art*, I blurted, and she smiled, not hesitating to tell me about the college's degrees in studio art, digital design, and art history. I left with a T-shirt, a pamphlet on the art department, and an admissions booklet with photos of happy, high-definition kids in glasses and beanies. I put the pamphlet and the booklet in my bottom drawer under my winter sweaters so Mom and Dad wouldn't see.

"A college fair," I tell Nai Nai, "a recruiter gave it to me. For free, of course. Not that I'm going. I just thought, you know . . . free shirt."

My grandmother can tell I'm tripping over my words, even if she doesn't know one American university from the next. She pokes my arm again, this time with surprising force.

"Nai Nai!" I gasp.

"If you want to do other things, you know, you should."

I scratch the undersides of my wrists. "I don't want to be anywhere but here, Nai Nai."

"That's not what I meant. In life. You're young. You're supposed to be having fun." She tilts her head back and looks up at the puffy summer clouds. "I had *lots* of fun in my day."

"*Nai Nai*," I laugh.

"I did! You know, in the fifties, times were tough. We had to flee to Taiwan. When we got there, we needed to celebrate. Or else we'd think too much about everything we'd left behind."

Nai Nai has told me many stories about her childhood. Born just as the war was beginning, she and her siblings used to huddle in makeshift bunkers and wait for hours, terrified of the bombings. She went to school in an abandoned mall and studied under candlelight with a jar of peanuts as supper. But she has never told me about Taiwan—only that they were the good years, bubbles of joy before she returned to China to reunite with her parents. My grandmother fiddles with my jacket on her lap.

"Your Auntie Lula and I hopped from one social to the next," she says. "The boys would buy us all sorts of things to get our attention. Necklaces. Gold bracelets. Ruby rings."

"Wow, you must have been quite the charmer," I joke.

"Oh, I was."

The flower petals twirl with the breeze and we both chuckle. Nai Nai cups my cheek in her small, smooth palms. I massaged her hands and feet with Eucerin last night so her skin wouldn't crack. I can feel the thick lotion on my cheekbones.

"I want the same things for you, my girl," she says, "I want *more* for you."

"What do you mean?"

"Joy." She eyes the letters on my shirt. "An exciting future."

I can't look at her face. All I can think of is Akil in Manga Palace, roaring with glee, telling the Yu-Gi-Oh! boys and the entire store that I could be anything I wanted, that I could be a real-life Winry Rockbell and fight battles, and save humans. I miss him so much, it hurts.

CeCe is racing toward us, the ruffles on her polka-dot dress flapping against her knees.

"Sissy!" she shouts.

I swallow Nai Nai's words and scoop my sister into my arms. Mom and Dad follow close behind.

"Your sister runs too fast," Mom says, wiping her damp forehead with a tissue. "We already made a loop."

CeCe rudely kicks the back of my thighs and I lower her to the ground.

"I'm hungry," she whines. "Can we get pizza?"

Pizza is my family's favorite food whenever we decide to go out. There is nothing as satisfying as bubbly cheese and sauce on a slab of pillowy bread. Especially when it's two dollars.

"Okay, you monster," Dad says. "Pizza it is."

The gardens may be beautiful, but on the other side of the fence, cars and bikers stream past families with bags of watermelons and plastic stroller covers. CeCe is tired out from running, so she hangs on to Nai Nai's walker and prattles on and on about how excited she is for first grade.

"There's math in first grade," I remind her.

CeCe flips her pigtails over her shoulders. "Shh, I'm doing the talking, sissy."

My sister, ever the boss. Maybe she should be the one to take over the restaurant. Maybe I can have the future Nai Nai wants for me after all. We find ourselves under a metal bridge, cars above us honking a steely wake-up call. My sister and parents race ahead once more as the pizza store comes into view.

I glance down at my phone. Ariel has texted us a picture of pastel houses with flat, powder-blue roofs. It looks beautiful in Busan. **Stunning**, I write. **Can't wait for the update later.**

**Ditto**, Everett says. And then I get another message from Everett, this time on a thread with just the two of us.

**Hey**, she types, **I didn't want to show you this but also I didn't want to NOT show you this**

I pause on the sidewalk, waiting with Nai Nai for the traffic light to change.

**What?** I type. **What is it?**

**It's probably nothing**, she replies.

**Just tell me, Ev**

She sends the photo. It's an Instagram story screenshot of Akil at a diner—a place that I don't recognize. My throat catches at his wide grin and brown curls flopped over his forehead. And then I take in the rest of the picture: the girl he is cheek-to-cheek with, her dewy skin and close-mouthed smirk. The same girl from the farmer's market, from Everett's high school, from that time in the restaurant, when she nibbled on two dumplings and scoffed in disgust. They look like they're friends. Or maybe—I can't bear to think—something even worse.

The traffic light changes and the pixelated walking man appears, signaling for us to cross. *Go*, I tell myself, *go, go, go.*

# 28
# Everett

Jia says it's perfectly fine for Akil to have friends or girlfriends or whatever he wants and she hasn't talked to him in weeks so she can't really blame him, but I know she's upset. I didn't want to show her the picture, really, but then I felt I had to. It's the Best Friend Code.

Madison must have known her sneer would get under my skin. She probably posted that photo to show how good she is at making friends, how chummy she is with the new kid now that we're no longer close (her fault, after being weird and rude at Lee's Dumpling House, something I can't bear to talk to Jia about and force her to relive). And of course, she and Akil were at Enzino's, Farrow's go-to diner, the fluorescent lights highlighting her off-the-rack Dior dress. She probably wanted to show him her favorite seat. When I get back to New York, and back to school, I'm going to give that Madison Pollack a piece of my mind. She and her

Dior dress and her Instagram stories and her Tesla that she barely knows how to drive can go straight to—

"Wow, you look beautiful."

Cheney is suddenly in my dorm room, model-worthy in his dress pants and freshly ironed button-down. I was so busy texting Jia that I temporarily forgot that we were going to Lucius Brown's annual summer dance together. I shove my phone into my purse. Now that he's here, the whole day seems to melt away.

"Thanks." I grin, adjusting my red body-con dress so that it lies perfectly against the curve of my hips. I have to agree with Cheney—I *do* look pretty amazing. My dress and ruby lipstick are well paired with the loose curls slinking down my shoulders and the black rhinestone sandals I bought at a sample sale in SoHo. Together, we're basically a power couple ready to sweep the Tony Awards.

Cheney laces his fingers through mine and we leave the dorm to head to the dance hall. Which is really just a wooden barn on the edge of campus, complete with breathalyzer tests at the door, since the administration caught wind of the drunken cast party debacle. I don't care *what* kind of party this is though. We could be milking cows in our dresses and I'd be perfectly happy. All that matters is the hottest guy on the planet, holding my hand. Jimmy and Millie (the understudy): the duo of the century.

When we arrive, the room is packed. I wait for everyone to notice us, but they're too busy dancing. So I survey the space. The counselors put in some effort and strung up lights on the ceiling. There's a punch bowl and a dozen boxes of supermarket chocolate chip cookies on a plastic folding table, and Ryan with his arm in a bag of sour cream and onion potato chips. Cheney pulls me to the center of the barn, where Valerie and the hair-whip girls are shimmying to some song I don't know. He grabs a fistful of dress and presses his hands against my waist.

"Hey," he says.

"Hey yourself."

His nose is touching my nose. I can see the summer heat pruning on his forehead. God, if we were in a movie right now, this would be the perfect screen grab. The best teen romance you've ever seen. His lips are *just* about to touch my lips when—

"AWW, Jimmy and Ching Ho are in lurvvvvvvv!"

Sofia's potato chip breath is on my shoulder, the lace on her sleeves rubbing against my skin. Valerie tugs on her arm, and they stumble backward.

"Oh my God," she says, "give them some space."

Sofia surrenders, giggling as she totters to the snack table. But the moment is ruined. Danny, the guy who plays Trevor Graydon III, thinks he can break-dance, which riles up a couple of girls, who immediately challenge him to a dance-off. I sigh, cuddling into Cheney's chest to make room for the crowd. Valerie winks at me. I'm glad we're sort of friends again, and that she's not mad I'm her unofficial understudy. In fact, she might even be impressed at my talent, now that I've finally had the chance to prove myself to everyone. Maybe Rae and Sofia gave her all the details on my incredible acting skills.

The song changes to "Mamma Mia," which gets everyone

going. And just in time, too, because Danny was truly about to sprain his ankle break-dancing. The girls stop poorly pirouetting as people pack onto the dance floor. Ryan ditches his sour-cream-and-onion chips to jump up and down on the perimeter. Cheney twirls me back to center stage and dips me dramatically. I laugh and don't even mind that my hair sweeps the dirty barn floor. With the twinkle lights and the rusty red walls, it feels like we're in a small-town rom-com. We shimmy and spin and do silly moves like the Sprinkler and a really awful Running Man. *This* is what summer is supposed to be like. This is what I dreamt of with Jia, lying on the couch in Queens.

When the song finishes, I'm drenched in sweat and also starving, so I lure Cheney to the snack table, where we stock up on cookies before heading out into the muggy Ohio night air. A couple of girls dash for the hay bales. Cheney and I stand in the tall grass, the full moon floating between us. I kick off my heels while he fumbles with the cookies before presenting them to me like he's a waiter at a Michelin star restaurant.

"Madame," he says.

"Ay yi yi," I tease, "you're going to drop them."

I relieve him from his duties and stuff them all in my mouth. God, I needed this. Whoever drove to the grocery store that's literally an hour away just to get store-bought cookies is a saint. I haven't had anything this yummy since the plane ride, when they brought out cheesecake for the first-class dessert.

Rae, Sofia, and Valerie join us on the grass. Sofia sips her punch and whispers that she thinks Garrett and Albany are hooking up, while I nod and pretend I have nothing to say on the subject, but really I have too many cookies in my mouth to speak. Okay, *maybe* I overshot my dessert intake. I chew rapidly so I can tell them that actually, Albany is hooking up with Mariah, and Garrett just has a sad, unrequited crush. But before I can spill the tea, Rae starts playing with my hair. She wraps a loose curl around her finger.

"Um," I say, glancing over at her rumpled dress and punch-stained lips. Her blood alcohol content literally has to be zero to get in here, so there's no way she's drunk. Does she just perpetually act tipsy?

Rae keeps my hair tightly wound around her thumb. "You," she says, jabbing my chest with her other hand, "look like a beautiful geisha."

I cough, the cookies scratching my throat. "What?"

"You know, like from that movie. The old one. What's it called?"

Sofia snorts. "*Memoirs of a Geisha?*"

"Oh yes! Duh." She smiles broadly like she expects a thank-you.

All I can do is blink at her. How in the hell do I look like a geisha? Is it the red dress? The lipstick? Is my foundation too light? Does Rae even know what a geisha *is*? It's like déjà vu from that night around the bonfire, when Sofia first uttered the character name Mrs. Meers and Valerie joked that she'd look great rocking a kimono. Except the only flames tonight are the ones licking my insides. This time, I say what I'm thinking.

"Geishas are Japanese," I tell her. "And I'm not Japanese."

It's clearly a clumsy comeback, because Rae just laughs and releases her grip on my hair.

"Please," Sofia butts in, "it's a compliment."

Cheney snakes his hand around the small of my back and I get ready for him to tell them what's what.

But he too just kisses the top of my forehead and says, "Yeah, Ev. My stunning geisha."

Is he serious? I can't tell from his signature smirk or the way he lets go of my back and hovers over my ass. My dress feels too tight. The air is sticky and thick, and I try to open my mouth to say something else, but no words come out. Valerie, who has been totally silent thus far, brushes off chip residue and swivels toward the dance floor.

"Oh my God," she squeals, "I think they're playing a slow song!"

Everyone races back to the barn to find their camp crushes. A singer is crooning through the speakers but I can't process a single lyric. Instead, I stand with my toes buried in dry grass and dirt, breathing in the swirl of hay and muffled laughter. When I look at the barn, I see Rae screeching with joy and the twinkle lights haloing her and Sofia's hair like they're angels, and not two girls who don't know a single thing about culture.

It really is just like that night at the bonfire. I'm such a fool. Nothing has changed since the moment I arrived at Lucius Brown. Not *Thoroughly Modern Millie*, not Abel and the cast's opinion of me, and most of all, not Cheney, who is somehow steering me into the barn and onto the dance floor. He drapes my limp arms over his shoulders.

"I believe," he says, his voice sickly sweet, "we were sorely interrupted before."

His lips hurtle toward mine and I move my head just in time for them to hit my cheek.

"O-oh," I stammer, "just, like, everyone's watching."

It's hardly true. Rae, Sofia, and Valerie are play-dancing together, and everyone else is either moping by the snack table, or successfully slow-dancing with their own camp flings. Ten minutes ago, I would've thrown myself at Cheney, happy to let the credits roll. But now? I don't want to be his leading lady.

I want to be with Ariel and Jia. Whenever I dragged them to my eighth-grade dances, we always pretended we were in music videos, showcasing our most dramatic pouts for the fake cameras until the chaperones asked us if we were unwell. Once, Jia kicked off her kitten heels and literally attempted to do a split on the maple wood floor. Ariel kept yelling that Jia was going to rip her tights, and I don't remember anything else but laughing so hard, my abs hurt for days. Those were the best parties, the best nights.

Cheney stares dreamily into my eyes, eager to make another move. I feel his needy, chapped lips push against mine and this time, I am too tired to make excuses. Instead, I close my eyes and imagine I'm back in the Hyatt ballroom with my friends, stitches in our sides, prancing until our feet fall off.

They were right, Jia and Ariel. It doesn't matter that I'm Millie's understudy or that I'm the best dancer in the cast or that I'm possibly Cheney's girlfriend. To everyone at the Lucius Brown Performing Arts Institute, I'm always Ching Ho. I'm always the geisha.

# 29
# Ariel

"This one," Haejin says, pointing to a song in the laminated binder. Her nail polish changes colors underneath the swath of purple and blue disco ball lights.

I shake my head. "No. Absolutely not."

Carl sticks out his bottom lip and whines into the microphone. "Please," he says, "pretty, pretty please."

The karaoke rooms in Geumjeong are small and kaleidoscopic, packed between grocery stores and nail salons. They're flashier than the ones in Manhattan's Koreatown. We used to go for Everett's birthday. She always picked show tunes, while Jia's go-to was the Spice Girls. Haejin says that I can't come to Korea without singing proper karaoke. So she dragged me here. University students fill the rooms next door. I can hear faint singing and the clink of soju shot glasses.

I've spent the past week with Bea's friends. We went to Nampo to munch on kebabs. We trekked from Imo's house all the way to Haeundae. I told them I couldn't go into any of the clubs or bars because I'm underage, but they surprisingly didn't mind. Instead, we strolled around town and lost ourselves to the thump of the music. Sometimes I had so much fun I forgot what Haejin and Carl did. I forgot about places like San Francisco, and Briston, and home.

Everett and Jia think it's time to get the truth about Bea's death. But every time I try, I see my sister drowning. I see her jewelry. The shell bracelets. The blue-glass necklaces. Carl gave them to me to keep. I see everything I don't understand. And then I can't find the words.

Carl's puppy-dog eyes are so wide, I think they might pop out of his head. "If you sing this," he says, "I will give you ten thousand won."

"You already owe me ten thousand won for the room," I tell him.

"Okay, I will give you ten thousand more won."

I shake my head. "My Korean is terrible."

The synthesizer starts pulsing, the music getting faster and faster. The countdown on the screen begins.

"Oops," Haejin says.

I groan, taking the microphone. Carl cheers and Haejin starts dancing like she's at a club. I wonder if Bea did this with them. We never did karaoke at home. I don't even know what her favorite songs were. Was she a K-pop fan like Haejin? Or did she prefer something cheesy and American like "Don't Stop Believin'" or "Sweet Caroline"?

I don't understand half the lyrics to So Chan-Whee's "Tears," but I scream them anyway. I'm a terrible singer. Everett would tell me I have no breath support. I will probably lose my voice tomorrow. If any Korean person saw or heard me, I'd be publicly ridiculed. But Carl is hugging my shoulders and Haejin is twirling around the room. When I get to the high notes, I give them my best shot and they erupt with applause. For the first time in months, I feel myself smile. The skin around my mouth is puckered and raw. I could stay in this room forever.

My phone jingles in my purse as the song ends. I hand the microphone back to Carl.

"I'll be right back," I say, "and when I am, you better have ten thousand won waiting for me."

Carl flutters his eyelashes. "Put it on my tab, darling."

I make my way out of the karaoke room and into the lobby. It's still brimming with Pusan college students in tennis skirts and leather jackets. The door swings open and a wave of fresh night air hits my face. I wander onto the street. Even outside, I can still hear muted, happy chatter. I pick up the phone without seeing who's calling.

"Hello?"

"Ariel." Umma's voice is stern but steady. Her screaming phase from last week seems to have passed.

"Oh," I say, "hi, Umma. It's early in New York."

My mother ignores my comment. Appa clears his throat in the background like he wants me to know he's there but is fully aware that my mother is in control.

"Your Appa and I need to talk to you," Umma says.

I picture them on speaker in the dining room, perfect posture, piles of plans and papers strewn across the table, all titled *How to Save Ariel from Ruin*. If I hang up now, they'll only call back angrier. So I inhale.

"Okay," I say, "what about?"

A piece of paper crunches against the phone receiver. I guess I was right.

"I called Briston and they said you can start on August twenty-sixth as planned. Although you will need to take your introductory STEM courses again since you never finished your precollege ones." Umma pauses for maximum guilt-tripping. "And you will have to find yourself a tutor if you are struggling. I already got some names from Mimi Ajumma's granddaughter—you know, the one who went to Briston and then Harvard Medical School. You may have graduated a year early, Ari-ya, but you don't know everything."

*I'm beginning to understand how Bea felt*, I want to say. But Umma would just start yelling. So I nod.

"Mm."

It is not a confirmation or a rejection of her plans. But it will suffice.

"We cannot make you come home," she admits, "but if you're not in Queens by August first, your Appa and I will be forced to use our vacation funds to come and get you. We will drag you on that plane if we must, Ari-ya."

This is like saying, *Oh, we're definitely not going to arrest you.*

*We're just going to put you in handcuffs, shove you in a cop car, and send you straight to booking.* At least my parents have settled on a date. At first, Umma insisted I come home immediately. *Now*, she would say during every call, *get on a flight now.* But we both knew I wasn't going to leave. I'd have to pack my things. Imo would want to drive me to the airport. The ocean would sob my name.

I respond with another "Mm." Appa sighs.

"Ariel," he says, "we are all so tired. You've already been in Korea for two weeks. We're giving you till the end of the month. That's more than generous."

Appa has always been the logical one. He loves geometry. He believes in the transitive property. If x, then y. If we give Ariel some more time, she will come home happily. She will start college and everything will be fine and dandy. We will forget this whole mess ever happened.

I used to play the same game with my sister. If I don't tell Appa and Umma that Bea snuck out at two a.m. last night, she will trust me. If she trusts me, then I can convince her to listen to them. I can persuade her to study a little more, party a little less. I can help her with her physics homework. I can get her on Khan Academy. I can mold her into my clone.

In this way, Appa and I are alike. We both make intelligent arguments for things that ultimately won't happen.

"Ari-ya?" my mother says. "Are you listening?"

"Yes, Umma." I stare at my shoes, open-toed wedges that Haejin let me borrow from her closet.

"So you will agree to come home by the first?"

Someone in the lobby screams with laughter. A group of boys start yelling the lyrics to a BTS song.

"Is someone there, Ariel?" Appa asks. "Where are you?"

I know my mother is analyzing every noise around me. "You're out," she confirms, her consonants slicing through the phone, "you're *partying*."

"I'm not partying."

"I recognize those sounds."

I don't understand what she means. And then I realize she's talking about her phone calls with Bea. Brief, and angry. Just like this. I hear the scrape of Umma's chair against the hardwood as she pushes it back.

"Your Imo is showing you a grand old time," she continues, "of course she is. My sister never could sit her butt down and do the work, huh? Always needed to have her fun."

My cheeks flush. Imo barely takes me anywhere. Sometimes we go out to a restaurant and eat cold sashimi at one of the tables on the sidewalk. She doesn't ask questions or tell me not to hang out with Haejin and Carl. She pats my head and changes my sheets. She lets me borrow her lipstick and tells me to text her when I'm on my way home.

"I'm not *with* Imo," I spit, my voice rising.

Immediately, I realize my mistake. The silence on the other end curdles in my chest. And then:

"Who are you with?" my mother hisses. "Tell me. Tell me now."

"No one," I croak.

"Clearly someone."

"Don't be stupid," Appa adds.

Their voices start to overlap. "You go all the way to South Korea," my mother says, the fifth time she's repeated this since I left. She usually trails off, afraid of what will come out of her mouth. But now she keeps going. "And you party, and you lie, and you argue. You're turning into a girl I don't know. You're just like—"

She can't finish. I know she can't. So I do it for her.

"Like Bea," I say. "Just like Bea."

I dig my toes into Haejin's wedges. The street corner whirs with motorcycle engines and happy shrieks and the roar of the ocean, farther away, in Geumjeong, but closer than ever.

"You don't know anything about her," I tell them. "I mean, how could you? You didn't even want to know her. And I didn't either. But Bea did amazing things here. She—"

"Stop," my mother shouts, "just stop."

"Umma, I—"

"Ariel." Appa's voice is quiet and shaky. "That's enough."

I've never talked to my parents like that. I've never talked to anyone like that. I wish I could explain. I wish I could ship every thought right to America. Instead, I inhale sharply and try to lower my pulse.

"I'm sorry," I say. "I have to go."

Umma sniffles. "I miss the old Ariel," she whispers. "She wouldn't have done this."

She's right. The Ariel from before, the one with the trophies, and the debate ribbons, and the good grades, achieved everything Umma and Appa wanted. She was obedient. She was happy. And she let her sister get on a plane and fly to South Korea. She let her fight, and flail, and cry. It doesn't matter what Haejin and Carl did or didn't do. I let her drown.

From: arielunderthesea_29@gmail.com

To: everetthoang24601@gmail.com; jialee@leedumplinghouse.com

1:12 AM

Subject: Late Night Thoughts

E and J,

Do you ever feel like everything's falling apart even when it's coming together? I'm getting to know Haejin and Carl better. I want to hate them. I had a plan. I was ready to confront them when the time came. But they're so nice to me. I can see why Bea liked them. I can see how tight they all were.

The more I stay, the more I can't seem to leave. My parents have given me a deadline. August 1st. It was pretty much a demand. But there's so much about Bee that I want to discover. Her jewelry is only the beginning. Also, I'm starting to really like Busan. Probably just because it doesn't smell as gross as New York. Haha. Anyway, I'm not going until I'm ready. I'll let you know when that is.

Love you both until the end of time.

XO,

Ariel

# 30
# Jia

I run my fingers across the first line of Ariel's email. *Do you ever feel like everything's falling apart even when it's coming together?* Nai Nai is in the living room, slurping up string beans and holding on to every word of the television's histrionic soap opera. In the afternoons, we do her physical therapy exercises together before walking outside with CeCe. We feel the sun on our skin, and watch the neighborhood dogs play in the park. All of the staff is back at the restaurant, so Mom gets her hour-long breaks again. She dips her tired toes into basins of hot water and peels back an orange so slowly, you can hear its skin crackle.

But I just want to bury my head under the covers. If I stare into the depths of my comforter, maybe Akil's face won't be imprinted on my brain. His face next to *Madison's* under the glare of the diner's yellow light. I shouldn't care. He can talk to whoever he wants. I roll over on my bed and imagine myself clicking into my camera roll and deleting the photo, but I know I won't.

Other than the park, I haven't been anywhere in days. The apartment walls are dark and dingy and I'm starting to note the way the wallpaper puckers at the edges where it meets the ceiling. The soap opera theme song plays on and on, a twiddling violin tune that pierces every corner of the apartment. When Nai Nai is taking her nap and CeCe isn't wreaking havoc, I open my sketchbook and redraw Itachi Uchiha's face, layering charcoal onto his irises so they become pitch-black holes.

And then, at four o'clock, I hear Mom's key click into the front door. I dash out of my room and pull off my sweatshirt, discarding it somewhere on the carpet. My bones are itchy and tired and seem to protrude from my shirt. I have to get out of here. I have to.

"Mom," I begin, tripping over my feet as I stumble down the hall, "do you think I could leave for like thirty minutes? Twenty, even. Just on my bike. I won't go far. I just need to—"

When I reach the kitchen, I see that my mother isn't alone. A woman in patterned scrubs stands behind her, rubber shoes squeaking on the tile as she slides them off her feet. Mom isn't wearing her good sweater like usual. Instead, she dons a linen dress and a cheery smile.

"Jia," she says, setting down her purse, "I want you to meet Danica."

The woman in the scrubs holds out her hand and I shake it.

"Hi," I say.

"It's so nice to meet you," she replies.

Danica has excellent posture and a businesslike handshake. She promptly places her bags on the table. She looks far too professional for our Flushing apartment covered in pots and pans and steeped in the leftover stench of dried pork.

"Danica is going to be helping out Nai Nai a couple days a week during the summer," Mom explains, "and then full-time once the school year starts."

Then she leads Danica into the living room, where Nai Nai is falling asleep to the tinny television voices. Gently, Mom shakes her mother-in-law's shoulder and Nai Nai's eyes flutter open.

I watch in awe as Mom repeats her explanation to Nai Nai, and Danica covers my grandmother's knees with the afghan from the couch. Words like *bathroom* and *anytime* and *physical therapy* fill the apartment. Nai Nai examines Danica's top and grins.

"So colorful!" she proclaims.

Danica laughs. "It's just my uniform."

As they get to know each other, my mother returns to the kitchen and turns on the tap, the water rushing into our silver tea-pot. She flips on the gas and scoops tea leaves into three mugs. I hover by the stove. I don't understand. Two weeks ago, my parents were panicking about hospital bills, rehab, and insurance, and now there is a medical professional in our apartment, nodding patiently as Nai Nai narrates every painstaking detail of the soap opera she's obsessed with.

"Mom," I whisper, inches from her cheek so Danica and Nai Nai can't hear, "how can we afford this?"

My mother twist-ties the bag of tea leaves closed. She doesn't look up. "Your dad and I discussed it," she says, "and we decided it's what's needed. We will handle the money. You don't worry about it."

She turns toward me, the creases on her forehead and around her eyes paper-thin.

"You need to focus on school. And in a few years, the restaurant. We should have done this months ago."

I nod silently. So she and Dad have been preparing. They're right, I suppose. I won't be able to take care of Nai Nai and the restaurant all at once. I have to be ready for my future. My mother lifts the bottom of my chin.

"You look tired," she whispers. "Go. Be back in an hour."

I leave the apartment in a daze. My bike wheels squeal under my sneakers. The line for the duck cart overflows into the bike lane, hungry customers breathing in steamy late-afternoon air and sizzling vegetables. At Flushing Meadows, I think about stopping, but my wheels drag me forward, past the skateboarders, and the baby parade, and the shamrock-green trees. When I reach the corner of Ascan and Austin, the underpass carries me to the other side. My bike knows where it's going before I do.

Forest Hills Gardens looks just like it did a month ago. Ornate lampposts line every block, and someone's golden retriever sinks under a vine-covered stone archway. The grass is neatly trimmed, and children in striped shirts run through the cul-de-sac sprinklers. I've never been here without Everett. I wait for someone to look my way or tell me I don't belong. But no one does. An elderly man in a straw bucket hat reads on his porch while a woman in Lycra shorts jogs past me. I stop at Everett's house on instinct and wonder if her brothers are home or if Watkins is at the kennel. And then I turn toward the other side of the street.

There he is. On the lawn, playing with his little brother. I
didn't expect him to be home. Masud runs through the grass, and
Akil smiles—that huge, dopey grin I missed so much. I unbuckle
my helmet. My bangs are slick against my forehead, and my thighs
are covered in bug bites that have ballooned into angry welts. I
look like a wreck. I should go home, shower, and do this all again
later. But then I think of Ariel, who could easily book a flight back
to New York and return to safety—to the cool concrete jungle
where there are no oceans or secrets, or dead sisters. Instead, she's
choosing to stay. I let out a shaky breath as Akil and I make eye
contact. He immediately sits up in the grass. I park my bike at
Everett's and nervously walk toward him.

"Hey," I say.

"Hi," he replies. He glances at Masud, who is shoveling up
mulch and throwing it onto the cobblestone pathway.

"Buddy," he shouts, "don't do that."

I stand awkwardly on the lawn while Akil picks up his brother
and deposits him on the porch.

"Go play inside," he tells him, and Masud dutifully disappears
behind their front door. Now it is just the two of us. Pollen drifts
onto Akil's sleeve, and I fight the urge to pick it off.

"It's been a minute," I blurt, which is an incredibly asinine
thing to say.

Akil gives me a pained smile. "Yeah," he says, and then, like
he's thinking really hard about it, "Yeah."

He is such a small boy surrounded by an enormous house. I
wonder what the view from his bedroom window is like. Maybe

it overlooks a pool, or a sprawling garden like Everett's, lush with pink roses and prickly thorns. Maybe he has parties in the backyard with Madison Pollack and the other girls, flipping grilled hamburgers, chomping on nachos, and talking about which classes they're going to take in the fall. Akil crosses his arms and steps forward.

"So," he says, "what's been going on with you?"

I shift in my sandals. "I—I don't know what you mean."

"But you do." He scoffs, shaking his head. "I texted you like a million times. If you don't like me, you could have just told me. I would have been fine with it."

He pauses, and I don't know how to respond. But then he continues: "Well, okay, I wouldn't have been fine—I'd have been pretty upset—but at least I would have had answers. And answers are really important, right?"

Akil's eyes dart back and forth across the top of my head, but he won't look directly at me.

"I mean, we—we *kissed*," he continues, "and I went home that night, and I was, like, just so freaking over the moon, and I thought you were happy. I mean, you seemed happy, but if you weren't happy, you could have picked up the phone. Or texted. Or literally made a TikTok. I would have taken anything."

I think he might cry. He has a horrible twisted expression on his face. So I don't know why I make it worse.

"You moved on fine," I hear myself say. "You have Madison."

Akil finally stares right at me, cocking his head like I'm an alien. "Madison? What does Madison have to do with this?"

"Never mind."

This was a terrible idea. I fight the urge to rush back to my bike and ride until the sky is dark and all the shopkeepers flick off their lights so I can see my reflection in the glass.

"No, seriously." Akil steps closer. "Tell me."

"It's nothing. Really. I should get home."

At this, Akil squints his eyes and pinches the bridge of his nose.

"Of course," he mutters, "you're not gonna tell me anything. Typical."

*Typical.* The word, razor-sharp, stings my tongue. I want to tell him that while he was touring the city, I was touring the hospital, willing Nai Nai to get better. I was watching her hobble down linoleum floors, teetering as she fought to regain the strength she lost—because of me, because of *us*. I chose fireworks and kisses and Akil over my grandmother's health. I know she's okay, but future Jia won't be given these second chances. The responsibility will be too great.

"You don't know me," I snap. "You don't know me at all."

Akil throws his hands up in the air. They swing like windmills.

"Maybe I don't," he admits, "but I *want* to. Don't you see, Jia? It's what I've wanted all summer."

I can't seem to catch my breath. Mom's break is almost over, and she'll be waiting for me to come home. CeCe will crawl her way back into my arms and whine until I dress up her dolls with her. And the bills must be counted, and the restaurant sign is still lopsided, and I belong there, not here.

"I need to go," I say again.

And with that, I rush down his driveway, my shoes crunching against the gravel. When I reach my bike, I rebuckle my helmet and push up my kickstand. I can hear Akil calling my name, but I don't look back. I ride until my legs are heavy and sore and the wind drags me home.

# 31
# Everett

"You look perfect."

*Perfect* is not the word I would use to describe the itchy blue satin jacket I'm wearing or the dragon-patterned docker hat sitting atop my braids. *Embarrassing* is a better word. *Inauthentic* is another. *Ariel rant–worthy* is a third.

Julie, the costume designer, swivels my shoulders toward a full-length mirror so we can admire this monstrosity in its entirety. It feels like there are bedbugs in my sleeves, or maybe flies, buzzing and buzzing and consuming my flesh.

Julie is oblivious.

"I used this costume for the last Millie I did, and I'm honestly astonished that my Ching Hos have the same measurements. What are the odds, right? Must be fate."

She blows a kiss to the greenroom ceiling like the theater gods really blessed us with cheap, boxy, vaguely Asian outfits. I fake smile back. It's all I've been doing this week. Like when Cheney kissed my forehead at dinner the other day. Or when Rae asked me if I lived in the "Asian part of New York." Ariel is in Korea wearing her dead sister's jewelry and trying to be strong, and Jia is juggling the restaurant, Akil, and her grandma's health, and all I can do is smile on cue and try to forget that all this theater cares about is the color of my skin.

I readjust the jacket and try to imagine any of the Ching Hos before me wearing this getup. Were they like Ryan, happily pretending to be Chinese? Or did they too disassociate every time they tipped their docker hats and kotowed to the evil Mrs. Meers? Did their hearts pang when they thought of their own friends, their own family, their own selves, and the struggles the real Ching Hos faced? The ones writers with their cigars and pinstripe suits could never understand?

I hear Abel call twenty over the greenroom's loudspeakers. Julie picks up her tote and rummages through its contents, emerging with her keys.

"Oh good," she says, "I'm starving. Ev, put your costume back on the rack, okay? There's a hanger with your name on it."

I nod wordlessly as she flounces out of the room, her keys jingling as she walks. Quickly, I unbutton my jacket.

In three weeks, this greenroom (which, contrary to popular belief, is not green but urine yellow) will be packed with cast members in fringed flapper dresses and cakey white foundation. Jacob will probably be sitting on the couch with Dorito dust on his jacket even though you're not supposed to eat in your costume, while Valerie will be donning a blunt-banged wig so she'll look exactly like a roaring twenties Sutton Foster. Everyone's parents and people from all over Ohio (Lucius Brown's theater productions are, like, the highlight of the summer here) will fill the auditorium seats and munch on overpriced snacks during intermission. The stage manager will call five minutes to curtain and we'll hurriedly squeeze each other's hands one by one so we won't have a bad show. The rush before we go on stage will be a collective high unlike any other—better than the weed I choked on that one time at a cast party. We'll remember this feeling for decades.

Except, as I stand in my sports bra and brown pants, I don't want to remember anything. I'd rather forget this summer entirely. Maybe Ariel can use her science skills to erase my brain and take me back to the Everett who would snap fifty selfies in her costume because she loved pretending to be someone else, who would cry after every show because she missed the unspeakable magic.

I slide off my pants and stumble into my leggings and tee. Folding my costume into the crook of my elbow, I walk back into the theater, where the racks line the side wall. A crowd is gathered around them, likely eyeing their own costumes and accessories. When I step closer, I spot Valerie's back heaving up and down, her hands curled to her mouth to stifle her giggles. She steps to her right and I make out the crowd's faces.

Rae, wearing Bun Foo's red satin jacket, too big for her body. Sofia, with chopsticks poking out of her hair like horns, the corners of her eyes messily elongated with black eyeliner. And Cheney, wearing a docker hat that matches the one resting in my hands.

"The American dreeeeeam!" Sofia sputters, laughing so hard, the eyeliner gets wet and smudges her skin. "Come on, I'll do yours."

I am motionless as she presses her fingers against Cheney's face and drags black kohl down his waterline. Abel Pearce is leaned over the piano sharing notes with Kayla, seemingly unaware of everything going down on the sidelines.

I am robot Everett. I am feel-nothing Everett. And then, at last, I am not.

"What the actual fuck?"

My voice ricochets against the empty rows as the group turns to me. I power down the aisle so I am two feet from Rae's eyeliner-smudged face.

"Do you think this funny?" I can hear myself getting louder. "Do you think you're so cool for being racist little shits?"

Abel Pearce steps away from the piano and walks rapidly toward me, his arms crossed.

"Miss Hoang," he says, "this behavior is unacceptable."

The old Everett would have cowered immediately at this chastising, at once again making a scene in public. But I am done with letting Abel Pearce get away with everything.

"No," I spit, "*this* is unacceptable."

There is so much more I want to say: about Abel's lies, about this show being ridiculous, about these costumes being a mockery of Chinese culture, about these awful people, and about this theater—this theater that was all wrong from the very beginning. It just took me this long to admit it.

"You suck," I snap. "You all suck."

I move to storm down the aisle, but Cheney catches my wrist. His grip is cold and firm.

"Ev," he says, "chill out. We were just joking around. Don't blow your top."

"Fuck you," I say. I drop my costume and it clatters at his feet.

"Miss Hoang."

"And fuck you, too. Fuck this camp."

Sofia holds her rib cage like she's been mortally wounded. Valerie's eyes fill with tears.

*Good*, I think, *good, good, good*. I want them to remember this moment. I want them to feel sadness and shame and fear. I want them to hate themselves as much as I hate myself.

"Everett." Abel Pearce steps closer. "You should know that disciplinary measures *will* be taken."

My laughter is demonic. Is this how Sweeney Todd felt? Is this why he started slicing and dicing everyone who wronged him to bits?

"Who cares?" I practically shriek. "I'm done with this place anyway."

I walk back down the aisle and fling open the theater doors.

"Everett, wait," Valerie calls after me.

But my roommate's fake sympathy can't save me now. I let the doors slam shut.

From: everetthoang24601@gmail.com

To: jialee@leedumplinghouse.com; arielunderthesea_29@gmail.com

10:01 AM

Subject: Urgent

My bestest and truest friends,

I'm leaving Ohio. Everything is terrible and everyone sucks and I can't stand it anymore, I really can't. You warned me and you were both right. Cheney is a douchebag and this entire institution is shitty and racist and I tried to reason my way through it the whole time. But I'm done making excuses.

I'm literally packing right now and trying to hurry as much as possible because the board of directors keeps calling me to arrange a "discussion" which is just a load of BULL. I don't want to discuss anything with Abel Pearce and his minions, especially since he'll just say, "Miss Hoang, maintain your composure" or some other condescending crap. Anyway, they can't force me to talk to them because this is NOT school, and I'm getting on a plane tomorrow!!!!

Ethan just finished his internship so I made him sign my release papers. I yelled at him to drag his butt to LaGuardia and pick me up and I think he knows actual shit is going down because he didn't even argue and said he'd come right away. Shocker, I know.

I love you both and I'll call you when I land. Going to drown myself in ice cream until then.

Hugs forever,

Everett

# 32
# Ariel

I open Everett's email under a flashing BBQ advertisement on Gwangalli Beach. If I close my eyes, I can feel the lights slink against my eyelids and hear purses and wallets slapping against thighs. It sounds just like Times Square. But then I remember that everyone is speaking in Korean. And if I walk fifty feet to my right, I'm on the sand, steps away from the ocean. I'm on the beach while my friends need me back home.

It must have been so difficult for Everett to leave Ohio. They must have pushed her to the edge. She's never missed a performance in her entire life. Even when she had acid reflux right before she went on stage. Even when Richie broke up with her over text during intermission.

Facing your fears is a key part of psychological development. When you're terrified of something, your amygdala pretends it's a bomb intent on total destruction. But if you look closer, it's just a cloud. It's only going to rain. Everett's already faced her fears. I look up at the BBQ sign. It's time to face mine.

Haejin and Carl linger under a storefront's overhang. Across the ocean, the bridge's lights reflect off the water. Carl holds his phone to our faces, aglow with a photo of a Korean guy with glass-cut cheekbones and a magazine scowl.

"What do ya think?" he says. "Cute or not cute?"

Haejin touches her nose to the screen. "Cute. But maybe *too* cute. Kind of intimidating."

Carl swings the phone to my face. "Ariel?"

I cock my head. "Who is this?"

Bea's friends curl into each other like Siamese twins.

"Some lad Carl fancies," Haejin explains. "They're in the same modeling agency."

"Glamorous. Does he live in Busan?"

"Seoul," Carl explains, "but that's only, what . . . three hours by KTX?" He bats his eyes. "Practically next door."

Carl kisses the stranger's glossy photo while Haejin rolls her eyes. "Oh, my love," she says, "always the hopeless romantic."

Her best friend lifts his hands to the sky, skimming the top of some poor woman's head. "All you need is love!" he declares while girls with their handbags stare and Haejin and I snicker.

If Bea were here, she'd arrange for Carl and cheekbones boy to meet up in an idyllic park with picnic blankets and a wine-and-cheese spread. Bea was addicted to setups and happy endings. She adored every romantic comedy from *When Harry Met Sally* to *Crazy Rich Asians*, ignoring my protests that the cookie-cutter formula was boring and clichéd. When she was fifteen, she decided that she was destined to meet a beautiful boy in ninth grade. The plan was for her and this fictional guy to date for four years before they got married. Their wedding would be at a villa in the south of France. I was going to be her maid of honor and wear blush pink—no objections allowed. She later realized that none of the Queens boys were remotely close to beautiful. She'd have to settle for Justin from health class, who cheated on every girl he dated and flunked the STD exam in more ways than one.

The ocean beats against the shore. Each wave sounds like a memory. Appa, reassuring my mother in the dining room as she hides behind her barbed-wire words. Imo, waiting for me to talk. Everett and Jia, worrying and wondering when I'll return home. My sister, flailing under the sea, time slipping away. *Come find me.*

I suck in salty air and Carl's cologne. "Why didn't you call?"

The pair snap forward like puppets. Carl glances at Haejin before looking back at me.

"Call when?" he says.

"You know when." My voice sounds steadier than I feel. "When Bea died. When my parents went back to Queens. You didn't call once. Why?"

Haejin's eyebrows crinkle like she has no idea what I'm talking about. But I refuse to let her feign ignorance. Not when we've spent almost every day together pretending to be friends.

"Ariel," she says, pinching the cuffs of her shorts, "let's go sit down."

"No. I want to talk now. Here."

"We will, I promise," Haejin replies, "but please, let's just sit down first."

Carl is already on the move, desperate to get away. I don't have a choice. So we walk to a layer of steps descending into sand. My flip-flops scrape the gaps between the wood. We crouch down, Haejin on one side, Carl on the other. Finally, Haejin speaks.

"Ariel," she says, "we wanted to call."

"*Wanting* is not the same as *doing*."

I am surprised to hear the bite in my voice. I've held it back for weeks, but now it sounds childish. Thankfully, the sky is too dark for Haejin and Carl to see my stinging eyes.

Haejin shakes her head. "No, we really *did* want to call. But we couldn't. We weren't allowed. I . . . I guess your parents didn't tell you."

"Tell me what?"

*Tell me what* is what a girl asks her boyfriend before he reveals he's been secretly married to someone else for five years. It's what the detective asks his brother who confesses that he was the murderer all along. I hold my breath.

"Your parents forbade us from contacting them," Carl begins quietly, "and you. At the hospital, they made it very clear that we could never talk to your family again. Not even your Imo."

"That's, um, why I was so surprised when you introduced yourself at Meokja," Haejin explains. "I figured you knew about the no-contact rule. But then . . . you seemed so willing to chat. So I told Carl that maybe your parents gave you permission."

"Yeah, now that I'm thinking about it, your parents didn't

want you in Korea at all, so *obviously* they didn't give you permission. But we had been waiting for so long to meet you. And to tell you about Bea," Carl says.

"And we also really like hanging out with you." Haejin half smiles. "So here we are. Upsetting your parents yet again."

The words burn in my mind one at a time—*parents, forbid, never, permission, Bea*. At once, I am on my feet. I pace back and forth.

"I don't get it," I say. "I don't *get it*. Why would Umma and Appa do this? What did—"

I pause. Umma hunched over the sink with her suitcases, fresh off the plane from Korea. All my questions: *who, where, how, Bea, I need her*. The sudden snap of her neck as she shook her head at me. *Reckless*, she told me, *Bea was reckless*. Appa in the study, shoving scholarship applications in my face, the unspoken message: *Make up for what your sister lost*. How could I not have known? How could I have missed all those puzzle pieces?

My parents saw what they wanted to see. I stare at what's in front of me. The circles under Haejin's eyes are blotchy and purple. She is wearing the friendship bracelet Bea gave her. Carl's forehead is creased into a lightning bolt.

I sit back down. My friends inch closer.

"Tell me about the day she died," I say. "Start from the beginning."

They nod. And then, they begin.

It was three days before Carl's birthday. Bea had cajoled a professional photographer into shooting promotional photos of her

jewelry. Haejin had just started classes for the fall. There were reasons to celebrate. Renting a pontoon was expensive. But it was the
last sunny day in September. Bea packed sandwiches in a cooler
bag and woke her friends up early. They traveled almost two hours
to Songjeong Beach, where the tourists were few and the water was
turquoise. They put on life jackets. They kept the boat a half mile
from shore, like they were supposed to.

In the afternoon, just as they were thinking of heading home,
Haejin and Carl wanted to go back in the water for one last swim.
They clipped on their life jackets while Bea kept hers off—she was
going to stay on the boat and eat her sandwich. She wanted to lie
in the sun, munch on deli meat, get a tan.

The current picked up. The waves grew higher. Higher than
surfer waves. Higher than the boat could handle. It flipped.
Haejin and Carl were screaming, their eyes drenched in salt. Up
ahead, they could hear people clamoring to dry land. They tried
to find Bea but they could not see her, could not search the water
while it was swallowing them whole. So they fled back to shore.
And they hoped she was there waiting for them. A better swimmer
than they thought, her bikini straps only tangled. She'd say it was
an adventure to add to their memory book. But Bea was not on
the beach. She was back with the boat, churning and churning in
the deep blue. The coast guards pulled her out thirty minutes later,
when the waves had died down and the ocean pretended there was
nothing lying in its center but seaweed. It was too late.

"Stop," I say, "just stop."

My feet sprint up the steps, and I crash into elbows and blue jeans. I see nothing but sand and Bea. Bea dead. Bea everywhere. The articles said, *The eighteen-year-old woman was not wearing a life jacket.* My parents said, *Your sister was stupid.* No one said, *Bea was just a girl enjoying her lunch, celebrating life. Bea was the last chocolate croissant in the box. She was an umbrella gifted by a stranger when it started to pour. She was pink hair dye on a boring Sunday. She was the first one to tell you that you had spinach in your teeth or a tag on the back of your shirt. She was an artist, a visionary.* She was my sister.

Haejin and Carl come up behind me. We are three ants under the storefronts and high-rises.

"It was a terrible accident," Carl says. "The current hadn't been that bad in years."

I can feel their breath on my neck. A tear drips down my shirt.

Haejin sniffles. "I'm so sorry, Ariel."

I want to tell them that I am sorry too—for all the ways I did not trust them. For all the lost time. Instead, I turn around and fold into Haejin's and Carl's arms. We cry together.

# 33
# Jia

It's a perfect summer day in Flushing. Usually, the end of July is a series of muggy, unbearable mornings that fade into gnat-ridden nights. But at eleven a.m. on the stoop of Lee's Dumpling House, the breeze brushes against my face and the clouds fluff overhead like jumbo marshmallows. I should be savoring this. CeCe is in the back with Lizzie, who is kindly teaching my sister how to make custard. Nai Nai and Danica are at a doctor's appointment. Mom and Dad are somewhere inside the restaurant—Mom at the hostess stand and Dad in the kitchen. Neither has asked for my help today. I am free, finally. And better yet, Everett is on her way back from Ohio, soaring over Pennsylvania to find her way home again. I want to squeeze the hurt out of her, but I know that's not possible. Just like with Ariel, Everett will have to rebuild her own world.

While I wait for her, I could go to the park or Manga Palace. I could walk over to the Goodwill around the corner and try to find a pair of thrifted jeans before the back-to-school rush begins. But all I actually do is wallow on the stoop and check my phone every five seconds to see if Akil has texted me. I replay the sting in my voice as I shouted at him: *You don't know me.*

*But I want to,* he'd said. He wants to. He *wants* to.

At the food cart next to the duck bao stand, Mr. Zhang hands out the last of his jian dui, the chewy sesame balls now tucked away in shopping bags. He's worked at this cart for the last twenty years, just like every other shopkeeper in Chinatown. They've all known me my entire life. When I was a baby, my parents told me that our neighbors were constantly bringing me gifts—knitted strawberry hats and hand-me-down pacifiers, packed red envelopes and stuffed animals. They did the same for CeCe twelve years later, even though they had bad backs and canes by then and couldn't always walk three flights of stairs.

Mr. Zhang wipes his forehead with a rag and smiles at me. It's rare that he sells all his jian dui so early. "A good morning," he confirms. "Made lots of money already."

"Yes," I say with a nod, "that's wonderful."

Even though Mr. Zhang and I mostly communicate in quick hellos and waves from across the street, he immediately notes the falter in my voice.

"Come," he calls, laying down his rag on the counter and beckoning me over.

It is rude to disobey your elders. So I dust the stoop soot off my shorts and shuffle to his cart. Up close, I can see red bean oozing out of pastry and smell the sweet aroma of fried dough.

"Pick one," he says, gesturing to the leftover desserts scattering his cart.

I shake my head. "I don't have any money on me."

Mr. Zhang scoffs. "For you, my Jia? Free."

*My Jia.* I'm still that fat baby in the strawberry hat even when I'm seventeen. I wish I could hug Mr. Zhang without it being strange. I think I will cry if I leave this place, even though I desperately want to go.

Mr. Zhang pushes his tongs into my hands, and I hold them tight. I settle on an almond cookie, feeling my way around its ridges before biting into its crunchy center. The crumbly dough and hot lard melt in my mouth.

"Mmm," I say, "delicious."

Mr. Zhang grins. "They were the first things I learned how to make."

"Really? In New York?"

"No," he says, "in Taiwan." He has this faraway look in his eyes, like he's lost in his younger self. "We fled during the revolution. Like your Nai Nai. I was eighteen or so. And there was hardly any food back in China, so I was very skinny. The Taiwanese probably thought I was some kind of animal."

I've heard snippets of my neighbors' lives before Chinatown, but not Mr. Zhang's. I bite into my cookie as noiselessly as possible and rest my elbows on the counter.

"In Taiwan, they had things like flour," Mr. Zhang continues, rearranging the pastries on his cart to fill up the empty space, "and sugar. And they weren't rationed. I could hardly believe it. I worked at a grocery store and took all my money and put it right back into the cash register. After I finished my shift, I would eat dinner and immediately start baking. I found a cookbook at the library and worked through it page by page."

He is giddy with excitement remembering his late-night bakes. They remind me of my own sketchbooks, filled to the brim with anime characters—the way the night sometimes curves into early morning, yet my pencil can't stop sketching.

"I became very good," Mr. Zhang says. He fiddles with his apron strings. "I wanted to open my own bakery in Taipei. But my father said there were better opportunities in America. So, I came. And I had to start all over again. I didn't even man the cash register. I swept the floors."

Dad always says I should be grateful that I'm just greeting customers and handing out menus when I'm working at the restaurant. He must be thinking of Mr. Zhang when he says this, and of his own story. When my parents came to America, they were dishwashers at an overcrowded hole-in-the-wall restaurant in Chinatown. Then Mom got pregnant while they were making $6.75 an hour and living in a studio with four other roommates. So my father went to night school and got his hospitality certificate while Mom worked until her water broke on the restaurant carpet.

Everyone on this block has similar stories of sacrifice. They all came to a country where they did not speak the language, where their degrees did not matter, where they were mocked and spit at just for the lilt in their voices and the small lines of their eyes. Over the years, they built a home—one I am so ashamed of, I cannot even show a boy down the street. I finish the last bit of cookie.

"Mr. Zhang," I say, "look where you are now. You've created something wonderful."

Mr. Zhang laughs at me. "It is just a cart," he says.

But we both know that it is so much more. Another slew of customers pour down the sidewalk and Mr. Zhang starts taking down orders and hurriedly doling out sweets. I slip out of the cart and find my way back to the stoop. The concrete scratches my thighs, and the car horns meld with the clatter of knives and spatulas from the surrounding food stalls.

I have spent so many months ashamed of this neighborhood and my place in it. I haven't wanted to share any part of China-town with Akil, and sometimes I don't even want to share parts with myself. It's easier to live in someone else's world, where I can pretend I belong. But I can't pretend anymore. My hands shake when I pick up my phone to text Akil.

Hi, I type, **I'm sorry for yesterday. I want to explain every-thing. If you're free, can you come over? I'm at Lee's Dumpling House. It's by the outdoor mall in Chinatown.**

I press Send. And then, I wait. Ten minutes pass. Fifteen, twenty. I think about wandering to the back of the store and watching CeCe pour creamy yellow custard into tart tins like I used to when I was six. But I don't want to move from the stoop. I don't want to miss him. Thirty minutes pass, and I figure he's likely busy, his phone hidden inside his jean pocket. *Or,* a voice in my head says, *he's given up on you*. I try to push the thought down so it doesn't devour me.

I'm just about to give up and head back to the restaurant booths when a neon helmet on a bicycle careens toward me. Akil skids to a stop, his shirt plastered to his chest, a trail of sweat dribbling down his neck.

"Sorry," he says, breathless, "I came right over and forgot to text back."

"Oh," I say, "hi."

"Hi."

It is just like the other day, only different. Akil chains his bike to the rack and I slide over on the stoop so he can sit beside me. He surveys the old Chinese ladies on their way back from tai chi, visors and yoga mats in hand, Mr. Zhang and his weathered skin and gray-speckled hair, the sign above our heads.

"This is cool," he says. "I haven't been to Chinatown yet. My dad said we should go for dim sum sometime, but we just haven't gotten around to it. Mostly 'cause he's on business trips all the time and my mom is legit not home until like ten p.m., so, like, I dunno when we would go. Maybe over the next holiday. When's that? Wow, like, Christmas." He glances at me, sheepish. "Sorry. I'm rambling."

"It's fine." I smile. "You do that when you're nervous."

"Ugh." He smiles back. "Cat's out of the bag."

I fold my arms over my rib cage so that my fingertips cling to my sides. "It's okay," I say. "I'm nervous too."

Akil tugs at his shirt collar. I take a deep breath.

"I wanted you to meet me here because . . . well . . . I live here. This is my family's restaurant." I point to the row of windows above the awning. "And that's where we live. When I'm older, they expect me to take over the store. I don't really think I want that, but I don't know if I have a choice."

Akil doesn't say anything, and I can't look at him, so I focus on the Chinese script draped over Main Street. "Every time I had to run off, it was because someone needed me at the restaurant. Or because I had to take care of my grandma, since she has Parkinson's. I wanted to tell you, but I . . . I just couldn't. I felt too embarrassed, I guess. I know this kind of life isn't what you're used to."

A motorcycle speeds past us, the roaring motor interrupting my thoughts. When the traffic light changes and it's farther away, I find the courage to meet Akil's eyes.

His shoulders are hunched, but he doesn't look angry or disgusted, or even sad.

"I'm sorry," he says.

I shake my head. "What? No. I'm trying to say that *I'm* sorry. For blowing you off, and for not being honest. Because I like you, Akil. Don't tell Everett, 'cause she'll make fun of me for years, but—a lot. I like you a lot."

Akil lights up, the freckles on his nose winging across his cheeks as he beams. "You do?"

"Yeah."

"I like you too," he says, "*a lot*. But really, I am sorry. I don't want you to ever feel like you can't share a part of your life with me just because we live in different places. And also, it sounds like you've been going through it this summer, and I was so worried about my new school and fitting into the Gardens that I didn't exactly think about what could be happening on your end." He scratches the back of his head. "That's why I was hanging out with Madison, by the way. Her mom and my mom are in a Farrow Facebook group, so she suggested I meet her and some other people since she knew I was so anxious about making friends. I sorta figured out what you were talking about yesterday."

"Oh," I say, "that makes sense." But like always, my face gives me away.

"You don't like her." Akil laughs.

"Well . . . not exactly."

The breeze combs through my hair so that it lies across my face like blinds: slivers of our knees on the stoop, tangy sauce drizzled over duck bao, a fragment of sandals, a pocket of fallen flower petals.

Akil gently places his hand on mine. "Maybe we should start from the beginning."

I flip over his hand and intertwine our fingers. "Okay."

I tell him about my parents—everything they fought for to get here, everything they expect me to be when I graduate from high school. I tell him about Madison and the debacle last autumn. I tell him about Nai Nai's fall the night we went to Citi Field, the guilt that gnawed at me. I tell him about the college brochures stuffed in my bottom drawer, my dreams of stone buildings and scribbled notes on wooden desks. It's the first time I've said it out loud: I want something different for my life. I want to arrive at a college and not know what my future holds.

As I speak, Akil nods and asks questions, careful not to interrupt. By the time I'm finished, his arms are cocooned around me, a human nest in this pigeon city.

"Thank you," he says, "for telling me all that. That sucks about your grandma, but I'm glad she's doing better. And I hope, like, you feel comfortable telling me more stuff in the future. I wanna be here for you, you know?"

I smile. "I know," I say, and I mean it.

Akil untangles his legs from mine. "And also," he sighs, "I didn't know that about Madison. Guess she's a friend I *won't* be making at Farrow."

"Well, don't write her off completely. Maybe she's changed." At least, I know I have. "So you don't hate me?"

He smirks. "I think I made that pretty clear ten minutes ago."

We lean in at the same time. His lips are as cool and soft as I remember. He still smells of sunscreen and a hint of chocolate.

I sit back, thankful for the throng of customers who have shielded us from Mr. Zhang. I can just imagine him spying on us from the food cart before toddling over to my parents and relaying the news that *Jia kissed some boy on the restaurant steps*. I'd prefer not to be murdered before the start of the school year.

"You know," Akil says, "you *could* try talking to your parents."

"Um, I don't think that will go very well."

"Maybe, maybe not." Akil shrugs. "But won't you feel worse if you don't? You can't fake it forever. You'll just be miserable. So

I think it's better to be honest with them, and, you know, with yourself."

"Wow," I laugh, "since when did you become so wise?"

Akil wiggles his eyebrows. "I should, like, start a podcast: *Akil Abboud Saves the Planet: One Piece of Advice at a Time.*"

"Yeah," I say, patting his leg, "we'll workshop the title."

The crowd starts to wane again, the street empty except for the shopkeepers, the straggling customers, and the pigeons picking at crumbs lining the food carts' wheels. Akil smooths down his shirt.

"So I have to confess something too," he says. "When I got your text, my little bro was having his birthday party in our backyard. I sorta ran out. My mom said it was fine because she's really into romance or whatever, but basically I need to get back before they cut the cake, otherwise *I'll* be sliced into bits."

"Oh my gosh." I picture little Masud with a bunch of seven-year-olds crowded around him, eagerly staring at a towering frosted cake. "Yeah, of course. Go. I'll text you later."

He stands up and walks backward down the stoop steps so he can watch me as he leaves. When he reaches the end of the sidewalk, his fingers weave around the bike's handlebars.

"You know," he says, "you contain multitudes, Jia."

"Wow, a literary scholar as well. You've really been busy this summer."

"Summer reading project," he says sheepishly. "But seriously. I mean it. You do. Whether you own a restaurant or become, like, president of the United States, you're one of a kind. And that's never gonna change."

I want to think he's joking, but he is completely stone-faced. I pull my hair behind my ears as he swings his leg over the bicycle seat.

"Don't be a stranger," he says.

"I won't," I reply, just as serious. "I promise."

He unchains his bike and takes off, his wheels curving around the corner. The leaves cheer so loudly, I feel them quaking in my bones.

# 34
# Everett

What is better than theater? Or jackass almost-boyfriends? A sunny walk, you say? A bubble bath? An excellent rom-com? ERRRR. Wrong answer.

The best thing in the entire world is my bed. And also, this pillow, and this duvet in which I can bury my face, and ice cream if I had it, which I don't, so I'll have to settle for leftover dipping chocolate from the time that Dad made chocolate-covered straw-berries for a Lillian's cocktail hour. After Ethan drove me home from the airport, I dumped my suitcases in the foyer and plopped myself right here. It's been an hour and I have not left. I texted Jia but she said she's helping her mom with something at the res-taurant and she'll be here soon. It's fine. Everyone in the world is busy—preoccupied with their happy little songs and flashy stage lights, and sparkly, insipid costumes. Like, none of my former camp friends have texted me once. Well, that's a lie—Valerie did ask *Are you okay?* but when I didn't answer, she fell back into radio silence. Cheney, Rae, Sofia? *Nada.* No apology, or *Wow, I'm a terrible boyfriend / friend / human being.* Even Watkins is uninterested in my sorrow. He licked my face a few minutes ago, so I thought he wanted to cuddle and be a nice, comforting dog, but it turns out that he just wanted chocolate. Well, I've got news for you, buddy. If you eat chocolate, you'll vomit and have diarrhea and you'll be miserable and then you too can join the club.

Ethan barges into my room in sweatpants and a ratty shirt because he immediately went to game with his friends as soon as we got home. He glances up from his phone and examines my sorry state.

"Yo," he says, "you have a surprise visitor."

I sit up. Jia must have finally arrived. But when he opens the door farther, a person who is decidedly *not* Jia enters my room. My mother.

I drop the dipping chocolate and it scatters all over my bed. "Mom?"

She looks stunning, as per usual, in a pale blue trench coat and stockings even though it's ninety bajillion degrees outside. Mom takes off her cat-eye sunglasses and picks up a piece of dipping chocolate that has rolled off the bed and onto the carpet.

"Evie," she says, "what's happened to you?"

I shrug. "I dunno. My life is ending, and the entire state of Ohio probably hates me."

"Ah," she replies, "my little drama queen, as always."

Ethan, who is still lingering by the doorway, just shakes his head and returns to his room. His ability to ignore me is possibly his best quality. Sean never can, so instead he just punches me in the arm. Good thing my other brother is still in Los Angeles, living his tech internship dreams.

I roll over on the bed so Mom can sit, but she just hovers by the duvet, continuing to gingerly scoop up chocolates and dump them back into the container.

"Aren't you supposed to be in Atlanta right now?" I ask.

My mom half smiles. "Yes, but I came home early once I heard about the incident. Ethan told me. And then Lucius Brown called, but I told *them* that we'd already paid full tuition so they have nothing to complain about. Also, whoever I was talking to was extremely rude and condescending, and I let them know."

I grin. Sometimes my mother really *is* a boss. I can't believe she flew across the entire Eastern Seaboard just to stare at her pitiful daughter wrapped in sheets that look like they've been smeared with poop. It almost makes up for all the musicals she missed because she was *on business*. Mom walks toward me and smooths back my flyaways. She used to do this when I was a kid—her trick to make me stop screaming every time I didn't get what I want. But this is different. As much as I love my mother being here, a simple hair pat won't fix Lucius Brown, or theater, for that matter.

"I'm meeting your father in Paris," she says. "We have a couple of events for the store and a charity gala we're attending. I'm leaving tomorrow morning. Why don't you come with me?"

"Where? Paris?"

"Yes. You need a good cheering up. We can do baguettes, the

Louvre, some shopping." My mother taps the bottom of my chin with a red fingernail. "You know, the works."

This is a very tempting offer. Bread and brie are my second favorite foods behind ice cream, and I bet I could find a nice pair of heels and a new purse in Triangle d'Or. But the thought of bumpy plane rides and Dad constantly making deals on his Bluetooth earbuds, and Mom repeating, *Oh, Evie, my drama queen* don't exactly scream *fun*. And even though I escaped Ohio, for some reason, I don't want to keep running.

"That sounds nice," I say, "but I think I'm gonna stay home for a bit. Catch up on TV. Make sure Watkins remembers I'm his favorite."

My mother laughs. "Well, okay, if you're sure. I'll be back in two weeks then, all right? Once all these meetings are over, we can talk for real."

Mom has never offered to talk about anything real, ever. I pull her in and hug her freshly ironed trench coat sleeves.

She smooths back my hair. "I love you, Evie."

"Love you too, Mom."

Just then, there's another knock on my door.

"Hey," a small voice calls from the other side, "it's Jia. Can I come in?"

She's here at last.

"Of course," I say.

Jia arrives lopsided because she's carrying approximately fifteen tote bags. Her cheeks have more freckles than before, her skin tan from the blazing New York sun.

"Hi, Mrs. Hoang," she says as my mother waves and disappears down the hall. She turns to me. "I'm so sorry I'm late. I was talking to Akil, and then my mom needed me to man the hostess stand for a minute because CeCe was acting up, but that minute turned into an hour, and eventually I told her I had to leave, and surprisingly, she let me. Anyway, now I'm here."

I have never heard that girl speak so quickly in my life. She dumps all her tote bags on the carpet while I process her words, one after the other.

"Wait," I say. "You talked to Akil? Are you guys good again?"

Jia smiles so wide, her face practically falls off. "Yes, we're great, actually. But I don't want to talk about me. Let's talk about you."

She removes buckets and buckets of ice cream from her bags, as well as paper bowls and plastic spoons, and a hundred takeout napkins. I survey the pickings. There's Cherry Garcia, and mint chocolate chip, and double fudge brownie—all my favorites.

"I thought you might want a little of everything," she explains, removing the container caps, "the theme being chocolate, of course. And it's not just from me. Ariel paid for most of it. She's really sad she's not here with us right now."

My eyes start to water. I may have the greatest friends in the entire world. Jia hands me a bowl with one scoop of each. The cherry and chocolate melt in my mouth, the perfect union of fudgy sweetness.

"You know," I say, "you could have just taken bowls from my house. We have plenty."

"Oh, no." Jia shakes her head. "Yours are too nice. What if I break them?"

To be fair, all our dishware was hand-painted in Morocco, so I understand her concerns.

Jia gracefully plops a dollop of double fudge brownie in her bowl and scoots my legs to the side, smoothing down a comfy spot at the rear of the bed. But if she thinks she's making room for herself, she's wrong. As soon as she sets down her ice cream, I fling my arms around her and we lurch toward the headboard.

"Oof," she says, "what was that for?"

I sniffle in her sleeve. "Just missed you, that's all. Five weeks is too long to not see your best friend."

She strokes my knotted braids. "I missed you too. More than you know." Then she fluffs up my comforter and props herself up against the wall, legs crossed. "How are you?"

I gesture to the chocolate streaks on my bed and my sweatpants, which reek of airport. "Clearly, excellent."

But I know that answer won't work for Jia. If she were Ariel, she'd push me into the shower and tell me to dry off and talk. But Jia is different. She'll sit with you for hours until she has to go home, covertly coaxing you to reveal you *really* feel. Jia Lee is the queen of gentle persistence.

"I'm sorry Ohio was so awful," she says.

I flip over so I'm on my belly, my cheek smooshed into the Tempur-Pedic mattress.

"It wasn't just awful. They were all . . ." I struggle to find the words. "Racist. Just flat-out racist. And the wildest part is they had no idea. Truly. I mean, they're sending me disciplinary phone calls without realizing that *they're* the ones who should be freaking disciplined."

Jia nods. "I can't even imagine what that was like."

"You don't want to."

"Is there anything you can do? Anything you can say to make them, I don't know, see the light?"

My baby hairs are matted to my forehead. I flop over and they spring up like leaf blades. "I doubt it. I mean, the director has his head stuck up his ass, so I feel like the board who runs the camp is probably even worse. To be honest, now that I'm really thinking about it, I don't even know why I did the show to begin with."

"How do you mean?"

I'm on my feet now, the ice cream container cap rolling between my palms like a Frisbee.

"Like, I *knew* it was bad. I knew it was all bullshit. I told Abel. I asked him to change stuff. And he completely blew me off. And then I asked him *again* once I got Ching Ho, so he threatened to put me in the ensemble, and I was so invested in being in this show that I just made a decision to stay silent. And suck it all up. I spoke that shitty fake Chinese. I listened to Rae completely butcher an 'Oriental' accent. I basically lived and died for theater, and I didn't care about the cost." I swing my head up to the ceiling. "Oh, and I, like, fell for a complete asshole. In conclusion, I made some *great* choices. So you know, maybe I'm to blame."

Jia's eyes narrow. "You are *not* to blame. Everett, don't for a second think—"

"No," I interrupt, "everything about the camp and the show was wrong. I should have been braver. A lot earlier."

When I look back at my beautiful, smart, compassionate friend, she is perched on my bed, cartons of ice cream surrounding her. I bite back tears and turn my head toward the window.

"Ching Ho was a messed-up stereotype. It was a super-degrading role. And it made me think a lot about you, about what your family and what every struggling immigrant has been through, and how this was just . . . a mockery of all that. And I couldn't see it—at least not fully, until now." I try to exhale. "I'm sorry."

Jia is silent. And then I hear her slide off the bed and walk toward me. Her fingers brush my sweatshirt. "Hey," she says. "It's okay."

"It's not," I whisper, "but I get it now. I *really* do."

"I know," Jia replies.

She kisses my cheek and we stare out at the cul-de-sac. Kids zoom past on their bicycles, laughing in the shadow of the trees. When I was in fourth grade, I did that too. I had a hot pink motorized scooter with streamers on the handles, a birthday gift I used to show off nonstop to Jia and Ariel. After school, I would speed past the stop sign, belting "So Much Better" from *Legally Blonde* to anyone who'd listen, even though that song is totally inappropriate for a child to sing on the street. In the back of my third-grade yearbook, I wrote that I was going to be an actress on Broadway. I begged my parents to hire a photographer and take headshots so I could audition to be one of the kids in *Matilda*. When I didn't get a callback, my dad pity-bought me a masterclass at Pearl Studios, where I tried to "network" and find my way to another open casting call. Back then, my dreams were just within reach. If I trained hard enough, and took a ton of dance classes, and made a bajillion connections, I'd make it. It was a winning formula. I didn't know yet about problematic musicals, or directors who ignored you, or fake friends who laughed at you, or boys who left you behind. I pin my hand to the glass, the other still grasping the ice cream container lid.

"If this is what real theater is like," I say, half to Jia, half to no one, "what the hell am I going to do?"

"Oh, come on," Jia replies. "I'm sure it's better elsewhere. You're a star at Farrow."

"That's Farrow," I argue. "It's a *high school*. It's a bubble. Lucius Brown was supposed to be the big leagues."

I crush the lid between my palms so the paper is warped and mangled.

"I guess I don't know if I belong on the stage at all," I finally admit. "I don't know if there's a place for me there."

Jia swivels my shoulders toward her. She places both hands on my plane-ridden, disgusting cheeks. "All right, Everett Hoang," she says in her most demanding Ariel voice, "if anyone belongs in theater it's you. So you're going to have some more ice cream, and then I'll tell you my plan."

She drags me back to the bed. "Eat," she insists, so forcefully I start immediately guzzling down Cherry Garcia without protest. It does numb my brain a bit.

When I'm finished, she declares: "You have exactly one more week to feel sorry for yourself."

I scrunch my nose. "And then what? I'm gonna quit theater and suddenly want to be an engineer?"

"No, silly. And then we're going to *do* something. We're going to fight the system."

"The system," I repeat.

"You said this isn't just one person doing something wrong," she says. "It's a group of people. It's a *mindset*. And we need to combat that mindset."

"Okay, but a *mindset* seems like a hard concept to battle."

Jia throws a pillow at my face, just missing my precious bowl of now soupy pink liquid.

"Okay," I say, "so we fight the system. What's the plan?"

She snatches away my ice cream, tossing it into a trash bag that she of course brought with her. But then her shoulders droop.

"Well . . . I don't exactly have a plan *yet*," she confesses, "but I'll come up with one. This is why we need Ariel."

I shake my fists at the ceiling. "O mighty Ariel, how we long for your wisdom!"

"And your PowerPoint presentations!"

We fake cry, and end up laughing, rolling in pillows and chocolate stains.

When we pause to catch our breath, Jia puts on her serious face. "You're a star, Everett," she says, "and no one can take that away from you."

I half smile, my head finding its place in the crook of her neck. I want to believe her so badly.

# 35
# Ariel

The ocean is bluer than it's ever been. From the bedroom window, I watch the waves rise and fall. They foam on the sand and crawl back into themselves. They are not beasts today. They have no blood on their hands.

Haejin and Carl have been calling every few hours to check in on me. They are a two-part act. Carl, with his stories about the awkward photographer and the love-struck makeup artist from this massive shoot he just finished in Osaka. Haejin's nonstop efforts to create a women's surf club. She wants me to join her, but I am too busy staring at my sister's jewelry, a line of pastels spread out on my bedspread. I offer to sign Haejin's petition instead.

There's a knock on the door.

"Come in."

Imo arrives with a steaming cup of jeontong-cha and a gold box under her arm.

"Ariel," she says, "how are you?"

She asked me the same thing this morning, over a plate of fruit and eggs. I know she's worried. She has heard me cry almost every day. Since that night on the beach, I can't seem to stop.

I slide the necklaces and bracelets back into the pouch. "I'm fine," I say, and then, taking the hot tea, "thank you."

Jeontong-cha is much sweeter than American tea. There's a richness to it. I sit on the bed while Imo puts the box on my desk. She turns the chair to face me, her back outlined by the water.

"Where are Haejin and Carl?" she asks.

I shrug. "Out."

"I see."

Imo pulls at the silver rings pinched around her middle fingers. Her eyes are trained on the floor. I've heard her late-night calls to Umma and Appa. Her whispers at dusk. This is it. She's going to tell me I need to go home. She's going to say that she's called my parents, booked my flight.

But my aunt just says, "I want to tell you a story."

She is completely stone-faced. Her red lipstick fades at the corners.

"About what?" I ask, sipping my tea.

Imo coughs into her chiffon sleeve. "Your mother," she says.

"I don't want to hear any stories about Umma."

I have all the information I need. She tossed my sister aside like a rotten fish, left for the sharks to ravage. Then she and Appa painted an angelic portrait of our new family—free of passion, and adventure, and girls who lived beyond their canvas walls.

"Please, Ariel." She sounds just like my mother. Except kinder, less angry.

Imo has let me stay in her apartment for months without saying a word. She has let me roam this foreign city, awaiting my return home with a fresh plate of fried fish and kimchi. I look at the blue, blue ocean behind her. I owe her this much.

"Fine," I say.

"Thank you."

I think she is going to talk about one of their phone calls, but instead, she tells me about the Korean National English Spelling Bee. Umma has mentioned it before. She loves to brag about how good at English she is. She picked it up very quickly in Korea. Her genes are apparently why I get such good grades.

Imo says that one year, both she and my mother were eligible to compete in the spelling bee. Imo was ten. Umma was twelve. Umma had been the reigning school champion for the past two years. The previous winter, she almost made it to Seoul for the national competition. My grandparents were proud of Umma's English skills. They would prepare her well for America, they said. An achievement like this could propel her to Harvard. Imo was not nearly as good of a speller. But she was competitive.

"Like Bea," Imo says.

Always eager to prove herself. So Imo studied her giant packet of words and surprised my grandparents by winning her classroom spelling bee. That meant she and Umma would be competing against each other. My grandparents thought Imo had beginner's luck, which Imo says, she did. She was not an innate speller like

Umma. She had not studied the Latin roots or the dictionary. But she had fire. So intense, she would not shut up about it to Umma. Imo practiced until they fell asleep on their side-by-side twin beds.

The day of the school spelling bee, Imo and Umma went round after round, spelling words like *peppermint* and *generosity* and *aerobics*. One by one, their competitors were picked off. Finally, it was just Umma and Imo. The two sisters fighting to make it to the next bee in Gwangju.

"I went first," Imo says. "My word was *sabotage*."

She spelled it s-a-b-a-t-a-g-e instead of s-a-b-o. She was out. Unless my mother spelled her word wrong too. Then Imo would have a second chance.

Umma's word was *malevolent*. Imo's heart sank. She'd seen it in the packet. Her parents had seen it in the packet. They sat up, excited for their eldest daughter's win. Except Umma glanced over at her sister. Then she butchered it. Completely. Imo was shocked.

"But I had no time to think about it too much," she explains. "I had to go up and spell my word."

It was *casserole*. She spelled it correctly. She sat down and Umma walked up to the podium to spell hers. If she got it right, they would keep going. Hers was *forfeit*. A classic *e* before *i* case that Umma knew well. She spelled it f-o-r-f-i-e-t. She was out. My aunt won.

"I couldn't believe it," Imo tells me. "I was so shocked that Seri would give up something like this. She had a real chance to go to nationals." But Umma just hugged my aunt and let her win.

At regionals, Imo got out on her second word, *eclipse*. She had to sit there for two hours and watch the other kids recite words that her sister could spell in her sleep.

"It was awful," Imo says, "for both of us."

She lets out a big breath, the ocean breeze echoing her sighs.

"So the point is," I say, "my mother made a crappy decision."

"No." Imo shakes her head. "The point is, Seri cares about her family so much, she will do anything to help them succeed. Even at her own cost."

"Not all the time," I snap.

Imo pauses. She glances down at the jewelry pouch hidden inside a bundle of comforter. "Ariel, all she wanted was for you and your sister to be happy. She would give her life to make it happen."

"Well, success and happiness aren't the same thing."

"No," she agrees, "but it's what she was raised to believe. It's what our parents taught her. Hell, it's what our entire church taught us. And when Bea came here, and left all of your mother's hard work behind, Seri thought she failed. And when she . . . she . . ."

"When she died," I finish.

"Yes," Imo murmurs, "when she died, that was the ultimate failure for your mother. For both your parents. She couldn't bear to think or talk about it again. It was too painful."

"Bea wasn't a failure," I say.

"Of course she wasn't. But now she can't have any kind of job, or a family, or whatever she might want in life." Imo places her hands on my knees. "Don't you see, Ariel? This wasn't supposed to happen this way. For your parents and for all of us, none of this was supposed to happen."

Her voice breaks. I can't bear to see her like this. So I rest the tea on the nightstand and hug her tightly, desperately. My aunt smells of perfume, and history, and my mother. She releases me and turns toward the desk. She picks up the gold box and places it in my lap.

"Take it," she says.

I obey. It is heavier than I expected. Its sides cave under my fingertips. I flip open the lid.

The first thing I see is a bracelet. It is made up of red, yellow, and orange arrows handmade with embroidery floss. It is the same one that Haejin has, expect the string is less worn. Underneath are knick-knacks: a navy blue hair tie, a sticky note in my sister's handwriting that says *eggs, milk, fish.*

"When I was setting up your room, I found these in a drawer," Imo explains. "I wanted to give them to you, but at the right time. I think, maybe, now is right."

I set each item on the bed, one after the other. They are a mini museum of Bea. I find a business card for Meokja at the bottom. Imo smiles.

"Bea's favorite restaurant."

"I know." I smile back. "I got their tteokbokki."

My aunt smooths down the creases in her pencil skirt and bends forward to get a better look.

"You know, one time she tried to get the chef to tell her the recipe. She brought me along and made it seem like it was a "business opportunity." Imo laughs. "Your sister, ever the entrepreneur."

I think about the sea-glass jewelry in the pouch beside me. Every morning, I take out the necklaces and bracelets and spread them across the bed. Then I come back at night and put them back one by one so I won't tangle the chains. I want to do more with them. I want to put them in a glass case and display Bea's work for all of Busan to see.

I place the business card next to the sticky note. There's one more thing on the floor of the box. It is hard to make out in our shadows. When I slide it between my fingers, I realize it's a photograph. In the light, I make out the faces. My mother, with her porcelain skin and oversized straw hat. Appa in a polo shirt and khaki shorts, his arm around Umma's shoulder. My sister in her bikini, mid-laughter. And me, wearing black shorts and a black crewneck, a hint of my swimsuit looped around my neck. My half smile is one of relief and hesitant joy. We have made it to Bermuda as a family. We are all in one piece.

I did not know Bea had a copy of this photo, had kept it all these years when there's one sitting on our windowsill, framed, next to the money tree. She had wanted it as much as she wanted the friendship bracelet and spicy tteokbokki. She missed my parents even when they barely spoke to her. And as angry as they were, they missed her too. They loved her. They love her still.

I have picked up so many pieces of her since I arrived. I have found her in every alley, and mountain, and ocean tide. Imo doesn't have to tell me. I put the photograph on the bed and close the box.

"Okay," I say. "Will you give me a minute?"

Imo smiles. "Gladly."

She walks to the door and gently closes it behind her.

When I press Call on WorldGab, Umma picks up on the first ring.

"Ari-ya," she says.

"Hi, Umma," I answer. "I'm coming home."

From: arielunderthesea_29@gmail.com

To: everetthoang24601@gmail.com; jialee@leedumplinghouse.com

11:35 AM

Subject: Important Update

E and J,

It's time. I'm leaving Busan. Don't worry—no one's forcing me to go. I think I just realized that I need to be home for the rest of the summer. With Umma and Appa. And with you. After all, I heard that Everett needs help taking down some theater jerks. I am at your service.

I'll be back in Queens on the 1st. Let's meet at the restaurant first thing? Jia, tell your mom that the avengers have assembled for dumpling folding. ☺

See you soon,

Ariel

From: jialee@leedumplinghouse.com

To: arielunderthesea_29@gmail.com; everetthoang24601@gmail.com

10:40 PM

Subject: Yay!!!


Dearest Ariel,

   This is the best news Everett and I have heard all day. We're truly sitting on her bed, jumping up and down. We can't wait to see you, hug you, and shower you with dumplings and fried pancakes.

   Hugs to our favorite world traveler and safe travels home!


Love,

Jia

From: everetthoang24601@gmail.com

To: arielunderthesea_29@gmail.com; jialee@leedumplinghouse.com

10:43 PM

Subject: STILL SCREAMING

Ariel,

   HELL YES. THE BRILLIANT ONE IS BACK.

XO,

Everett

P.S. Hope your PowerPoint skills are still sharp.

# 36
# Everett

"Yo, real talk," Ethan says. "Why is Abby so obsessed with Henry when he's a complete asshole?"

While I eagerly await Ariel's arrival, I'm watching the final season of *Objection*, a very over-the-top but delightful courtroom drama. Ethan's sprawled out on the recliner while Watkins snoozes at the foot of the couch, sometimes opening one eye to peek at the five mostly empty containers of Oreos on the coffee table. This morning, I promptly kicked my brother out of the living room (contrary to popular belief, the television is *not* just for video games) to catch up on the trial lawyer Abby Clearwater and her exciting love life. Of course, she has a crush on her colleague and competitor, Henry, who happens to be charming, extremely hot, and ridiculously cunning. And of course, *of course*, her best friend, Greg, is secretly head over heels for her and would probably propose to her on the spot if he knew she was interested. It's high-class television.

Ethan whined for fifteen minutes but then plopped himself back on the recliner and has not gotten up since. As for me? I'm greatly enjoying my blanket cocoon and sweatpants/Oreo situation. Why deal with my problems when I can worry about Abby's?

I lick the frosting from the inside of an Oreo and twist my blanket fort toward my brother.

"He's not an asshole," I say. "He's just, like, competitive. And also, he and Abby have amazing chemistry."

Ethan flings his arms at the TV. "Dude, he's literally taking credit for her work right now! That's some messed-up shit."

Okay, to be fair, Henry *is* standing in front of the senior partners and presenting discovery on a case that he stole from Abby. Our heroine cowers in the back of the room like she just got hit by a semitruck halfway through the meeting.

"Um, maybe he'll redeem himself?"

Ethan shakes his head. "No, man, he can't come back from this. He's a total douchebag. She should drop him and get with Greg."

I smirk through my Oreo crunching. "I thought you didn't care about this show *at all.*"

Ethan kicks my shin so hard, it crashes into the coffee table.

"What the fuck." I grasp my leg in pain. "I could have broken something."

My evil brother stretches out in the recliner. "You know, Ev, you and Abby are kinda alike. Extremely annoying, highly dramatic, and lovesick to boot."

"You forgot ambitious, brilliant, empathetic, stylish, beautiful . . ."

Ethan snorts, and I'm tempted to kick him back, but I don't. I can't get in a wrestling match with my brother when there's only seven minutes left of season two. Once upon a time, I did emulate all of Abby's superior qualities (and come on, dramatic people are the most interesting to be around). But now, with the blanket wrapped around my face so tightly that I look like a cupcake spilling out of its wrapper, I'm not so sure.

At least the emails from Lucius Brown have finally stopped. And Jia sent me a text this morning about our takedown, also known as the nonexistent-PowerPoint-because-we-haven't-worked-on-it-whatsoever. What am I going to do, print it out and mail it to Abel Pearce and his minions? Get them on video-chat and start presenting? Yeah, right. Anyway, when Ariel comes home, I'll utilize her expertise then. I can't believe that in a few days, my best friends will finally be in one place. Thank God.

"Oh, here we go."

I emerge from my theater doldrums to find Abby Clearwater sauntering to the front of the room, the only woman in an office stuffed with men in boring black suits. The city skyscrapers around her flicker and darken. Ethan rubs his hands together and we both lean in. *This is* my *work*, she says, *not Henry's*. She snatches the laser pointer from her nemesis / maybe lover and underlines her evidence, iterating every little detail she knows about the case and even refuting some of the crap Henry got wrong in his less-than-stellar analysis. She is calm, cool, and collected, reveling in the senior partners' slack jaws and frozen eyebrows.

"What a badass," Ethan murmurs, and the partners agree.

They thank Abby for her work and give Henry a polite but biting dressing-down before leaving the room. Now it's just Abby and Henry, alone at last (although, to be fair, the entire office can see them since the walls are glass). Will they fight? Will they make out? You truly can never tell with these shows. But Clearwater just opens the door and walks back to her office. She doesn't even look at Henry and the camera zooms in on his guilty face to highlight her lack of interest in his excuses. She's presented her evidence and that says enough. Now he's left to deal with it.

I sit up. For once, I think Ethan is right. Maybe Abby and I really *are* alike. Abel Pearce and his jerks have spoken their minds. It's time to speak mine. I whip off the blanket so fast, my sweatshirt flies up my stomach.

"Dude," Ethan says, "you good?"

But I'm not listening to him. I dig between the couch cushions until I find my phone and Jia's and Ariel's profile pictures appear in tiny green circles.

**No PowerPoint needed**, I text. **I know what to do.**

With my blanket dragging behind me, I stumble up the stairs until I reach my room, which unfortunately has not cleaned itself. There are ice cream bowls everywhere and used napkins all over the floor and dried plant leaves scattered on my desk because I am a bad plant mom and have not watered my pothos. I peek under my bed, behind my dresser, and in the dark pits of my closet.

"Aha!"

My laptop reveals itself from the hidden sleeve inside my backpack, which I had angrily tossed when I got back from camp. I dust it off and set it on my desk in front of the window. The kids are back in the cul-de-sac. If I focus hard, I see myself out there too—the girl in the streamer scooter with her two French braids, belting the afternoon away. I open my email, my fingers shivering against the keys. I know I have to do this. For Abby Clearwater. For Ariel and Jia. For ten-year-old Everett. For the Everett I want to be. So I begin.

To the Lucius Brown Performing Arts Institute Board of
Directors:

I know you've been waiting to hear from me, so I might
as well reintroduce myself. My name is Everett Hoang. To
refresh your memories, I'm the girl who went out screaming
at a rehearsal about a week ago. It was definitely not my
finest moment, and I really should not have told anyone to
fuck themselves, so for that, I apologize.

But I do not apologize for the reasons behind my anger.
When I came to Ohio, I was so excited. Like, "Barbra Streisand
just asked you to perform at her Carnegie Hall concert"
excited. All I wanted was to learn from and perform with some
of the most talented actors in America, ones who'd hopefully
become my colleagues on Broadway one day. I was ready to
do anything to be the best actress I could be, and looking
back, my eagerness may have clouded my judgment.

Over time, I realized that Lucius Brown Performing Arts
Institute—and I mean the production, the casting directors,
the actors, the script, the costumes, and, by connection,
yourselves—created a racist and hostile environment. Yes,
actively freaking racist. Let's talk about all the reasons why:

*Thoroughly Modern Millie* is a problematic show on about
six hundred levels. Mrs. Meers, the musical's villain, is a

white woman pretending to be a Chinese woman trying to traffic white girls to "the Orient." This makes it seem like Asia is a place where trafficking regularly occurs, which is a rude and unfounded assumption. Also, the musical allows a white actress to blatantly mock an Asian person, which just—how can you not see this is wrong? And her minions? First of all, you didn't even cast Chinese people to play the "henchmen," and second of all, these characters encourage super racist stereotypes about Chinese immigrants. They are not just laundry men speaking in broken English. You could have either chosen a different show to produce, or revamped the musical to address these problems. After all, you supposedly created this program to "push boundaries," as director Abel Pearce bragged about during orientation.

I voiced these concerns to Abel and to my fellow cast members tons of times. And no one listened to me. In fact, my director outright refused to utilize any of my suggestions and subsequently threatened to put me in the ensemble if I did not "like my part." Meanwhile, the actors constantly spewed ignorant, racially charged insults that I pretended were fine, but really were not fine at all. At the end of the day, the environment you created was harmful.

You hired an all-white production team and an all-white cast. You didn't care how said white actors portrayed harmful stereotypes. And really, when it came to me, you never cared about how talented I was. I could have busted my butt ten times over at that audition and in those showcases. My fate was already sealed. You just cared about my face. The shape of my eyes. To you, I was just an Asian body to slot into the role of Ching Ho. Mission accomplished.

Maybe you'll trash this letter and toss me aside as some annoying teenager, but before you do, I ask you to read this one more time from the beginning. Think about all the things you could do better, like reaching out to more diverse actors and choosing a more thoughtful musical.

As Millie would say, it's time to become thoroughly modern. It's not that hard. I'm asking you to make the effort.

Sincerely,
Everett Hoang

# 37
# Jia

Squished between my best friend and my boyfriend on the hot metal bench, I pretzel my legs as Everett narrates her letter to the Lucius Brown Performing Arts Institute. With every question mark and air quote, I imagine spotlights exposing each board member's hiding place on stage. Akil rests his elbows on his knees, his hands cupping his chin. If Everett was lacking a rapturous audience in Ohio, she has one now.

The sidewalk in front of Lee's Dumpling House is pockmarked with gum stains. CeCe sits on the front stoop, batting her eyelashes as customers coo at her gap-toothed smile and handful of dolls. She is our unwitting mascot while Nai Nai snoozes upstairs and my parents juggle menus and plates towering with cui pei doufu.

Everett finishes her letter, jumping to her feet and offering a slight curtsy. We clap, and even CeCe—who thankfully thinks that Akil is just Everett's neighbor and is too young to ask questions—stomps her sneakers against the concrete in applause.

"That was, like, awesome," Akil says.

"I'm really proud of you," I tell her.

Everett grins, her nose ring glinting in the sun. "You're gonna have to hear it again when Ariel comes home."

"Gladly."

In just twenty-four hours, the gang will finally be back together. Emails, texts, and hurried WorldGab messages will be replaced with snuggly blankets and feet draped over each other's thighs on our fifth watch of *To All the Boys I've Loved Before*. We'll stuff as many midnight Clue marathons (Ariel always wins) and neighborhood bike rides into our four remaining weeks of summer. We'll remember that when the wind changes, Everett will be back on stage and Ariel will return to the California palm trees. All that anticipation, joy, and missing makes my toes ache.

Two girls in Doc Martens and honey dresses wave to CeCe before walking inside the restaurant, the blast of the fan blowing out into the street.

I fiddle with my earrings. "Have they answered you yet?"

Everett shakes her head. "No," she says. "Ugh. What if they never do?"

"It's only been a day," I reassure her.

Akil sits forward. "Yeah, and even if they don't, you basically skewered them. That has to mean something."

"Yeah." Everett rakes her fingers through her hair. "I guess."

I know how much Everett wants change. What she said last

week in her room still blossoms in my belly: *I get it now, I really do.* Whether with theater or with obnoxious girls who turn up their noses at our dumpling house, Everett will always fight for what's right. She will always dream of a brighter, better world. And I will too. Tentatively, I pick up my backpack from underneath the bench. I pull out ten college brochures unearthed from my bottom dresser drawer. Everett looks at the glossy papers folded in my lap.

"You ready?" she asks.

I bite the inside of my cheek. "Ready as I'll ever be."

"You're gonna be great," Akil insists, squeezing my hand.

I hope so. I didn't fully devise this plan until last night. Everett and I talked through it over the phone, when my parents were long asleep and CeCe and Nai Nai were snoring in their bedroom. She and Akil are here for moral support. I look over at my sister, who is completely oblivious as she rolls her dolls in mystery dirt.

And then, the restaurant door swings open. My parents appear on the stoop, fresh off their newly instated Friday-afternoon breaks now that Lizzie has been promoted from head chef to kitchen manager. Mom airs out her sweater, damp from the humidity. I clutch the brochures with all my might as CeCe pushes aside her dolls and wraps her grimy fingers around Dad's leg.

"Oh," he says, "I didn't know you were out here."

"Hi, Mr. and Mrs. Lee." Everett waves. "It's great to see you again."

Mom eyes the brochures and then Akil. "Nice to see you too. How was camp?"

"Erm, could have been better, to be honest."

But she isn't really listening. My mother walks down the stoop, one loafer at a time, staring right at Akil. "Have we met before?"

Before he can open his mouth, I say in a quick line of succession, "No. He's Everett's neighbor and new to Queens, so we're showing him around Chinatown."

It is a mostly true lie. And Akil knows that I'm not ready to introduce a boy to my parents just yet—I can only spring so many surprises on them at once. Dad surveys the flashy college names sprawled out on my jeans: *Geneseo, Hunter, City College of New York, Lehman.* If I could disappear beneath the grate right now, I would.

He shakes CeCe off his leg and points. "What are these?"

I gulp. "Um. Something I wanted to talk to you about actually."

"And on that note," Everett says, jumping to her feet and practically yanking Akil's arm off, "we should probably get going. We have to . . . feed Watkins. Okay, bye!"

My entire family watches them toddle down the street like Akil is the dog being dragged on Everett's leash.

"Let's go upstairs," Dad says, his words clipped, "and discuss this?"

I nod. Stuffing the stacks of college brochures under my armpit and pulling my backpack over my shoulder, I follow my parents and sister through the side door and up the apartment stairs. When we arrive, CeCe races into the living room. Danica emerges from Nai Nai's bedroom and, noticing the tension between us, grabs her keys and bag and smartly slips out into the hallway.

My parents pull out chairs from the kitchen table. I place the brochures in front of them like they are playing cards and this is merely a game. If only my hands would stop trembling.

"So," I begin, pretending I'm reading through the script I wrote with Everett last night, "I want to tell you that I love this restaurant. And I love our neighborhood, and the life you've built for CeCe and me here. But I've been thinking about it all summer, and I . . . Well, I just don't know if this is what I want for my future. To stay here, I mean. I've been doing some research. And I want . . . I want . . ."

*Breathe, Jia, breathe.* I think of Akil on his bike, the trust in his cool gray eyes as they bored into mine. *You contain multitudes.* I inhale the musty apartment air and the saddle-stitched, glossy paper.

"I don't want to go to community college. I want to go to a four-year school."

"Jia—"

"A four-year *public* university. One that could give me a full scholarship. I did some research and you can go to almost any state school for free now. If I do all the paperwork, I think I could even try to get free room and board." I run my hands along the brochure bindings. "These are just options, but I want to look into them."

For a moment that seems to descend into hours, my parents say nothing. Finally, Mom speaks.

"I knew there was something up with you this summer." She drums her fingers on the table. "You've been going out so often and you don't seem that excited about restaurant stuff anymore."

"Really?" Dad says.

Mom elbows his shoulder. "Ai ya, you never notice anything."

My mouth feels dry and tears sting the corners of my eyes. I am so proud of what my parents have created. Prouder than I've ever been. And I *want* to love the smell of steam-dried dishes, the clean lines of an ironed tablecloth. I want to want my future so badly.

Dad crosses his arms. "And what would you study at this four-year school?"

"Business maybe." At that, my parents light up. "Or maybe something else. Art or English or psychology like Ariel. I really don't know."

"Jia," Dad says, "we came to this country to give you a good future. A solid one."

"I know. I just . . . I want to keep my options open."

The clock on the wall seems to tick louder and louder. When my parents don't respond, I think about melting into the tile.

"I'm sorry," I say. "I don't mean to upset you."

Mom gets up from her chair. I worry she is going to haul me into my room, but she just pours water into the teakettle and sets it on the burner. She touches the curls swathing her neck.

Quietly, she says, "I understand."

"You do?"

Dad and I both gape at her as she lifts a mug from the cupboard.

She opens our year-old tin of dried tea leaves from our aunties in Canton and spoons them into the cup.

When she turns to us, Dad's brows are knitted and my eyes are wide.

"When I was in grade school, I wanted to be a writer," she says. "In English too. My teachers said I was talented. I thought I could go to an American school and get real good. I wanted to be like that man who writes all those sad British stories. Charles Dickens."

She sets down her mug. "But my parents didn't think it proper for a girl to be interested in the arts. So I went to school for finance, married your father, and moved to New York. By then, we had piles of debt, and the dream went *poof*."

In another world, I see my mom typing away on a sleek silver laptop, pages filled with paragraphs of smooth English words. I see her as I see myself: dreaming away afternoons, pencil sketching impossible stories, waiting for our fire escapes to ferry us away.

"You never told me this," Dad says, the edge in his voice giving way to hollow surprise.

Mom shrugs. "Not too important anymore."

The teakettle begins to hum while Dad surveys the brochures still piled on the table.

"I think," Mom continues, "that my parents wanted what was best for me. They wanted to make sure I had enough money to be happy. We want that for you too." She pauses. "But maybe there are other options. More than one way to be happy."

Dad shakes his head. "Then who will take over the restaurant, huh? Your baby sister?"

"Ai, Jia is seventeen. She'll be too young anyway when she finishes community college. Not mature enough."

It's not meant as a compliment, but I hold it close to my chest.

"And we have Lizzie for some time at least. She's a good worker."

I look at my mom—her crow's feet and tired black eyes—and my mesmerized dad, trying to see a different woman than the one he married. The teakettle whistles its finale.

Dad pulls the Stony Brook brochure toward him and unrolls its folds, sticky from my fingers pressing too hard into the paper.

"Long Island," he says hesitantly. "Nai Nai would like the beach."

I think I might burst. "Yes, she would."

He thumbs through half a dozen of them—bearcat mascots and Comic Sans statistics. He squints at the fine print fees as Mom pours her tea.

"All right," he says, "but just schools in New York, Jia. And you'll have to apply for those scholarships you talked about."

"Scholarships, financial aid, the whole works. I promise."

My parents are not sentimental, but I fling my arms around them anyway. We topple into a messy pile of cardigans and hugs.

"I love you," I say.

"Ai ya, Jia. We love you too."

# August

From: arielunderthesea_29@gmail.com

To: everetthoang24601@gmail.com; jialee@leedumplinghouse.com

12:05 AM

Subject: Home


E and J,

I'm back in Queens. Well, to be more specific, JFK. I'm in a taxi on my way home. It's weird being back. The city is so empty at night. You can't hear the ocean here. Just our good ole East River.

Haejin and Carl came with my aunt to drop me off at the airport in Busan. They were very sweet and gave me Choco Pie for the flight. I ate approximately ten in transit (whoops) and have exactly two left for you. One day, maybe we can all meet up with Haejin and Carl in the city or in Korea. I think you'd like them.

I can't wait to see you tomorrow. I'll be at the dumpling house bright and early. With an abundance of hugs. And gifts from Korea. ☺


See you soon,

Ariel

# 38
# Ariel

In the darkness, I make out the tree in our front yard. The house's all-brick façade. The gas station at the end of the corner. It feels like years since I've been home. The jewelry tucked inside my cross-body bag jingles when I walk. I roll my suitcase up the driveway and the foyer light turns on. Umma and Appa are waiting for me.

I open the garage door and turn in to the mudroom. Umma is already beckoning me inside with whispers of *Go, go, you'll wake up the neighbors.* Once the garage door is closed and everything is locked, she pulls me into a hug. It is so sudden, I trip over the wheels of my suitcase. My mother is angry at me, I know. But I am now her only daughter. I hug her back.

Appa flicks on a light in the living room. I notice that the money tree is still where it is, the curtains still closed. But there is one change. The photograph peeks out from its hiding spot. There is a sliver of my sister in view.

"Do you want to eat now or later?"

It is the first question my mother always asks any time Bea and I return home. Whether you are coming back from a half-day drive or you are flying across the world, the question is always *What will you eat? How much pork will make you remember us?*

I rub my eyes. "Later's fine. Thanks."

My father busies himself. Fluffing pillows. Moving a magazine on the coffee table from one side of the glass to the other. I have followed their orders. I have come home. Now they are at a loss.

Umma grips my suitcase handle and swivels its wheels toward the hall.

"Why don't you shower and go to bed?" She pats my sweater. "You must be tired."

She is giving me an out. Even though she has stayed up, has watched the taxi roll in from down the block, she is telling me to sleep Korea away. We will talk in the morning. She will hand me the new Briston schedule and we will forget about this whole summer.

But the jewelry is still sitting in my bag, looped over my shoulder. And Bea is fresh on my mind. Her head thrown back on the pontoon. Her silky laughter in every department store. Her peach-and-blue necklaces shining in the sand. I prepared a speech on the plane, scribbled on a cracker napkin when everyone else was sleeping. I am trying to remember it all but it seems to disappear the more I think about it.

"I know it's late," I finally say, "but I want to talk to you. About Busan. And Bea."

Appa looks at Umma and then back at me. My mother puts her hands on her hips.

"Ariel," she says, "not now. I don't want to fight."

"I don't want to either. Ten minutes. Ten minutes and then I'll shower and go to sleep."

My parents don't respond. We hover around the coffee table like we are in a Western standoff. Umma tightens her bathrobe. Appa pinches the bridge of his glasses. So I make the first move. I take a seat on the couch. I used to study here, and eat Cheetos, and listen to Bee and Umma fight. Now, under the haze of the streetlamps, our living room is another planet.

I settle deeper into the couch. "Before I left," I say, "I talked to Imo. About Bea, and about you."

Umma scoffs. "What did she say? Something horrible, I bet."

"No." I shake my head. "She actually defended you."

My mother tries to hide her surprise. Appa walks over to the recliner, the backs of his legs hovering over the cushions.

"Go on," he says.

"She told me that you always wanted Bea and me to be happy."

"Of course we did," my mother says.

"I know. And in your minds, good grades, and a college education, and a steady job were things that would make us happy. I get that. I mean, I believed that too. But I think Bee was different. In Busan, she had her own way of being happy."

"Bea behaved poorly," Umma snaps.

"She was a little rash," I admit, "but she was also nineteen. And we've all behaved poorly."

"Ari-ya, don't be dramatic."

"I'm not. We *have*. I shouldn't have up and left San Francisco without telling you first. You both kept Haejin and Carl from me.

And you cut off Imo." I swallow the needles in my throat. "I know you wanted to shield me, but that hurt a lot. Bea was your daughter, but she was also my sister. I'm glad I went to Korea because there was so much I didn't know about her."

I move to the coffee table and unzip my bag. The jewelry glimmers under the dim lights. I spread out the necklaces and bracelets like they're on display.

"She made these. She told Haejin and Carl that she was inspired by the pastel houses in Gamcheon Village. And by Grandpa's sailing."

I explain how she loved the sea. How she charmed the locals, planned photoshoots, created a website layout, and diagrammed shops across South Korea and New York City.

Appa says, "She was going to come back to New York?"

My mother doesn't say anything. Instead, she looks away from the coffee table and pretends she's engrossed in the money tree's browning leaves. I touch the hem of her bathrobe.

"Umma," I say, "please."

She won't move. Appa hesitantly crouches to the floor. He runs his hands along a series of turquoise beads.

"She made all these?" he asks.

I nod while my father stares at the glass like they will bring him back into the past. Umma is still examining the tree. Her fingers pinch the corners where green meets shriveled brown.

"Ari-ya," she whispers, "I can't do this right now."

It's the first slightly honest thing she's said all night. I stand up. My amygdala is a siren. Epinephrine flows through me like a strong tide.

"You don't have to look, then," I say, "just listen, for a second."

Umma clenches her fists, and I wonder if she is going to yell or walk away or tell me to go to bed so we can sleep away the hard stuff like usual. But she just stays clenched, unmoving. So I keep going.

"Bea had dreams," I say. "They weren't the ones we wanted. But she had them. She liked to party. She liked dancing. She had friends, *real* friends, people who cared about her. She liked the beach and the ocean, and bikinis, and sunshine. She wanted to be happy and she wanted you to be proud of her, and she wasn't sure how to do both at the same time. But she tried."

Umma sniffles. A river brims in her eyes. She tries to wipe it away.

"Umma," I say, "don't. We *should* cry about Bea. We *should* talk about her. This is the one part of Bee we have left. I want to celebrate it." I feel my own tears falling, trickling down my neck. "Come on, please."

At last, she relents. She bends down so that she's face-to-face with the jewelry. Her hand brushes against mine and it takes me a moment to realize what she's trying to do. My mother cups my palm in hers. She squeezes and I squeeze back. We sit like this, an unfinished family in the dark, kneeling around the colors of the sea.

Appa holds up a necklace to the light. "They're beautiful," he says, "really something."

I nod. Tears plop onto the table like clear glass beads. I'm not sure whose they are anymore. My mother leans her head against mine.

"I miss her," she chokes out. "I miss her so, so much."

I hold her tight and she buries her face in my hair. "I know," I say. "Me too."

Appa presses the necklace to his heart. My sister smiles from the water. *I'm here*, she says. *You found me.*

# 39
# Jia

"She's returned!" Everett shrieks.

When we yank open the creaky restaurant door, Ariel grins at us from under her baseball cap and a stack of presents. She looks the same—no makeup, skin-cut nails, gold studs she's worn since she got her ears pierced in fifth grade. But somehow, as Everett smooshes our favorite jet-setter against her chest, Ariel seems different. Her eyes wrinkle when she smiles; her cheeks are rosy and plump. I join in on Cuddle Central until Ariel pries herself from our bodies and shakes out her sun-streaked hair.

"Next time you pull a Thelma and Louise, we're coming with you," Everett says, dragging Ariel and her presents to a nearby booth.

Ariel laughs. "I could say the same for you."

The chefs start to trickle in, the whir of refrigerators and fryers humming awake as Everett chatters about Ohio, corn, and Cheney (who she has successfully blocked on four different social media platforms). Light yawns through the windowpane and I head to the back, ferrying bowls of meat and dumpling wrappers between the kitchen and the booth. When Mom hands me the water, she brushes her fingers against my wrist, her touch light but tender.

"You're off the hook today," she says, "but don't stay out too late."

The water sloshes between my palms as I reach out to hug her.

"Careful," she scolds, "you still have dumplings to make. And you don't want to get water on that outfit."

She eyes the lavender dress I put on today, the one with the ruched bodice and sheer sleeves. "I assume you'll sleep over at Everett's then?"

"Yes," I say, "but I'll be home in time for dim sum tomorrow."

"Hmm. And is your friend going to be there? Akil?"

She turns to the fan and presses her face to the blades so that her curls blow in the artificial air. Thank goodness she's not looking when I blush.

"Um, I don't think so. No."

My mother shrugs, like she doesn't care either away. "Okay," she says, her face still bent toward the fan. "Go back to the girls."

I shuffle to the booth, speechless. Perhaps my mother is less oblivious than I thought.

When I return, Ariel and Everett are scrolling through photos of the Jagalchi fish market, jumbo carp lined up on trays like candy bars. I organize our assembly line, listening as the sky turns starburst orange.

Everett is the first to grab a dumpling wrapper, dabbing her fingers with water and lining its circular rim.

"You're supposed to put the water on *after* you do the meat," Ariel says, purposefully plopping the ground pork in the center of the dough.

Everett shakes her head. "No," she protests, "water first."

"Well, Jia is the expert."

The two look at me expectantly.

"Either works," I say. "It doesn't make a difference."

Everett groans. "Why do you have to be so fair all the time?"

I roll my eyes. Nothing has changed. And yet, everything has.

We continue our assembly line, folding our rows of pork-filled envelopes until our fingers grow tired. Meanwhile we chatter constantly—about Everett's letter (Abel Pearce and his minions have still not responded) and whether or not I should invite Akil over because Ariel is dying to meet him (absolutely not). When our plates are full with dumplings, we carry them to the kitchen and watch the chefs drown them in boiling water.

Ariel beckons us back to the booth, picking up gifts from the floor.

"For you m'lady," she says, plopping a silver tissue-papered package into my palms.

She hands Everett a small rectangular box and we both dive in. Everett emerges with a pink neckerchief decorated with white flowers.

"One hundred percent silk from Korea," Ariel says, and Everett gasps, immediately tying it around her neck.

"A modern-day Audrey Hepburn," I declare.

She does a series of poses, her lips puckered, hands on her hips. I know she's still upset about Ohio, but it's good to see her glowing.

"Your turn, Jia."

My friends nod excitedly as I meticulously peel off the tape and flatten the tissue paper.

"Just like Umma," Ariel says, pinching my sweater and chuckling.

"We shall wait another millennium for Jia to unwrap her present."

"Ha ha, very funny," I say, but I stop when I see what's inside.

The most beautiful blackwood colored pencils lie before me. When I flip back the paper lid, the pencils glide into my hands, chalky and smooth as I roll them between my fingers.

"Wow, thank you."

Ariel wraps her arm around my back. "So you can draw the hottest anime men in all the land."

"I won't disappoint you."

"As hot as *Akil* though?" Everett winks.

"Oh, shush."

At that, Everett grabs my phone and shows Ariel *more* pictures of Akil, as if she hasn't flipped through two dozen already. There's the selfie of us at Flushing Meadows, perched on the ledge of the Unisphere, a pigeon flapping between us. There's Akil in Manga Palace, takeout chow fun dangling between his lips. There's a video-chat screenshot of his thumbs-up when I showed him my detailed college spreadsheet last night.

"This one's my favorite." Ariel smirks, pointing to a photo of my boyfriend mid-sneeze.

Everett snorts. "Him at his most attractive."

The kitchen door swings open and Lizzie appears with egg tarts, a secret treat, still warm and flaky. On the count of three, we bite into sweet, sugary egg and hot butter. Ariel finishes first and grabs a napkin from the dispenser, wringing it between her hands.

"So," she says, "I have to tell you guys something."

"You're not, like, moving to France, are you?" Everett groans.

"No. Although from what your parents have said, Paris sounds pretty nice."

"Not worth it. Trust me."

I pull at my bangs. "What is it?"

Ariel looks at Everett, cheeks ballooning with tart, and then at me, wide-eyed and frozen in place. "I'm going back to Busan. In September. I'm going to stay for the year."

"The *entire* year?" I hear myself ask. "But what about Briston?"

"I'm deferring enrollment. I'll go next fall. My parents and I had a long, long talk about it. I don't think we slept at all last night." She laughs nervously. "They have some stipulations, like I need to take a couple of online courses, and call them all the time, and come home during the holidays, but mostly . . . they're on board."

Everett's jaw hangs open, egg still dissolving on her tongue.

"I'm not just going to hang out at the beach. Although that's definitely a perk."

Ariel slips a bracelet off her wrist. I hadn't noticed it before, entangled with a zigzag embroidery floss bracelet. She lays it on the table—an aquamarine sea-glass rock resting on a shiny, silver chain.

"Wow," I say, "Bea made these? They're even more beautiful in person."

Ariel smiles. I can imagine the pastel cottages that inspired her sister's art, their grandfather's ships on the cerulean sea. It's like Bea's here with us, even though she's not.

"I'm going to finish what she started," Ariel says, sliding the bracelet back onto her wrist.

"You're going to open a jewelry store?"

"Not just by myself. Bee's friends are going to help, and actual professionals who she was in contact with in Busan. I'm going to get it up and going with a website and a storefront, and then Haejin and Carl said they'd take over. And who knows, maybe then, we'll have already expanded to New York."

Everett gasps. "Oh my God, you're, like, a real-life business woman. We should buy you a suit."

"Definitely no suits," Ariel laughs. "We're going for a bohemian vibe."

We stare at her in awe. I know we are thinking of so many things: Ariel taking Korea by storm, photoshoots and models, her toes in the sand. And how Bea will be in every bead, every charm, every bracelet. I can almost hear her now, floating through us, full and bright.

"I couldn't have made this decision without you," Ariel says. "You've been here for me all summer. And I know that I wasn't always the easiest to reach." She bites her lip. "This time, it will be better, I promise. We'll video-chat all the time. Even more now, since I'll be up at all hours of the night taking virtual classes."

I nod, egg splattered on my chin. Everett blinks back tears. Just months ago, Ariel sat in this same vinyl booth, here but not here, always slipping from our grasp. Now, she is practically an adult. Tears start to prick my bottom lashes too.

"Wait, not both of you crying." Ariel dabs her crumpled napkin on my eyes.

"Sorry," I say, "I'm just happy for you. I think that Bea would be really proud."

"Ugh," Everett sobs, "group hug!"

She throws her arms around us, and we collide—our plates knocking against each other, tarts threatening to spill all over the floor.

Ariel scrunches her nose. "I love you guys, but you are *so* cheesy."

"Cheesy is what makes us great." Everett kisses her cheek and then mine. "My fabulous friends, all together again."

"A reason to celebrate," Ariel says. "We should do something special." She scoots forward and I nod, the taste of sugar and aquamarine dreams still on my lips.

Everett leaps up, hands clasped. "I have just the thing."

# 40
# Ariel

Everett has packed the most elaborate brunch I've ever seen. Jam and brie, a baguette, frosted sugar cookies, and things I've never even eaten before like figs and truffle butter.

After we left the restaurant, we rode our bikes to the Trader Joe's on Metropolitan. Jia and I wanted to go inside, but Everett insisted that we wait for her in the parking lot. She said we would ruin her *vision*. So she gallivanted around the store by herself while Jia and I went to Petco. We cooed at kittens and rescue dogs, and talked about Akil and Haejin, art and Busan. Forty-five minutes later, Everett emerged with four vinyl grocery bags, and miraculously, a picnic blanket.

Now she is buzzing. She lays out the gingham quilt on a patch of grass in Flushing Meadows and arranges the spread of goodies in the middle with the cheese unwrapped and the jam unscrewed so they look Instagram-able. Jia takes pictures so that the sunlight hits the scones at just the right angle. We joke that we should become influencers. Jia the photographer, Everett the visionary, and me, the statistician. I think I will stick with Bee's jewelry project.

I wasn't expecting to ask Umma and Appa about Korea last night. I was going to bring it up after we had slept away our tears. But Appa was still sitting at the coffee table, clutching Bea's necklace. Umma's face was curled into something like a smile—real and strange and almost happy. So at six in the morning, I recited the second part of my airplane napkin speech. I said I wanted to defer enrollment and go back to Busan for the year. I laid out a plan. I gave them my word that I would return. And after a lengthy discussion, somehow they believed me. They trusted me.

I breathe in sunburnt grass and creamy brie. I love Busan, but it will never compare to a New York summer. The chubby Asian babies and their bucket hat–clad mothers are back in droves. The skateboarders are dangerously close to running us over. The Unisphere looms above our heads. Everything in this moment is right. Except for Everett, who is aggressively cutting the baguette with a plastic knife.

Jia drapes her dress over her thighs and leans forward so that the chiffon brushes against my arm. "Is she okay?"

We eye Everett from across the gingham like we are the audience and she, the knife-wielding carnival act. Crumbs spew in every direction.

"Ev," I say, reaching out to touch her sleeve, "you good?"

"Maybe I can grab a real knife from somewhere," Jia adds. "There's probably a corner store that will lend me one."

Everett stops cutting. My hand stills on her shirt. She wilts, like all the energy from her Trader Joe's trip and picnic arrangements has seeped out of her.

"I guess I thought that if I just distracted myself, I'd get over it," she confesses.

Jia catches on before I do. "The letter," she says. "They haven't responded, have they?"

"Nope."

The knife falls onto the blanket as Everett abandons the baguette and inches toward us. I pretzel my legs and she falls into them, her braids folded over my shorts.

"What were you hoping they'd say?"

Everett sniffs. "I don't know. I mean, they weren't . . . going to, like, admit all their wrongdoings or whatever. But some acknowledgment would have been nice. A step in the right direction, you know?"

"Yeah," Jia empathizes, "they wanted you to answer their messages *so* badly but when you finally did, they didn't want anything to do with you."

"They're cowards," I declare.

They really are. What they did to Everett this summer was horrible. And probably something that happens everywhere. I sit forward, my stomach bumping the back of Everett's head. It *definitely* happens everywhere.

"Ow," Everett yelps.

"Shush," I say. "I have an idea."

Everett gathers her braids in her hands and bobs up so she's facing Jia and me. "It's too late for a PowerPoint presentation."

"A *better* idea," I clarify. "Okay, hear me out. We'll make a TikTok. Ev, you already have an account, so it's perfect. You'll talk about what happened at Lucius Brown, we'll show your letter, and then, I don't know, we'll create some kind of call to action. We can make it snappy but pointed, and more about theater than just Lucius Brown. That way, you can illustrate the real systemic problems."

Everett scrunches her nose. "A TikTok?"

"Come on, it's brilliant, Ev," Jia says. "You'd be fighting the *system*." She looks off at the looming Unisphere, her eyes glittery and faraway. "We'll post, wait a couple hours, and then *boom*. You'll go viral."

"Have any of us ever gone viral?" Everett says doubtfully.

"Well, no," I admit.

Jia presses her hands against her knees. "It'll be fun. It'll be *cathartic*."

Our favorite theater girl stares at us for a moment, picking at the grass. "Okay, fine," she says.

Jia claps and more crumbs go flying. We get to work. Everett and I tackle the script while Jia runs through video logistics. I give up on the plastic knife and tear off a piece of baguette. Paired with a dollop of truffle butter, it melts in my mouth— cool and light. When we've eaten our way through the bread and stuffed ourselves with sugar cookies, we admire our work. Everett does one beautifully acted run-through before we start rolling. Jia smooths out the gingham blanket and sits on her knees, the phone steady between her fingers. I count down: *three, two, one.* When Everett finishes talking, I add her letter and splice together each section. And then, as the sky turns fiery orange and the moon drifts beneath the clouds, I hover over the Post button.

"Ready?" I ask.

"I don't want to see it after," Everett moans. "Just press the button and log me out."

"But what if you get comments?" Jia protests. "Or a bunch of likes?"

"I don't care."

"But—"

"Send it out into the universe!" she shouts.

A couple of skateboarders in beanie hats and baggy jeans glance at us in amusement. I press Post. Everett screeches and buries her head in the blanket. Jia covers her eyes. I click out of TikTok and place the phone facedown on the blanket.

"Well, if we're not going to check, we need a distraction." I lift up Everett's head from the blanket. "What's next?"

# 41
# Everett

Dizzy Cat is packed because it's the last cabaret of the season. Swanky older ladies from Manhattan pull their husbands onto the dance floor while college students gossip about their summers in the corner booths. We arrive fashionably late after demolishing even more food at my house. Jia orders a Shirley Temple and pulls down the sleeves of that showstopping lilac dress she unearthed from the back of her closet.

"There you go, girl," I cheer, clinking the glass of my club soda with her Shirley Temple. "To reuniting."

"And to business deals," Jia says.

"And to taking down the man," Ariel adds, tipping her cup of lemonade.

The cabaret starts at ten, but the dancing's already begun. Misty Coolidge (my favorite of the Dizzy Cat performers) croons "Big Spender" in a flapper dress and maroon lipstick, her fingers grasping the silver microphone. The Jones brothers make waves with their trumpet and saxophone riffs. Even though the only people dancing are the divorcées swaying with mojitos in hand, I drag my friends to the center of the wooden platform. We twirl and twirl until we're tripping over each other. Jia mimes an excellent trombone solo and Ariel and I link arms for a campy Charleston. I am sweaty and mushy and delighted, and I don't even care about TikTok, or theater, or my armpits, which are 100 percent leaking right now.

The pianist takes the mic at five minutes to ten and unveils a clipboard and a jar of ballpoint pens. "For you brave souls and Broadway wannabes, your time is now." He rests the clipboard on the stage in front of the microphone and boogies back to the piano.

I walk over to the pool table and am downing a cup of water (turns out you really *can* get a workout from doing a box step fifty times in a row) when Ariel pokes my ribs with a cue stick.

"Um," I say, "I'm pretty sure that's not what that's for."

She waves the pool stick like it's a wand and not an extremely dangerous object that might very well take my eye out.

"What are you waiting for? Put your name on the list."

Jia absentmindedly wrestles with a pair of billiard balls while some mildly irritated college guys cross their arms and mutter behind her.

"Oh," she says sheepishly, "sorry." She drops them onto the table. "Everett? Aren't you going to go up and sing?"

It's a valid question. I've never *not* sung at a Dizzy Cat cabaret.

There was the time I even whipped out some gloves and an old Elizabeth Bennett costume and rapped "Satisfied" for an audience of tipsy thirty-year-olds. It was truly an iconic moment. But I haven't peeped a single note since the Lucius Brown debacle.

I gulp down the last of my club soda and attempt to slink away. Ariel whips me around anyway, her clammy hands grasping my shoulders.

"Hey," she says, "what's wrong?"

"Nothing," I answer quickly, but Ariel, as per usual, doesn't buy it.

She squints and taps the edge of the pool stick. "You're not going to let those Lucius Brown douchebags get the best of you, are you?"

"Of course not," I say, and then, recognizing that my best friend is a walking lie detector: "Well . . . I don't know."

I *shouldn't* let Abel Pearce, and Cheney, and the hair-whip girls, and the drone of the musty Ohio bugs stop from me singing, or doing anything. I've done my part. I wrote the letter, we made the TikTok, I'm back with my best friends dancing just the way I wanted to all summer. But it all feels like it amounts to nothing. I mean, my email is likely lost in the abyss, and God knows who saw my TikTok. Probably some eleven-year-old who's left a nasty comment. There's always an eleven-year-old to drag you down.

I play with the hem of my skirt. The thought still gnaws at me: *There's no place for you here. This is what it will be like, always.* Abel Pearce is one of the most well-regarded directors I know. If he doesn't see the problem, if he doesn't see *me*, who will?

Ariel releases my shoulders and opens her mouth to give some very intense debate response that will likely take years to finish when Jia hesitantly steps forward, her phone pressed between her palms.

"Hey," she whispers, "you're a star. In fact, so much of a star that . . ."

She shares a knowing look with Ariel.

I fight the urge to grab Ariel's pool stick and jam it into Jia's arm. "You weren't supposed to check!" I screech.

"You said *you* didn't want to check," Jia screams, darting around the pool table as I chase her. "There were no rules about *me* looking."

The college bros scowl at us like we are the worst things to happen to New York City. Jia stumbles into the corner, hands on her hips as she catches her breath, Ariel close behind.

"I'm not a runner," she pants. "You win."

I weave my fingers through my post-braid waves, cascading down my shirt like a lion's mane. "Show me," I blurt. "Wait, don't show me. Well, actually—"

"Everett," Ariel interrupts, shoving the TikTok in my face, "just look."

There are 30,000 views and 10,000 likes, which isn't exactly *viral*, but is still a respectable number. But most breathtaking are the comments. The hundreds of comments. I scroll through them, the cabaret walls around me fading into night.

*I had this exact experience at a different theater!! Message me GIRL the stories I have to tell. Thanks for speaking out*

*I'm so sorry this happened*

*Funny enough, I was just looking at Lucius Brown for next summer and I've never clicked out of a website so fast—*

*Thank you for talking about this, no one does*

There are more and more, flooding every inch of the screen.

"Oh my God," I say.

"You're literally getting more comments every second," Ariel says.

She's right. We refresh the page and a handful pop up. I can't believe it. I keep reading each one again and again, trying to remember that these are *real* people. Aspiring actors and actresses who have been through this exact same thing. The entire summer, Abel Pearce made me feel young and foolish. My ideas were bad, my outburst uncalled for. Cheney and my so-called theater friends mocked me or ignored me. I was completely and utterly alone. But now, as more comments appear and hearts scatter the screen, I realize I'm not. I'm actually, really not.

Later, when Ariel and Jia have passed out and it's only me and the moon and the cul-de-sac where little Everett used to ride her bike and have big dreams, I'll write back to each commenter on TikTok. Maybe I'll even start a virtual support group or something. Better yet, a committee. A union. Do they have those for teenagers? Whatever I do, the possibilities seem endless.

I look up from the phone to find Jia's and Ariel's proud and beautiful faces. I fall into their embrace.

"Go out there and kill it," Ariel says.

The pianist and the clipboard are still waiting by the stage. I've missed the high notes and the microphones and the spotlights. I've missed my moments in the sun. When I walk through the crowd to the front of the room, my fingertips seem to crane toward the pen. I hover over the clipboard before signing my name in one cursive swoop. The pianist beckons me over, and I whisper my song selection to him. He nods and flips to a page in his binder before standing to address the crowd.

"Please welcome our first performer of the night." He booms, and then turns to me. "Take it away."

The audience cheers. Ariel and Jia roar so loudly, you'd think we're at a football game instead of a cabaret.

I wrap my fingers around the microphone. "Hi," I say, "my name's Everett Hoang."

The piano keys tumble into the opening melody.

And then, I sing.

# 42
# Ariel

"Gosh," Jia whispers, "I forgot how beautiful her voice is."

She's right. I forgot too. Everett dives into a current of low notes. I squeeze Jia's hand and she squeezes back.

Bea would love this. Dizzy Cat only started cabaret nights a few years ago, and she never made it here. I can see her in wedge heels, her hair pulled back, singing a raunchy version of "Someone to Watch Over Me." She always had a nice voice even when she was trying too hard to be Marilyn Monroe.

Now that we are older, Bee would be so excited to watch Everett and Jia grow up. She'd happily stuff her face with fried pizza and show off Jia's drawings to all her friends. On lazy afternoons, she'd bring Everett with her to chat up the coffee shop baristas. At night, she'd snuggle in bed with me after a daze of partying, her breath blowing faintly on my shirt.

I roll the bracelets down my wrist. One for her past—for her friendship with Haejin and Carl and her life in Busan. And one for her future—for the one I will keep alive.

I miss her. I miss the parts of her I will never know. I miss the woman she never got to be. But I will come back for her, always, even when the tide has changed, and California calls my name.

There's an ocean of Bea everywhere, I think. I keep my hand in Jia's and listen close.

# 43
# Jia

After a night of dancing, we sprawl out on Everett's front porch steps and watch the moths circle the lampposts. The girls whine until Akil finally stops by. He and Everett bond over their new school while he rests his head in my lap and dangles his feet over the mulch. We move on and talk about everything and nothing—K-dramas, what Busan will be like in the fall, blueberries or strawberries, the merits of the Q train versus the R. The number of taxicabs whirring past start to dwindle, and through the window, we can see Watkins snoozing in the living room.

Akil yawns. "I should probably get going," he says, clambering to his feet and pecking me on the lips.

He jogs down the driveway and through the street as we wave goodbye. When his garage door shuts behind him, Ariel snickers. "Adorable."

"Gross." Everett teases, elbowing my rib cage.

I shake my head. "Satisfied?"

"Very."

Everett takes Akil's spot, draping her hair over my dress. Peering into the unzipped purse stuffed between my legs, she wrinkles her forehead.

"Are those dumplings in your bag?"

"Oh," I say, "yes."

Gingerly, I lift the small container onto my lap, thankfully still intact. When we left the restaurant, Mom handed me six leftover dumplings as a snack for our sleepover. I meant to transfer them to my backpack with my pajamas and toothbrush—the one currently flopped over Everett's couch—but in our buzz of excitement and tears, I forgot.

Ariel examines the creamy brown canoes through the plastic. "I can't believe you brought these all the way to Dizzy Cat."

"Well," I say with a shrug, "they're very hearty. Dancing and subways have nothing on them, right?" I pat the container top and release its edges.

"I'll get chopsticks," Everett says, running inside.

She returns with wooden ones every restaurant in Chinatown throws in the bottom of your takeout bag.

"Perfect."

We dig in, one by one.

There are three parts to every perfect dumpling. Ariel lifts her chopsticks to the lamppost light and carefully squishes the skin. Everett devours the meat in one go, juice sliding down her chin. We've walked so many paths alone this summer, and we'll keep trekking in the autumns and winters to come. But for now, we're together—three queens under the same Flushing sky. I take a bite.